PELICAI

THE LIGHT

Peter Mason is well known for his lively radio programmes with the Australian Broadcasting Commission's Science Unit and for his books Genesis to Jupiter and Cauchu – the Weeping Wood.

His research career began at the age of eleven, when he silvered copper coins for his friends, and it almost terminated in the same year with an unexpectedly effective experiment on the combustion of hydrogen.

Graduating from London University during the war, he was sent to a laboratory on the Channel coast designing radar sets for the invasion of Europe. As soon as the war ended, he left to pursue more peaceful avenues of research, working on optics, building and roadmaking materials, rubber and plastics, and becoming fascinated by the borderline between living and non-living things. His growing interest in biological molecules brought him to C.S.I.R.O. in Australia to study the proteins of wool, and in 1966 he was invited to take up the foundation chair of physics at Macquarie University.

Peter Mason is a Corresponding Member of the World Federation of Scientific Workers. His current research lies in trying to discover how the cells of the brain control the temperature of the human body.

The Light Fantastic

Peter Mason

PENGUIN BOOKS

Penguin Books Ltd, Harmondsworth, Middlesex, England
Penguin Books, 625 Madison Avenue, New York, New York 10022, U.S.A.
Penguin Books Australia Ltd, Ringwood, Victoria, Australia
Penguin Books Canada Ltd, 2801 John Street, Markham, Ontario, Canada L3R 1B4
Penguin Books (N.Z.) Ltd, 182-190 Wairau Road, Auckland 10, New Zealand

First published by Penguin Books Australia 1981
Published in Pelican Books 1982

Printed and bound in Great Britain by
William Clowes (Beccles) Limited,
Beccles and London
Set in Italia

Contents

List of figures & tables

Introduction

We all know what light is; but it is not easy to tell what it is.
Samuel Johnson, 1776

The Lacemakers. A spherical flask of water is used as a lens to condense the light from a candle on the fine lacework.

I have a poignant childhood memory of a dimly lit room in which young women in long, old-fashioned dresses, are sitting making lace. A candle is their only source of illumination. In front of the candle stand glass globes filled with water. Their purpose is to collect the feeble rays of the candle and focus them into a small pool of light. The young women are leaning forward, holding their intricate lace work as close to this point of light as they can. I stare in wonder at their pale, sad faces and at each shining globe that is their lens.

The scene is still and quiet, for the girls are wax figures. The 'candle' is actually electric, and the room is part of an exhibition of Lighting through the Ages, in the Children's Gallery of the Science Museum in London. The exhibits range from primitive oil lamps, thousands of years old, to modern fluorescent tubes. They show how the progress over the last hundred years has made it safe to walk the streets at night, how it brought a blaze of light to the cities and places of entertainment, and expanded our lives by lighting up the long winter nights in our homes. *The Lacemakers* is the star exhibit. It shocks us with a glimpse of the bad old days when science was first being pressed into the service of production. Although the use of a water-filled globe as a lens to condense the light into the working area was an ingenious optical device, it was used not to help the young women but to exploit them. A little girl would be sent to the lace school at the age of five and she would probably leave the trade with ruined eyesight before she was twenty.

The rest of the exhibition redressed the balance by showing how the new forms of lighting brightened the workplaces, as well as the homes and the cities, liberating the workers of England from the gloomy conditions of their dark, satanic mills. But I was left with the haunting memory of the lacemakers' faces, the wonder of the glass ball concentrating the light, and a puzzlement about how such a brilliant invention as the lens could produce such a terrible result.

The Light Fantastic is a patchwork story of the wonder and magic, the science and the technology of these brilliant optical inventions. They have changed the whole pattern of human life, and their influence upon the lives of ordinary people is indeed the thread that weaves the story together. As just one example, the introduction of gas and electric lighting brought in its train a social liberation. Cities sprang into life when darkness fell. People who could afford this illumination in their homes found that a new dimension had been added to their lives. The coal miners and the workers in the gas and electricity supply companies, on the other hand, found their lot becoming intolerable and they joined the growing swell of industrial unrest.

The first gas lamps that flickered in the streets of Georgian London lit the way to an extraordinary scientific laboratory just a few hundred metres off Piccadilly, the Royal Institution. It had been set up by the American adventurer Benjamin Thompson, who had recently been created Count Rumford of the Holy Roman Empire, with the aim of closing the gap between science and industry. In its laboratory Thomas Young demonstrated that light was some sort of wave motion, and one of his successors, Michael Faraday, established connections between three apparently unconnected things – electricity, magnetism, and light. All of this work was gathered up by the Scotsman, Clerk Maxwell, into a comprehensive theory with breathtaking implications. The light waves were both electric and magnetic in nature and they travelled through space at the almost incredible speed of 300 000 kilometres per second. And, as if that weren't enough, ordinary visible light was claimed to be merely one particular example of these 'electromagnetic' waves. Many other forms of 'invisible light' should exist, waves that did not produce any effect upon human vision. Perhaps they would be found to have spectacular properties of their own, health-giving or death-dealing for instance.

Such ideas were too revolutionary to be taken seriously by Maxwell's contemporaries but nine years after his death Heinrich Hertz succeeded in generating invisible waves that could be detected at a distance – the waves of radio. His discovery was taken up enthusiastically by the Italian inventor Guglielmo Marconi, and soon the signals of S.O.S. were speeding from ships in distress across the oceans of the world, saving thousands of lives each year. Soon, also, ordinary homes would be filled with music, news, and entertainment from all parts of the world, all cheaply available at the turn of a switch. First as a means of communication, then of entertainment, and more ominously as an integral force in modern warfare, radio made as great an impact upon the lives of individuals as had public and domestic lighting. Modern life is scarcely imaginable without artificial lighting, radio or its offspring, television.

The most important device in the realm of visible light was not strictly an invention: the lens had been present in the eyes of animals for millions of years before the human race existed. In the times of Mohammed, eye diseases were prevalent in the Arab countries and the Islamic surgeons gained a clear understanding of the function of the lens. Their knowledge filtered through into Europe where the medieval invention of spectacles came as a priceless blessing to clerics and craftsmen, as well as to countless millions ever since.

From spectacles came telescopes, just in time to meet the needs of the trading and fighting fleets of the European superpowers. Using lenses to see the very big and the far away, however, turned out to be less important than using them to see the very small. Through the work of a gifted Dutch amateur, Anton van Leeuwenhoek, such tiny secrets of life as bacteria and spermatozoa were revealed. The science of light had increased the powers of vision and it now gave a vital new dimension to biology and to medicine.

In the late nineteenth century the microscope was brought close to perfection by a group of craftsmen and scientists in the small German town of Jena. Out of this group came the great optical company of Carl Zeiss. Its greatness lay not simply in the quality of its optical products but equally in the care it took of its workers at a time when exploitation and grinding poverty were the rule. The Carl Zeiss Foundation survived the two World Wars before it divided like an amoeba. There are now two quite independent and first-class optical companies, one in each of the East and West divisions of Germany. Both are called Carl Zeiss, and both are still operating essentially under the enlightened charter set up by the Foundation in the nineteenth century.

The nineteenth century was really a Golden Age for the light fantastic. Two of its inventions became pillars of the modern way of life: photography, of both still and moving pictures, and the once mysterious X-rays, yet another form of invisible light, which have become an everyday tool for the doctor and dentist. And here the scientific detective story begins. For although the wave theory of light explained how camera lenses focused a picture on a photographic plate, no one knew how the black-and-white image was actually formed, nor did anyone understand just how the X-rays were produced by the X-ray tube. A vital clue seemed to be missing.

In 1905 the mystery was resolved by Albert Einstein, who showed that light waves can, in appropriate circumstances, best be considered as a stream of individual particles which he called *photons*. Out of this concept came a deep understanding of atomic structure, which could explain how vision works, why the sky is blue, the ruby red and the grass green, and which paved the way, for better or for worse, to such inventions as the atomic bomb and the laser. The idea of photons was Einstein's greatest contribution to science and it justly brought him a Nobel Prize.

Light is as basic to our universe as matter. Although we shall probably never find a fully satisfying answer to the question 'What is light?', we now have an understanding of it that is complete enough for most practical purposes. It has provided some of the most powerful tools for the primary job of science, to improve the condition of humanity. Yet at the heart of the modern scientific revolution we find a disturbing reminder of an earlier age. In a brightly lit room in South-East Asia, rows of women are peering intently down microscopes, assembling the microchips required for our sophisticated electronic devices. Their working lives are short because of the damage this work inflicts upon their eyesight. The image of the lacemakers returns in oriental dress. The scientific revolution still has quite a way to go.

1

Switching on the Light

Electric lighting comes to homes and cities

The winter evening settles down
With smell of steaks in passage ways.
Six o'clock.
The burnt-out ends of smoky days.
And now a gusty shower wraps
The grimy scraps
Of withered leaves about your feet
And newspapers from vacant lots;
The showers beat
On broken blinds and chimney-pots
And at the corner of the street
A lonely cab-horse steams and stamps.
And then the lighting of the lamps.

(T. S. Eliot, 'Prelude I', *Collected Poems 1909-1925*, p. 21)

Ikhnaton receiving light from
the Sun God

/

Will the Sun rise again?
Will our old friend the Dawn come back again?
Will the power of Darkness be conquered by the God of Light?
(from an Indian Veda, ca. 1500 B.C.)

The Vedas are the hymns of the ancient wisdom still chanted by Indian priests at dawn and at sunset. There are over a thousand Vedas and they show how the people of that early civilisation sought to solve the mysteries of life and destiny. They sing of their worship of the elements and the forces of nature, above all of the Devas, the Bright Ones, the gods of light and of goodness. The later oriental religions, including Christianity, kept a special wonder for the sun and the stars or, more generally, for the origins of that perpetual mystery, light.

And while the Vedas were still being written, the worship of the sun was being lifted to a supreme position in the already ancient civilisation of Egypt. The Egyptians had a huge pantheon of gods to fit all occasions – Isis and Osiris, Horus the child, gods with human faces and gods with the faces of animals – but above all they worshipped everything connected with the sun. When the young High Priest of Aton, the Sun God, became the Pharaoh Amenhotep IV in 1375 B.C., he immediately set about founding a new religion and a new era of love and happiness, all based on worship of the sun.

The audacity of this teenage Pharaoh was breathtaking. He found himself, an ardent pacifist, suddenly at the head of the greatest superpower of the day. He promptly cut the generals down to size, refusing to fight the wars which they told him were needed to retain the outer reaches of his empire in Syria and Palestine. His attacks on the wealthy establishment were still more devastating. He made mortal enemies even before he came into head-on collision with the powerful priesthood of Thebes, dedicated to the worship of Amon, the Hidden One. As part of his challenge to their control, he changed his own name from Amenhotep ('Amon is satisfied') to Ikhnaton ('it pleases Aton'). Every reference to Amon was hewn out from the stone monuments of Thebes and that great city was abandoned in favour of Ikhnaton's new capital of Akhetaton, now known as Tel el-Amarna, 500 kilometres down the Nile.

But Ikhnaton had cut too deeply into the powers of the military-theological complex of his time. When he was only about thirty years old he was removed from the throne, his great new city Akhetaton was abandoned, and within a short time few physical traces of his benevolent sun religion remained.

During his reign Ikhnaton did not succeed in persuading his people to worship only the Sun God, or to accept the ideas of pacifism and internationalism, or even to abandon pomp and circumstance in favour of directness and the pursuit of truth. But his philosophy took root in the world of art: Egyptian artists started producing works of simplicity and naturalism, in refreshing contrast to the stylised, artificial art of the past. Poets and song writers flourished and Ikhnaton himself wrote one of the most famous songs of all, the 'Hymn to the Sun':

You have made the far skies so that you may shine in them,
Your Disk in its solitude looks on all that you have made, appearing
    in its glory and gleaming both near and far.
Out of your singleness you shape a million forms – towns and villages,
    fields, roads and the river.
All eyes behold you, bright disk of the day.

                                            (from Moore, *Suns, Myths and Men*, p. 28)

The hymn praises the sun for inspiring the animals and the plants, and for giving its blessings equally to all people on earth. Ikhnaton also devised the symbol for this Sun God, a golden disk radiating its light down to earth, with each ray ending in a human hand to signify the gift of life.

But what could one do when the fiery Sun God went down over the Indus or the Nile at the end of the day? The priests and the Pharaohs, the rich and the powerful, would make tiny images of him in their palaces or homes, burning olive oil in lamps of earthenware or bronze using wicks made from vegetable fibre. For those who were neither rich nor powerful it was a case of the dictum later expressed by St John: 'The night cometh when no man can work.'

A thousand years later domestic oil lamps were glimmering in the cities of ancient Greece and Rome, while natural gas was illuminating mines and houses far away in China. With the Christian era, candles came into fashion, gaining a religious significance as well as providing the main source of artificial lighting throughout the Middle Ages. But they were never cheap. Writing of the life of William Oughtred, the seventeenth-century mathematician, Aubrey showed how domestic lighting could be a serious problem for the educated classes: '. . . his wife was a penurious woman and would not allow him to burne candle after supper, by which means many a good notion is lost.' Even in 1827 candles were a luxury at the comfortable English establishment of Haworth Parsonage. Mrs Gaskell records an argument between the old servant and the Brontë sisters as to whether or not a candle should be lit. The servant emerged victorious and no candle was produced. Today the western world is lit by electricity, but about half the world's inhabitants still use some kind of flame as their only source of light at night.

The night cometh when no man can work, and in the early cities people couldn't go out either, unless they were wealthy enough to be accompanied by lantern-bearers and a bodyguard. To go out to supper in ancient Rome without having made a will was, said Juvenal, simply carelessness. Darkness was the friend of villains, and even in eighteenth-century England the situation had not improved much. In 1744 the Lord Mayor and Aldermen of London issued a warning that '. . . divers confederacies of evilly disposed persons, armed with bludgeons, pistols, cutlasses and other dangerous weapons, infest not only the private lanes and passages, but likewise the public streets and places of public concourse.'

The scientific and engineering achievements of the nineteenth century changed the face of the world. And none of these achievements had more direct effect on the lives of ordinary people than gas and electric lighting, the transformation of night into day.

Street lighting with gas, obtained by distilling coal, was demonstrated successfully in London in 1807. It was hailed at once as a valuable means of reducing crime, and over the next twenty years some fifty thousand gas lamps were installed in that city alone. Gaslighting in the home became enormously popular – 'Better to eat dry bread by the splendour of gas', enthused the Rev. Sydney Smith, 'than to dine on wild beef with wax candles' – and supplying gas for lighting soon became a profitable business.

In England the gas companies, as public utilities, had won the coveted right of limited liability. (In other forms of enterprise it was still held that the investors had a responsibility for the debts that their business might incur.) The gas companies also had the backing of a law which, although it recognised trade unions, nevertheless enabled Lord Justice Brett in 1872 to send the gas-stokers' leaders to prison for a year, merely for preparing to strike.

From the very beginning of the century, though, there was an even brighter prospect than gaslighting. Alessandro Volta made the first electric battery in 1800 and presented it to Napoleon. At the Royal Institution in London Humphrey Davy built a huge battery of no less than two thousand cells. He showed how a platinum strip could be heated electrically and maintained at a glowing white heat, a foretaste of the incandescent lamp. In 1807 he used his battery for his celebrated discovery, by electrolysis, of the elements sodium and potassium, but he soon returned to the electrical production of light and proudly demonstrated a brilliant arc of light between two carbon rods ten centimetres apart.

Another fifty years of development was necessary before either the incandescent light or the arc light could be considered a serious method of lighting. But Davy did find an immediate solution to one long-standing problem. The use of candles and lanterns with naked flames had often led to catastrophic explosions in the coal mines owing to the presence of the dreaded firedamp, a gas consisting mainly of methane. The flint mill, an invention stemming from a lecture given by Sir James Lowther to the Royal Society, was a pathetic answer. Sir James had explained that sparks were much safer than flames when firedamp was around:

it is to be observed that this sort of Vapour or damp Air will not take fire except by Flame; Sparks do not affect it, and for that Reason it is frequent to use Flint and Steel in Places affected by this sort of Damp, which will give a glimmering Light that is a great Help to the Workmen in different Cases.

The flint mills were operated by little boys, who had to keep an iron wheel rotating all day long, at the same time pressing a flint against it to produce a shower of sparks that was supposed to provide light for the miners. Many thought it safer and better to work in the dark. Mr Spedding, who designed the mills, introduced them in 1730 but was later killed in a pit explosion. The famous Davy Safety Lamp was a small cylindrical oil lamp with the flame totally enclosed by a metal wire

Flint mill for lighting a coal mine

gauze. In reasonably still conditions, with air speeds well below two metres per second, the gauze conducted the heat of the flame away and usually prevented an explosion. If the firedamp concentration was high, the lamp itself would give a warning because the gauze would start to glow a dull red.

This particular bit of technology was welcomed by the mine owners, who used it to justify sending miners down in pits hitherto considered unsafe. The net result was that mine explosions actually increased in the years following the introduction of the Davy Safety Lamp.

Only after a cheap and robust filament had been invented could sealed electric lamps be developed for use in mines. They were safer because the hot filament was sealed inside a glass globe out of contact with the explosive gas. Later on, they were built directly into the miner's helmet, leaving both hands free and concentrating the light just where it was needed. But the real future of incandescent light lay in domestic lighting, and for such widespread service more was needed than just the ingenious invention of the filament. A source of continuous electric power was required. Even for arc lighting, a better source was needed than the banks of batteries that had supplied some impressive but uneconomic demonstrations in the streets of Paris and London. Michael Faraday's fundamental discovery of electromagnetic induction in 1831 provided the key. Faraday found that when a coil of wire is moved through a magnetic field an electric current flows through the coil (see Figure 1.1). Translated from the laboratory of the Royal Institution into the world of industry, this principle gave birth to the electric generator, the machine that would both light and power the world.

The most important electric generator, the *dynamo*, was invented in 1866 by a Prussian ex-artillery officer named Werner Siemens. This machine is self-excited: its magnetic field is provided by electromagnets which are themselves energised by the current from the rotating coil. Dynamos and arc lighting developed together in Germany, France and Britain. And in the United States, thirty-year-old Thomas Alva Edison, fresh from his success with the telephone and the phonograph, awoke to the commercial possibilities of a light that would be less intense than the arc and thus suitable for indoor lighting in homes and in shops. Characteristically, Edison attacked not just the problem of the power supply, or that of finding a suitable filament, but the creation of an entire lighting system — its science, its technology, its economics and its public relations. On 20 October 1878, he gave an interview glowing with optimism and promise to the New York *Sun:*

'Are you positive', the reporter inquired, 'that you have found a light that will take the place of gas and be much cheaper to consumers?'

'There can be no doubt of it,' he replied.

'Is it an electric light?'

'It is', he answered, 'electricity and nothing else'.

(cited in Hughes, *Thomas Edison*, p. 22)

At that time he did not actually have a lamp, but he did have a project for lighting New York City from twenty central generating stations to match the conventional distribution systems for gaslighting. The implications of this interview created shock waves in both scientific and financial circles. The shares of gaslighting companies fell — not just on Wall Street but on the European stock exchanges as well. It was hardly by chance that the interview took place immediately after the formation of that part of the system intended to raise the finance, the Edison Electric Light Company.

In proclaiming that 'the subdivision of light is all right', Edison deliberately contradicted the widely held belief that it would not be possible

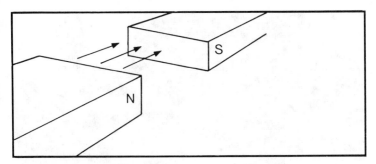

(i) A magnetic field exists between the poles (ends) of magnets.

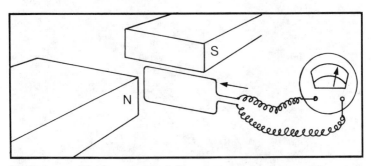

(ii) Moving a coil into or out of the field produces an electric current.

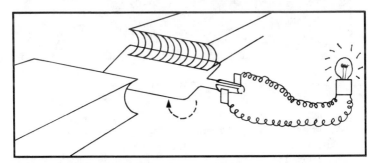

(iii) Rotating a coil in the field produces a continuous electric current.

Figure 1.1: Faraday's electromagnetic experiment

Edison clocking in on his seventy-fourth birthday

to light a large number of lamps from a single generator. He was relying upon the law given sixty years earlier by George Ohm, well known today but evidently not fully appreciated by Edison's critics, that the electric pressure applied to a lamp (measured in volts) and the current flowing through it (measured in amps) are very simply related to its resistance (measured in ohms):

$$\text{voltage} = \text{current} \times \text{resistance}$$

Although leading scientists on both sides of the Atlantic still maintained that subdivision was impossible, Edison went ahead with his system in which each house would be supplied with the same voltage. The lamps in each house would be connected in parallel so that any one of them could be switched on and off without affecting the others. These ideas had come to him in 1878 after watching a demonstration of dazzling 500 candle-power arc lights in Connecticut. He wrote:

What had been done was not practically useful. The intense light could not be brought into private houses. I saw that it had not gone far and that I had a chance. I came home and made experiments, two nights in succession. I discovered the necessary secret, so simple that a boot-black might understand it. It suddenly came to me like the secret of the phonograph. It was real, it was no phantom – the subdivision of the light is all right.

(cited in Chirnside, *Sir Joseph Wilson Swan*, p. 10)

Edison designed generators that would supply electricity at a high voltage but he proposed also to use lamps of high resistance so that, according to Ohm's Law, the current would be kept low. He wanted the energy supplied to be turned into light rather than heating up the rest of the wiring system, as would happen if high currents were used. Using a low current also meant that the wires could be of much smaller diameter, thereby saving a considerable investment in copper.

The only thing, in fact, that was lacking was a suitable high-resistance filament. And that was where Edison had gone right out on a limb. The only lamp he had working, the one he had shown the *Sun* reporter, had an expensive and short-lived platinum filament with a low resistance. Unknown to him, though, Joseph Swan in England was already demonstrating carbon-filament lamps to delighted audiences at his local scientific institution, The Literary and Philosophical Society of Newcastle-upon-Tyne.

It is hard to avoid making a caricature of the contrast between these two men. Edison, the dynamic, get-rich-quick American inventor and folk-hero; and Swan, the self-effacing, nature-loving, pharmaceutical chemist whose amateur scientific interests led him to brilliant inventions in photography, electric lighting and synthetic fibres. Perhaps the most striking feature they had in common was their lack of formal education: both had finished school at the age of twelve. But Swan described his own education in terms worthy of a born technologist or an Ionian Greek:

I was an inquisitive boy . . . I roamed about with my elder brother John and we did not shut our eyes in sleep. In these excursions I had seen lime kilns and a factory for making crucibles. I can remember from the time I was four years old how lime was made . . . and within a year or two I had been in a glass house and seen the red hot 'metal' twirled about the end of a long tube, blown and rolled and shaped into a bottle . . . I had seen the inside of a pottery and had watched the working of the potter's wheel and the making of cups and saucers; knew how they were kept apart in the kiln . . . and had been in the tunnel groove where the clay was found. I had paid clandestine visits to the copperas works where the green sparkle of the crust that linked the great square pits astonished and delighted. I knew the brick field . . . I knew how hemp was heckled and spun into yarn and how this was made into ships' cables.

My education was according to common rule rather neglected but I owe very much of my true education to that neglect.

(cited in Chirnside, *Sir Joseph Wilson Swan*, p. 2)

In Swan's early experiments he soaked strips of paper in treacle or tar and carbonised them by heating them in a pottery kiln. Although the resulting carbon filaments were mounted in glass bulbs and evacuated as thoroughly as possible, there was still sufficient oxygen and volatile material left to burn them out quite rapidly. Swan saw his chance when Sprengel introduced the mercury pump in 1865 and conceived the technique of 'outgassing', which has been of incalculable value in subsequent vacuum physics, especially in scientific instruments, valves and television tubes. The carbon filament was heated to incandescence and maintained in that state while the bulb was being exhausted. Within an acceptable time the volatile components had been distilled out of the filament and the bulb, which was then sealed off.

When Swan first switched on a carbon lamp at a public lecture in February 1879, he was clearly getting a bit irritated by the bombastic claims being made by Edison. His lecture breathes something of the excitement of the times:

During the last few months, no subject, scientific or even popular, has occupied so large an amount of public attention as the electric light. Not only have men of science been discussing it but, one may almost say, everybody has been talking about it, from one end of the country to the other. The subject had for some time been gradually acquiring importance and gaining more and more attention from scientific and practical men, but the crisis, if I may so call it, was reached in October of last year when the following telegram from Mr Edison to his London Agent was fulminated – 'I have just solved the problem of the Electric Light indefinitely.'

(cited in Chirnside, *Sir Joseph Wilson Swan*, p. 9)

And Swan proceeded to read a statement by Edison reported in an American newspaper:

When the brilliancy and the cheapness of the light are made known to the public – which will be in a few weeks or just as soon as I can thoroughly protect the process – illumination by carburetted hydrogen will be discarded. With 15 or 20 of the dynamo-electric machines recently perfected by Mr Wallace I can light the entire lower part of New York City using a 500 H.P. engine. I propose to instal one of these light centres in Nassau Street, whence wires can run up town as far as the Cooper Institute and be laid in the ground in the same manner as gas pipes. I also propose to use the gas burners and chandeliers now in use. In each house I can place a light meter whence these wires will pass through the house, tapping small metallic contrivances that may be placed over each burner. The housekeepers may turn off their gas and send the meters back to the Companies whence they came.

(cited in Chirnside, *Sir Joseph Wilson Swan*, p. 9)

The crash in gas company shares resulting from such proclamations was so severe that the British government set up a parliamentary committee of inquiry including such notable scientists as Tyndall, Faraday's colleague at the Royal Institution, and the panjandrum of British science, Lord Kelvin. The report of the committee relieved the feelings of anxious gas shareholders about the possible threat posed by Edison's schemes for lighting homes by electricity: . . . while these plans seem good enough for our transatlantic friends, they are unworthy of the attention of practical or scientific men.' Swan, however, had no such illusions about the future of electric lighting. He was simply concerned about Edison's beating the gun in claiming authorship of the design of the lamp filament. He wrote a restrained reply to an article in *Nature* pointing out that fifteen years earlier he had carried out experiments identical to those now described as original contributions by Edison. He added 'I am now able to make a perfectly durable lamp by means of incandescent carbon', referring to his new development of a material which he called 'parchmentised thread'. To make this 'thread', he treated cotton with sulphuric acid, converting it into a transparent, plastic fibre which when washed and dried resembled catgut. The dry fibre was then drawn through a die to make a uniform filament ready to be carbonised.

The year 1881 marked the coming-of-age of electric lighting. It was also the year of *Patience*, Gilbert and Sullivan's operetta satirising the dandified aesthetes of the period — the Whistlers and the Wildes — as well as the brutal and licentious soldiery, the Soldiers of the Queen. The successful opening in London in April was quickly followed up by productions in New York and Sydney. Richard D'Oyly Carte, the producer, ensured its success in America by sending Oscar Wilde on a lecture tour so that American audiences could be introduced to the concept of an exquisitely attired poet sporting a green carnation; he presumably thought such publicity either unnecessary or undesirable for the visit to Australia. On 10 October, Carte moved *Patience* to a new and splendid theatre in the heart of London, the Savoy. The Prince of Wales attended the glamorous opening night but the show was stolen when the dim gaslight was extinguished, Carte closed a switch, and over a thousand gleaming electric lamps burst into light.

'I have been convinced', Carte wrote in his prospectus, 'that electric light

SPECIAL NOTICE.

THE arrangements for the production of the Electric Light are not yet perfected. The contractors hope to be able to light the *auditorium* by electricity this evening; but the *stage* will be lighted by gas as usual, as will also the Theatre generally, should everything not be ready. It has never before been attempted to light nearly so many as 1,200 incandescent burners as a single undertaking. A few days longer will probably perfect the arrangements, and the fact will be advertised.

R. D'OYLY CARTE,
Proprietor and Manager, Savoy Theatre.

A light and airy young thing   Early Effects of Electric Lighting

This Room Is Equipped With

Edison Electric Light.

Do not attempt to light with match. Simply turn key on wall by the door.

The use of Electricity for lighting is in no way harmful to health, nor does it affect the soundness of sleep.

in some form is the light of the future . . . There are several extremely good incandescent lamps, but I finally decided to adopt that of Mr J. W. Swan, the well-known inventor of Newcastle-on-Tyne. The enterprise of Messrs Siemens has enabled me to try the experiment of exhibiting this light in my theatre. About 1200 lights are used, and the power to generate a sufficient current for these is obtained from large steam-engines, giving about 120 horsepower . . . This is the first time that it has been attempted to light any public building entirely by electricity.'

(Baily, *The Gilbert and Sullivan Book*, p. 188)

In the following year Edison's power stations in London and New York were brought into commission. The age of domestic electric lighting had begun. Ambitious householders immediately converted to the new system and displayed notices on the walls of their rooms proclaiming that they were in the vanguard of fashion.

After the initial shock of the new electric rival, the gas companies were again doing quite nicely, but the gasworkers were not. Long hours, poor pay and other hardships were common enough in industry at that time, and the gasworkers had their full share of atrocious conditions. The response in England was recalled by Will Thorne, a man who received no education as a child, and who was taught reading and writing by Karl Marx' daughter, Eleanor. He subsequently became the Member of Parliament for West Ham, and years later he described the turning-point which came for him in 1889 at the Beckton Gasworks in London:

Generally the men had no food, because when they left home they did not know that they would have to stay on and work later. There was a big canteen adjacent to the works where sometimes food and drink were obtainable, but when the eighteen-hour shift was finished, the men living at Poplar and Canning Town ... had a walk of nearly four miles. This caused a great deal of annoyance and, on top of other slave-driving methods, caused the men to get desperate. They were almost prepared to go on strike, even though they had no union behind them. I saw the time was ripe ... A few of us got together; I gave them my views and we held a meeting on March 31st, 1889 ... A resolution was passed in favour of a gasworkers' union being formed, with the eight-hour day as one of its objects ...

After the meeting was over we started to take down the names of the men who wanted to join up. Eight hundred joined that morning. The entrance fee was one shilling, and we had to borrow several pails to hold the coppers and other coins that were paid in ...

The news of the meeting spread like wildfire; in the public houses, factories and works everyone was talking about the union ... For months London was ablaze. The newspapers throughout the country were giving good reports of our activities. They were curious to know what we wanted and what we were going to do.

I knew what we were going to do. I kept in mind all the time my pledge to the men at the first meeting. To work and fight for the eight-hour day – that was my first objective, soon to be won.

(cited in Hobsbawm, *Labour's Turning Point, 1880-1900*, p. 79)

The time was, indeed, ripe. Even in that obscure corner of the lighting industry devoted to making matches, conditions were recognised as intolerable. In an oral history of the London underworld, Arthur Harding recounts his early life with his parents and five other children living in a single room, his father a drunken beggar and his mother paying the rent by making eight gross of matchboxes at 1s 6d a day for the firm of Bryant and May. That was in 1890.

At Bryant and May's main factory in London, 700 unorganised 'match girls' surprisingly and spontaneously came out on strike. Emotions had been aroused by a fierce denunciation of their work conditions by Mrs Annie Besant, a socialist who later went to India and became President of the Indian National Congress. To her astonishment the women at Bryant and May's read her article and struck. Their immediate grievance was a deduction of a few pence from their wages, which they thought unwarranted, but it was their discontent with their work conditions that gave them solidarity and the strength to win their fight.

These were symptoms of a new stage in the Industrial Revolution. Western Europe was harnessing the forces of science and prospering as never before. The enterprises of England, France and Germany were pouring out wealth in profusion, and the uneven distribution of that wealth was the very mainspring of their capitalist systems. Sir Humphrey Davy had laid it clearly on the line while he was Director of the Royal Institution: 'The unequal division of property and labour, the differences of rank and condition among mankind, are the sources of power in civilized life, its moving causes and even its very soul.'

'Devil take the hindmost!' became the watchcry of the industrial entrepreneur, who latched on to the fast growing industries, newly stimulated by the discoveries in electricity, chemistry, and optics. 'We shall not be the hindmost' was the response of the workers in those industries, and they started organising themselves into trade unions with the avowed aims of a legal minimum wage, an eight-hour day and a guaranteed right to work. A long, continuing war began between the unions, the employers, and the government.

One particularly savage battle in this war, the British General Strike of 1926 in support of the coal miners, showed the importance that artificial lighting had acquired in the life of a modern nation. The trade unions called out their most powerful battalions on the first day of the strike: the transport workers, whether on land, sea or in the air; the whole printing trade; the metalworkers; the chemical workers; and the general building workers. The electrical and gas workers supplying power for industry were also called out. The only major exceptions were sanitary and health workers, builders working on hospitals or houses, and the workers engaged in supplying gas or electric light. It is intriguing to speculate whether the list would be different were there a general strike today. Would the workers in radio and television, for instance, be exempt?

While all this union activity was going on, a completely new industry, the production of synthetic fibres, had emerged quite unexpectedly from a superior method of making carbon filaments. Swan's method doubled the efficiency of the lamps but it also produced what for once could accurately be described as a spin-off. And in the long run the spin-off turned out to be far more important than the product itself. Swan first made fine filaments by squirting a sticky solution through a small hole in the way that a spider spins its web. This idea had been suggested in 1664 by Robert Hooke, a brilliant physicist and curator of experiments to the Royal Society. Swan started with cellulose, a natural polymer whose long-chain molecules are packed together side-by-side to form the tough fibres of plants and trees. The pure cellulose − in this case white blotting paper − was dissolved in a zinc chloride solution and squirted through a die into alcohol. As cellulose is insoluble in alcohol, the solution coagulated in threads which were then drawn to the required size through a second die. Heating the threads to about 1500°C gave finer and more uniform carbon filaments than any other process yet devised.

But if the process is stopped just before the carbonisation stage, a fine, colourless thread of extremely high strength and of any desired length is produced. Swan recognised that he had found a potentially valuable fibre for textiles. He had some of it crocheted into lace for a display at the 1885 Inventions Exhibition in Paris, and though he himself went back to working on lamp filaments there was a great future for the fibre. This 'artificial silk', as it was called before the generic term *rayon* became popular, established itself in the first decades of this century as the leading synthetic fibre. At the same time the carbon in filament lamps was being superseded by tungsten. Today, surprisingly, forty-five carbon-filament lamps are still kept at the National Bureau of Standards in Washington; these lamps are there not just to record history but also to provide the International Standard of Light Intensity.

The main factors governing the growth of the electric lamp industry were the initial cost and the length of life of the lamp. But the efficiency with which the input energy was converted into light energy was also important, and Table 1.1 shows clearly the continuous development of improved sources of light.

The dramatic increase in efficiency shown by the gas-discharge lamps was achieved only after at least eighty years of trial-and-error research. When sources of high voltage and good vacuum pumps became available in the nineteenth century many scientists combined the two to investigate the colourful phenomena produced by electrical discharges in glass tubes containing different gases at a low pressure. In 1910 Georges Claude in France made the first red neon display tubes. In the 1920s, following his further work with argon, krypton and other gases, the big cities were ablaze with the brightly coloured messages of the Consumer Age.

Source	Output (lumens per watt)
Candle	0.1
Gas mantle	2
Carbon arc	7
Electric lamp	
early carbon filament	2
squirted cellulose filament	3
tungsten, vacuum	9
tungsten, gas-filled coiled coil	15
Domestic warm-white fluorescent lamp	64
Sodium vapour discharge street lamp	150

From the consumer's viewpoint the efficiency also depends upon the cost per watt of the power. Illumination with candles bought in a developed country may cost ten thousand times as much as an electric lamp *for the same amount of light.*

Table 1.1: Efficiency of light sources

But these colourful discharges were of little use for ordinary domestic lighting. In the light of a mercury vapour lamp, for instance, a face takes on a greenish hue with nearly black lips. We really want to see everything in sunlight, the 'white' light that Newton decomposed into the spectral rainbow colours with his prism. The light from a gaseous discharge contains only a very few colours — mostly blue and green in the case of mercury vapour. So an ingenious way was found of adding further colours to make the light 'whiter'. But a large part of the energy of the discharge was in the form of ultraviolet light, invisible and therefore wasted from the viewpoint of lighting. The trick is to coat the inside of the tube with a fluorescent powder which can absorb the ultraviolet and convert it into visible light. The lamp is made more efficient — for the same wattage it is brighter — but more significantly its colour has been changed. Starting with a basic 'phosphor' powder, such as zinc or cadmium sulphide, the colour can be adjusted by adding small amounts of antimony for blue, manganese for yellow, and so on.

The addition of a phosphor is also responsible for the surprising but justifiable claim that some detergent powders can 'wash whiter than white'. A white shirt will retain a small amount of the fluorescent ingredient; when daylight falls on it the invisible ultraviolet is converted into visible light so that the treated shirt really does look brighter.

Until recently the blending of ingredients to produce any particular colour of a fluorescent lamp was a kind of black magic achieved by chance and enshrined in trade secrets. But the theory of colour vision put forward by Thomas Young early in the nineteenth century has prompted the development of a novel and very promising type of fluorescent light. Young concluded that all of the complex colours we perceive are broken down by the receptors in our eyes into combinations of only three basic colours, which are then interpreted by the brain as the appropriate colour sensation. This astonishing insight could not be tested until the necessary microanalytical techniques were developed in the 1960s, but it was then found that Young was correct. However, the three basic colours were not pure colours each of a single wavelength: one was primarily in the blue-violet range, the next was in the green and the third was in the orange-red.

Having discovered the colour ranges, the next trick was to find three phosphors whose light outputs would match the colour sensitivities of the three kinds of receptors in the retina. Phosphors based on strontium, yttrium and europium seem to give a good match and tubes made from such phosphors look as bright as normal tubes although using only about half the power. Moreover it is reported that when they are tested in department stores the meats look redder, the fabrics brighter, the dollar bills crisper, and the smiles of the sales people broader.

This development, like that of the laser, the hologram or the atomic bomb, is one of those rare achievements that come from a fundamental understanding of the problem and can hardly be achieved by trial and error. The laser, in particular, required a deeper understanding of light than the nineteenth century yielded. Yet this concentration of optical engineering upon such subtleties as colour matching emphasises how successful the nineteenth-century scientists and inventors were in solving the basic physical problems of lighting houses, streets, theatres and cities. It takes a conscious effort to remind ourselves what life was like before this technological revolution took place: what a winter's day really meant when the darkness that set in by late afternoon was not lifted for fourteen or fifteen hours; and why Shakespeare's plays were only performed in the daytime. Today the primary problems in lighting are of a different kind − economic, engineering, social, or political: how, for example, to provide good lighting for the millions who are still lacking it?

But to understand the light fantastic we must go back, back to the beginning of the nineteenth century, to the discovery of the wave nature of light, the prelude to the exploitation of the waves of 'invisible light' especially the waves of radio or of X-rays.

2

The Young Phenomenon

Light as a wave

To the passenger drooping over the ship's rail, the ocean seems to consist entirely of waves.

2

March the seventh 1799 was a bright spring day in London town. For nearly an hour the carriages of the nobility and the gentry had been drawing up in Soho Square and allowing their elegant passengers to descend into the home of Sir Joseph Banks, President of the Royal Society and popularly known as 'The Father of Australia'. The last carriage had now gone and the turbulent crowd that had gathered to watch and to cheer or jeer at the spectacle was being dispersed by the footmen. In the huge reception room, the light from its chandeliers gleaming on the glass cases of strange plants and insects acquired on his voyages to far-away Canada, Australia and Iceland, Sir Joseph was addressing fifty of the country's most eminent and philanthropic citizens.

Each had donated fifty guineas to become a proprietor of a project which was, Banks reminded them,

a Proposal to form by Private Subscription, an Establishment for Feeding the Poor, and giving them Useful Employment . . . connected with an Institution for introducing and bringing forward into general Use of new Inventions and Improvements, particularly such as relate to the Management of Heat and the Saving of Fuel . . .

(cited in Bence Jones, *The Royal Institution*, pp. 44-5)

In the previous century Francis Bacon had envisaged a world uplifted by the benefits science could bring — *A New Atlantis* he had called his utopia. But the situation was now more urgent. Poverty and unemployment were widespread. The new textile machines had so far brought more suffering than benefit. There was a crying need not only for the

Statue in Munich of Benjamin Thompson, Count Rumford of the Holy Roman Empire, Knight of the White Eagle

humane advancement of science but also for a more generous system of education so that everyone could gain advantage from the new technology. Satisfying these needs would be central to the work of their institution — the Royal Institution as they hoped it would be called, given the gracious approval of His Majesty the King. And now Banks had

pleasure in introducing to them the author of this great proposal, a
worthy successor to Francis Bacon himself, Sir Benjamin Thompson,
Count Rumford of the Holy Roman Empire, Knight of the Order of the
White Eagle.

For the man who now stood up — adventurer, physicist, social
reformer in Bavaria, exiled from his native America for fighting with the
British against the rebellious colonists — this moment was the crowning
point of his colourful life. His dream of launching the first institute of
technology was about to come true. Eagerly and with great conviction
he expounded his vision:

**Our Institution will have the great purpose of bringing together the natu-
ral philosopher and those engaged in arts and manufactures in order
to improve industrial and domestic efficiency. This noble objective will
be achieved in two distinct ways: first by mounting a permanent though
changing exhibition of manufacturing aids, model kitchens and domestic appliances such as fireplaces. The industrial processes of brewing,
distilling, cement manufacture, spinning, weaving and agriculture will
be represented. Working models of that most curious and most useful
machine, the steam engine will be displayed. All such models will be
provided with specifications, work drawings, the name of the manufacturer and the price.**

**The second endeavour will lie in the provision of a well-equipped
laboratory and a large lecture room where the application of scientific
discoveries to the improvements of arts and manufactures in this
country, and to the increase of domestic comfort and convenience, will
be taught. Lecturers of the first eminence in science will be engaged to
teach on subjects such as:**

> **Heat and its Application to the various Purposes of Life**
> **The Combustion of Inflammable Bodies**
> **The Management of Fire and the Economy of Fuel**
> **The Means of making Dwelling Houses comfortable and salubrious**
> **The Methods of procuring and preserving Ice in Summer**
> **The Chemical Principles of Tanning, Soap-making, Bleaching,**
>   **Dyeing and other manufacturing Processes . . .**

                    (cited in Sparrow, *Knight of the White Eagle*, p. 111)

Despite Rumford's impassioned advocacy there was opposition right
from the start. Voices were heard warning of the dangers of educating
the lower orders beyond their station in life. More serious was the

hostility of the manufacturers who were never likely to divulge their valuable secrets by supplying working models with drawings of their best designs.

'Your object' said one, **'is one that every practical inventor ought to discountenance. You would destroy the value of the labour of the industrious; by laying open his invention you would take away the great stimulus to invention ... this would be ruinous to individuals and would ultimately interfere with the commercial prosperity of Britain ...'**
(Sparrow, *Knight of the White Eagle*, p. 129)

The wealthy industrialist Matthew Boulton thought that the Count's philosophy had got the better of his judgement:

To the philosophical dilettante who employs only his time and talent in pursuit of knowledge the fame of his discoveries may be a satisfactory reward, but to the manufacturer who expends his Capital as well as his skill and labour with a view to Emolument, the possession of his improvements can alone afford him a proportionate remuneration.
(cited in Sparrow, *Knight of the White Eagle*, p. 128)

Nevertheless the proprietors at the meeting supported the proposals, partly because a technically competent workforce was clearly going to be needed for the coming age of the machine, partly as a genuine attempt to alleviate human misery, and partly because the Institution could act as a safety-valve for the unpredictable consequences if the sufferings of the lower orders became unbearable. All of these reasons were congenial to Rumford. He was a dyed-in-the-wool Tory, and appeared to be delighted when King George III agreed to be the Patron of this Royal Institution. But behind the appearances he must surely have feared for the future of his brainchild under the patronage of the despotic monarch who was ruling England like a police state, forbidding public meetings and locking up or transporting to New South Wales anyone who ventured to speak out against him. A less desirable patron of the kind of institution that Rumford wanted could scarcely be imagined. Buckle's famous but merciless description of George III portrays him to be lacking in the very qualities that the Institution most required:

Every liberal sentiment, every thing approaching to reform, nay, even

the mere mention of inquiry, was an abomination in the eyes of that narrow and ignorant prince. Without knowledge, without taste, without even a glimpse of one of the sciences, or a feeling for one of the fine arts, education had done nothing to enlarge a mind which nature had more than usually contracted.

(Buckle, *History of Civilization in England*, I, p.360)

Thus it was that the Royal Institution of Great Britain was launched, and it got under way in splendid style with lectures on physics, mechanics and chemistry to packed-out audiences. An additional lecturer was needed and Rumford appointed a young Cornishman, only twenty-two years old, who had just published a paper entitled 'An Essay on Heat, Light and the Combinations of Light'. This was Humphrey Davy, the future inventor of the arc lamp and of the miners' safety lamp, President of the Royal Society, and discoverer of sodium and potassium. (It is often said, however, that his greatest discovery was Michael Faraday.) The Minute Book of the Institution for 23 February 1801 shows the managers' resolution

That Mr Humphrey Davy be engaged in the service of the R.I. in the capacities of Assistant Lecturer in Chemistry, Director of the Chemical Laboratory and Assistant Editor of the Journals of the Institution and that he be allowed to occupy a Room in the House and be furnished with Coal and Candles and that he be paid a salary of One Hundred Guineas per Annum.

(cited in Sparrow, *Knight of the White Eagle*, p. 123)

Perhaps it was the long evenings spent by candlelight that motivated Davy to invent arc lighting, the first form of lighting by electricity. But this was a minor affair compared to the complete revolution in the understanding of the nature of light brought about by Rumford's next appointment, a twenty-eight-year-old doctor named Thomas Young. And though Young was not the best man for the job — he stayed for only two years — he was certainly the best man to lead this revolution.

'Phenomenon Young' he was called by his fellow students at Cambridge and a phenomenon he was, almost from the day he was born, the first of his Quaker parents' ten children. Young was reading fluently by the time he was two, and had read the entire Bible twice by the time he was four; the next year he began writing and made a start on Latin.

Sacred to the Memory of
THOMAS YOUNG, M.D.

Fellow and Foreign Secretary of the Royal Society,
Member of the National Institute of France;

A man alike eminent
in almost every department of human learning.
Patient of unintermitted labour,
endowed with the faculty of intuitive perception,
who, bringing an equal mastery
to the most abstruse investigations
of letters and of science,
First established the undulatory theory of light,
and first penetrated the obscurity
which had veiled for ages
the Hieroglyphics of Egypt.

Endeared to his friends by his domestic virtues,
Honoured by the world for his unrivalled acquirements,
He died in hopes of the resurrection of the just.

Born at Milverton, in Somersetshire, June 13th, 1773,
Died in Park Square, London, May 10th, 1829
In the 56th year of his age.
(memorial in Westminster Abbey; by Gurney)

At seven he was sent to school, though his powers of self-education perhaps made this experience superfluous. By fourteen he knew Latin, Greek, French, Italian, Hebrew, Arabic and Persian. He read widely in literature and the classics, mathematics, physics and biology. He studied the construction of scientific instruments and learned how to use a lathe, to mix colours and to bind books.

At nineteen he went to London to study medicine and made his first important discovery — how the human eye can focus sharply on a nearby object then immediately on one that is far away and see it with equal sharpness. This marvellous *power of accommodation* we take for granted when we are young but it sadly declines as we grow older. Young explained this focusing mechanism so convincingly and with such a wealth of physiological detail that he was elected a Fellow of the Royal Society when he was twenty-one.

During the last year of his medical course, now at Göttingen, Young wrote a thesis on the physical and mathematical theory of sound. As an aside he proposed an alphabet of forty-seven letters which he claimed could express every sound that the human voice can make. But his interest in wave motion had been aroused and in 1799 he made so bold as to read a paper to the Royal Society in which he argued the case that light, just like sound, was propagated as some sort of wave motion. Too bold, perhaps, because nothing could be said to the scientists of the eighteenth century that appeared to contradict the great Newton, any more than in the Middle Ages the great Aristotle could be contradicted, or, in earlier times still, the great Pythagoras. The lecture aroused furious opposition. Young avowed that he would prepare and present a fuller and more convincing account of his theory, but he was then occupied with his practice as a physician and it was fortunate that Rumford came along just at that moment and snapped him up for his two-year spell at the Royal Institution.

Phenomenon Young now moved swiftly into action. He proceeded to demolish the theory that a beam of light consisted in a stream of fiery particles, the theory that had been supported by Newton. He praised Newton's achievements as superb for their time, reserving his scorn for those who had for so long simply followed blindly in the footsteps of Newton. He also praised Hooke's work, saying that Newton was superior to Hooke only in his mathematical ability. He let Newton down very lightly:

From the time of Empedocles and of Aristotle, philosophers have been divided in their sentiments respecting the nature of light ... Newton employed the system of the emanation of separate corpuscles. The novelty and importance of his experiments, and the ingenuity of his arguments, quickly silenced all objections; yet few later opticians have been willing to admit the whole even of his essential hypotheses: although scarcely any attempt has been made to substitute more satisfactory ones in place of those which have been abandoned ...

(Young, Notebook 16, XV, 'Of the Nature of Light')

One of the strongest objections to the particle theory, Young remembered, had been the argument that when two beams of light crossed each other the particles would surely crash together so that the light would be scattered in all directions. But common experience showed that two crossed light beams did *not* obstruct each other: each beam carried straight on as if the other were not there. Young asked himself how two beams of light would overlap if they were more like waves than particles of light. He took analogies from his own researches into sound and from observations of tides and water waves. In these cases two waves meeting at a point can either give an increased effect or cancel each other out depending on which way they are actually waving at that point (you can study this on a lake or in a bath). In Young's words, when

. . . the elevations of one series coincide with those of the other, they must together produce a series of greater joint elevations; but if the elevations of one series are so situated as to correspond to the depressions of the other, they must exactly fill up those depressions, and the surface of the water must remain smooth.

Now I maintain that similar effects take place whenever two portions of light are thus mixed; and this I call the general law of the interference of light.

(cited in Arons, *Development of The Concept of Physics*, p. 620)

Young knew that with this *theory of interference* he had come very close to the true nature of light. All of those beautiful investigations of the colours of thin films, of oil on water, of insects' wings or Newton's rings, for which Newton had needed such contrived explanations, now fell into place (see Figure 2.1). Light inescapably had the characteristics of a wave motion.

Within a few months of joining the Royal Institution Young presented his celebrated paper 'On the theory of Light and Colours' and he went on to test and apply the theory in other situations. He showed how the wave theory could explain the puzzling phenomenon of *diffraction*, the slight but important departure of the directions of light rays from the straight and narrow paths that the particle theory allowed them. Light passing a straight edge or shining through a tiny hole in a card, for example, is bent ever so slightly away from its original direction. Differently coloured rays are bent by different amounts and a careful examination using white light reveals that the edge of the hole is bordered by narrow coloured fringes. Newton had looked for such possible evidence of wave-like nature but − possibly owing to a deficiency in his eyesight − had failed to find it. Others had observed the fringes, but Young now used them to estimate the wavelengths of light waves of different colours:

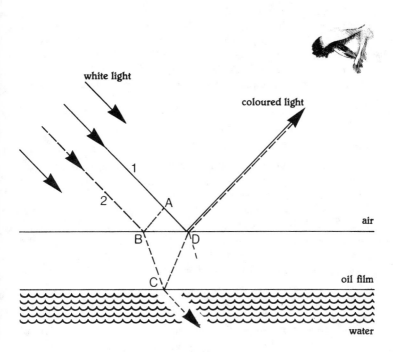

Figure 2.1: The brilliant colours of oil films or soap bubbles

White light is reflected from a thin film of oil on water. Rays 1 and 2 are in step as far as the line AB. Ray 1 then goes on to be reflected at D towards the viewing eye while ray 2 follows the path B to C to D to the eye.

At AB the rays are in phase (i.e. their waves are in step).

Ray 2 takes longer to reach D than ray 1 so the two rays are somewhat out of phase. For a certain thickness of oil film and angle of viewing, the green components of the two rays will be *exactly* out of phase: they cancel each other out and the eye sees the light with mainly the red and blue left in it, i.e. it sees a light purple patch. Other thicknesses and angles give rise to the different colours seen in oil films and soap bubbles.

Modern camera or binocular lenses have a purplish 'bloom' on their surfaces because they have been coated with a transparent film just thick enough to cancel 5 per cent or so of the yellow-green light which would otherwise be reflected at each surface. A typical ' lens ' may contain ten separate component lenses, of different glasses, and it would normally lose well over half the incident light by reflexion. 'Blooming' the surfaces cuts this loss down to only about 10 per cent.

But it will be found that one universal law prevails in all these phenomena. Where two portions of the same light arrive at the eye by different routes, either exactly or nearly in the same direction, the appearance or disappearance of various colours is determined by the greater or less difference in the lengths of their paths; the same colour recurring when the intervals are multiples of a length ... In air this length, for the extreme red rays, is about one 36 thousandth of an inch, and for the extreme violet, about one 60 thousandth.

(Young, Notebook 16, XIV, 'Of Physical Optics', 376)

Light was behaving as a wave, with a wavelength − the distance between successive crests of the wave − ranging, in modern parlance, from about 700 nanometres (nm) for red light (one thousand million nanometres equal one metre) to 420 nm for violet.

This fundamental scientific achievement did not mean that Young was being disloyal to the avowedly practical aims of Rumford's Institution. On the contrary, in the two years of his stay he also worked out the theory of colour vision, devised the formula for measuring kinetic energy, and lectured on the principles and practices of such diverse matters as mechanics and dynamics, the strength and elasticity of materials, architecture, the use of wheels and ropes, hammering, forging, drilling, hydrostatics and hydrodynamics, pumps and fountains, spiders, carpentry, and his old favourite, the physics of sound. All of these he wrote up on request in the form of two huge volumes, well over a thousand pages of text and illustrations, including nearly five hundred articles on mathematics. Alas when *Dr Young's Lectures in Natural Philosophy and the Mechanical Arts* finally appeared in 1807 it was too late for Young to get the £1000 which he had been promised on publication − the publishers had gone bankrupt.

But in 1803 Young performed an experiment of classic simplicity which put the wave-like nature of light beyond possible doubt; it remains a key experiment even in the twentieth-century discussions of light in terms of the quantum theory of matter and radiation. He made a small hole in the window blind to serve as a tiny, homogeneous source of sunlight. Then he pierced a card twice with the point of a pin and placed it so that sunlight from the hole in the blind could pass through the pinholes onto a screen (see Figure 2.2). There, right in the middle where the images of the two pinholes overlapped, was the conclusive evidence he had been seeking: the area was crossed by a series of coloured bands with exactly the same curved (hyperbolic) shapes as the rippled patterns on the surface of a lake where two sets of water waves meet. Young had proved that the two beams of light from the two pinholes must indeed be two beams of light *waves*. And from the geometry of that simple arrangement he showed again that the wavelength of violet light is about 400 nm while the red waves are nearly twice as long.

What a triumph for Young! It must surely have brought immediate glory to his Institution. In fact it wasn't and it didn't. Science, scientists and society are not like that. His papers to the Royal Society were ill received and he was strongly criticised, though more for his presumption in opposing the particle theory of Newton than for his own arguments. His position at the Institution had been already weakened by the unfortunate lack of success of his lectures. After Humphrey Davy, Young appeared to be dull and didactic. He was acutely aware of this weakness and was reduced at times to an apologetic state that many must have felt but few have made so bold as to express:

I am conscious how ineffectual it would be for me to attempt to show that this course of lectures has been all that it ought to have been; and how unnecessary it is on the other hand to assure you that I have not been wanting in my efforts to make it less defective. To prepare fifty lectures on subjects so widely detached from each other, and often so obscure and so little understood in themselves, is a task which instead of four months might well occupy as many years. Under the weight of so anxious and laborious an undertaking it has not been possible for

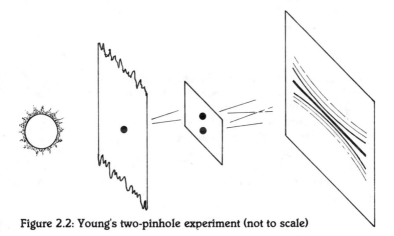

Figure 2.2: Young's two-pinhole experiment (not to scale)

me to arrange a single lecture to my own satisfaction, and my audience has perhaps often been fatigued with insipidity or disgusted with inelegance . . .

(cited in Cantor, 'Thomas Young's Lectures
at the Royal Institution', pp. 92-3)

At this time, the managers of the Royal Institution were not interested in the least in Young's plans for his next series of lectures. They were fully occupied with sabotaging Rumford's aims of helping the poor and increasing industrial efficiency; their own aim was rather to provide an intellectual playground for the fashionable and well-to-do. Ironically they succeeded, without realising it, in creating one of the world's great centres of fundamental research, a centre which would become illustrious through the work not only of Davy and Young, but equally of their successors: Faraday, Tyndall, Dewar, the Braggs, both father and son, Bernal and others. The irony lies in the fact that the nineteenth and early twentieth centuries were exactly the right periods to explore the fundamentals and thus lay the basis for achieving Rumford's aims on a far wider scale than he could ever have imagined. Such a cornucopia of dividends — from electroplating, new elements, wave optics and colour vision, through transformers, dynamos and electric motors to dyes, colloids, X-rays and the structure of crystals — is unlikely ever to be provided again by basic research in physics and chemistry.

Blind to these possibilities, the managers turned against Young. Their hostility was not even softened by his proposal that the Institution should provide a scientific education for upper-class females:

The many leisure hours which are at the command of females in the superior orders of society may surely be appropriated with greater satisfaction to the improvement of the mind, and to the acquisition of knowledge, than to such amusements as are only designed for facilitating the insipid consumption of superfluous time.

The Royal Institution may in some degree supply the place of a subordinate university of those whose sex or situation in life has denied them the advantage of an academical education in the national seminaries of learning.

(cited in Bence Jones,
The Royal Institution, p. 241)

The managers became increasingly alienated from him, and in April 1803 they turned down his requests for a rise in salary and for the appointment of a librarian. Young promptly resigned, though his action was probably more in recognition of the new direction of the Institution rather than a response to these particular pinpricking issues. England was now in a state of unrest. Intolerable conditions had provoked a mutiny in the Navy; trade unions had been outlawed and any attempt to organise the workers was met with imprisonment or public whipping. In the face of falling wages and rising unemployment the Somerset shearers had started a movement to wreck the new labour-saving machinery. In such an atmosphere it is understandable that as soon as Rumford had gone abroad the managers moved swiftly to annul what they saw as his dangerously radical plans. The intended school for mechanics was abandoned, the men working on the demonstration models were dismissed, and Rumford's apparatus and workshop were destroyed. Webster, an architect who had given up his practice to join Rumford and had drawn up the plan for the school for mechanics, wrote:

I was asked rudely ... what I meant by instructing the **lower classes** ... I was told likewise that it was resolved upon that the plan must be **dropped as quietly as possible**. It was thought to have a dangerous political tendency, and I was told that if I persisted I would become a **marked man!**

Count Rumford left England about the same time, certainly neither rewarded nor thanked in proportion to the good he had done ... In short it might seem as if the managers had resolved that the Institution should **not** be for the application of sciences to the common purposes of life.

(cited in Bence Jones, *The Royal Institution*, p. 194)

So by the time that Young gave his November lecture to the Royal Society on his crucial two-pinhole experiment he was again a scientific amateur, back in his physician's practice where he seems to have been scarcely more successful than he had been as a lecturer. What would become of the wave theory of light?

For fifteen years it looked as though the wave theory was doomed to extinction. For although Young had shown how beautifully interference fits in with the wave theory, he was completely stumped by the old stumbling block of wave theory – *double refraction*. A crystal of cal-

Figure 2.3: Double refraction

cite, also known as Iceland spar, has the strange property of making you
see double (see Figure 2.3). A ray of light meeting the surface of a plate
of calcite splits into two, and two parallel rays emerge from the far side.
And these two rays are mysteriously different. If, for instance, you put
on a pair of polaroid sunglasses and look at a bright point of light through
a calcite crystal you will in general see the *two* rays as clear points of
light; but if you slowly rotate the crystal you will find that in different
positions first one of them and then the other will disappear. This sort
of observation (though not with the aid of polaroid sunglasses!) had
strengthened Newton's argument against Huygens, the champion of
the wave theory in the seventeenth century. Newton pointed out
triumphantly that the alleged light waves must have some 'sideways'
property to account for the changes observed as the crystal was turned.
It was all right to suppose that his particles could have 'sides' – perhaps
they were flat, thin things – but a wave was a wave; on the strength
of his knowledge of sound waves, he assumed that the oscillations must
be forwards and backwards in the same direction of the wave itself. They
could not be from side to side. It was not perhaps surprising that Newton
overlooked Hooke's proposal that the light waves were *transverse*

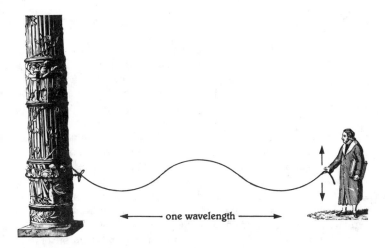

Figure 2.4: A transverse wave

waves, the kind of waves which have exactly the sideways properties
required (see Figure 2.4) because there was a deep antagonism between
the two men. But it is surprising that Huygens did not recognise this as
the key to the success of the wave theory he advocated. It is positively
astounding that it took even the phenomenal Thomas Young fifteen
years after carrying out his crucial two-pinhole experiment to realise that
Hooke's proposal of transverse waves could solve all the problems.

It was not until April of 1818 that Young wrote to his friend, the French
physicist Dominique Arago, comparing the motion of light to the waves
that pass down a stretched cord when the end is shaken up and down,
the very analogy that Hooke had used in 1671. This time, however, there
was already prepared and waiting a young Frenchman, Augustin Fresnel, who scooped up the idea and used it to establish wave theory
beyond even the strident objections of the leading scientists of the
French Académie. Fresnel showed that the idea of transverse or 'polarised' light waves accounted for diffraction and also explained the strange
behaviour of light passing through calcite. 'Polarisation' unfortunately
has other meanings, both in science and in politics, but its use in describing the behaviour of light stems from some observations made by
Colonel Malus, an engineer in Napoleon's army, who was playing with
a crystal of calcite one evening in Paris while he was watching the setting
sun reflected in the windows of the nearby Luxembourg Palace. He
could see two images of the red sun through the flat plate of crystal,

and he noticed by chance that one became brighter while the other became dimmer as he rotated the crystal.

Fresnel explained this surprising observation by supposing that the light rays had been given a sideways, polarised character simply by being reflected from the glass windows of the Palace. An ordinary beam of light, he said, contains countless polarised rays each vibrating in a sideways direction to that of the light but all at different angles to each other. No one at that time knew just what these vibrations were, but it was clear that calcite acts like a screen which lets the vibrations in one particular direction through into one beam, and the vibrations at right angles to that into the second beam. Similarly polaroid spectacles screen off reflected light, which is vibrating in one particular direction, and that is why they can be used to look right through the surface of the sea or a pool from which dazzlingly bright sunlight is being reflected.

In 1818 Fresnel gave the *coup de grace* to the advocates of the particle theory. He had begun to study diffraction in 1815 while in prison for fighting with the small army which tried to block Napoleon's return after his escape from Elba. By 1817 the particle theorists of the Académie had become so confident that they proposed the subject of diffraction for the next year's contest, certain that the prize would be won by a particle theorist. During the scrutiny of the entries, the mathematician Siméon Poisson noticed a consequence of Fresnel's strange and unlikely wave theory: a circular disk placed in a parallel beam of light should throw not merely a circular shadow with narrow diffraction fringes around it, as all agreed, but it should also show *a bright spot right in the middle of the shadow!* One can imagine the wise Academicians having a good old chortle over this. But it was no longer the Middle Ages; Poisson immediately arranged with Fresnel to have an experiment set up, and there, wonder of wonders, right in the middle of the dark circular shadow was the predicted bright spot of light. The Académie prize was immediately awarded to Fresnel.

Over the next eight years Fresnel developed the mathematical wave theory of light so thoroughly that the particle theory was vanquished, not to be heard of again until the twentieth century. Fresnel, now thirty years old, was elected into the Académie but, as he wrote to Young, he had none of that sensibility or that vanity which people call love of glory: 'all the compliments that I have received from Arago, Laplace and Biot never gave me so much pleasure as the discovery of a theoretic truth, of the confirmation of a calculation by experiment.' His health, though, was failing and a sad note to Young apologises for his delay in replying owing to a very grave indisposition: 'I have not yet at this moment

sufficient strength to write a letter.' In a belated recognition of his stupendous achievements the Royal Society awarded him its Rumford medal.
Arago, to whom Young had entrusted the job of delivering the medal,
found him dying and a week later he was dead.

And what of the phenomenal Doctor Young? Among his manifold
activities he had taken a particular interest in a large, black stone slab
that had been unearthed at the Nile Delta town of Rosetta by Napoleon's
soldiers in 1799. The Rosetta Stone was inscribed in Greek and also in
Egyptian characters — both the demotic, or popular, style and the mysterious hieroglyphics of the priests. Young worked on the Egyptian text,
identifying the name of Ptolemy V among other words, and he succeeded in making a major contribution to the decipherment of Egyptian
hieroglyphics in general. It was to a large extent through the work of
Young, the champion of the wave theory of light, that we were able to
penetrate ancient Egyptian history, to discover the young Pharaoh Ikhnaton and to learn about his Sun God, Aton, whose life-giving rays had
turned out to have all of the intriguing characteristics of waves.

3

S.O.S.

The discovery of radio and television

From a long view of the history of mankind — seen from, say, ten thousand years from now — there can be little doubt that the most significant event of the 19th century will be judged as Maxwell's discovery of the laws of electrodynamics.

Richard Feynman, 1963

"S. O. S."

PUNCH (*to Mr. MARCONI*). "MANY HEARTS BLESS YOU TO-DAY, SIR. THE WORLD'S DEBT
TO YOU GROWS FAST."

3

Michael Faraday believed in the unity of nature. His abiding dream was to discover connections between the great forces of the physical world — particularly between electricity, magnetism and light. In 1845, after the relationships between electricity and magnetism had been clearly established, he succeeded in demonstrating a relationship between magnetism and light. Shining a beam of polarised light through a block of glass placed between the poles of an electromagnet, he found that the direction of polarisation changed the instant that the electromagnet was switched on. A similar experiment, however, using a source of electricity instead of the electromagnet failed to reveal the connection between electricity and light that he had hoped for.

Twenty years later, though, Faraday's dream of unification was transformed by his young friend, James Clerk Maxwell, into a grand mathematical theory. It received a triumphant experimental verification, but only after both Faraday and Maxwell had died. Maxwell's memoir, *A Dynamical Theory of the Electromagnetic Field*, expressed the whole existing knowledge of electrical and magnetic phenomena in a complicated form which he later concentrated into the set of four equations shown (in a modern notation) in Figure 3.1.

These equations brought a longed-for clarification to the hitherto mysterious subjects of electricity and magnetism. Ludwig Boltzmann, one of the century's outstanding physicists, contemplating Maxwell's equations, was moved to quote from Goethe, 'Was it a god who wrote these lines . . .?' They compress a wealth of knowledge and experience into a mere four lines, and the principles they thus encapsulate govern the operation of electric motors, dynamos and transformers, as well as the transmission of signals by telegraph, radio or television. The great surprise was that they also governed the behaviour of light.

49

$\nabla \cdot E = \frac{\rho}{\epsilon_0}$ relates electric field (E) to electric charge (ρ)

$\nabla \cdot B = 0$ relates magnetic field (B) to 'magnetic charge' (which doesn't exist, so always zero)

$\nabla \times E = -\frac{\partial B}{\partial t}$ a changing magnetic field produces an electric field

$\nabla \times B = \epsilon_0 \mu_0 \frac{\partial E}{\partial t} + \mu_0 j$ a changing electric field or an electric current produces a magnetic field

ϵ_0 is an electrical constant, the permittivity
μ_0 is a magnetic constant, the permeability

Figure 3.1: Maxwell's equations

Maxwell's equations predict the existence of electromagnetic waves travelling with a speed of $\sqrt{\frac{1}{\mu_0 \epsilon_0}}$.

Maxwell took measurements of μ_0 and ϵ_0 that had already been made for the electrical industry and calculated the speed of these waves to be 300 000 kilometres a second. This was so close to the speed of light that he concluded that light is an electromagnetic wave.

The 'electromagnetic field', in Maxwell's words, is 'that part of space which contains and surrounds bodies in electric or magnetic conditions.' His equations describe the interaction of magnetic and electrically charged bodies, whether at rest or in motion, but the surprise that would have gladdened Faraday's heart came only at the end of the memoir when Maxwell showed how waves of combined electricity and magnetism can spread out through space. If an electrically charged body is shaken up and down, it creates a varying magnetic effect, a 'magnetic field', which moves outwards at a definite speed. As this magnetic field varies, it automatically creates a changing electric field at right angles to itself. But the changing electric field creates yet another magnetic field, and so on and so on. These inseparable electric and magnetic vibrations travel outwards together through space carrying the energy of the original shaking with them as they go.

The electric and magnetic vibrations are automatically at right angles to each other; and both are at right angles to the direction in which this 'electromagnetic wave' is moving, as shown in Figure 3.2. Maxwell

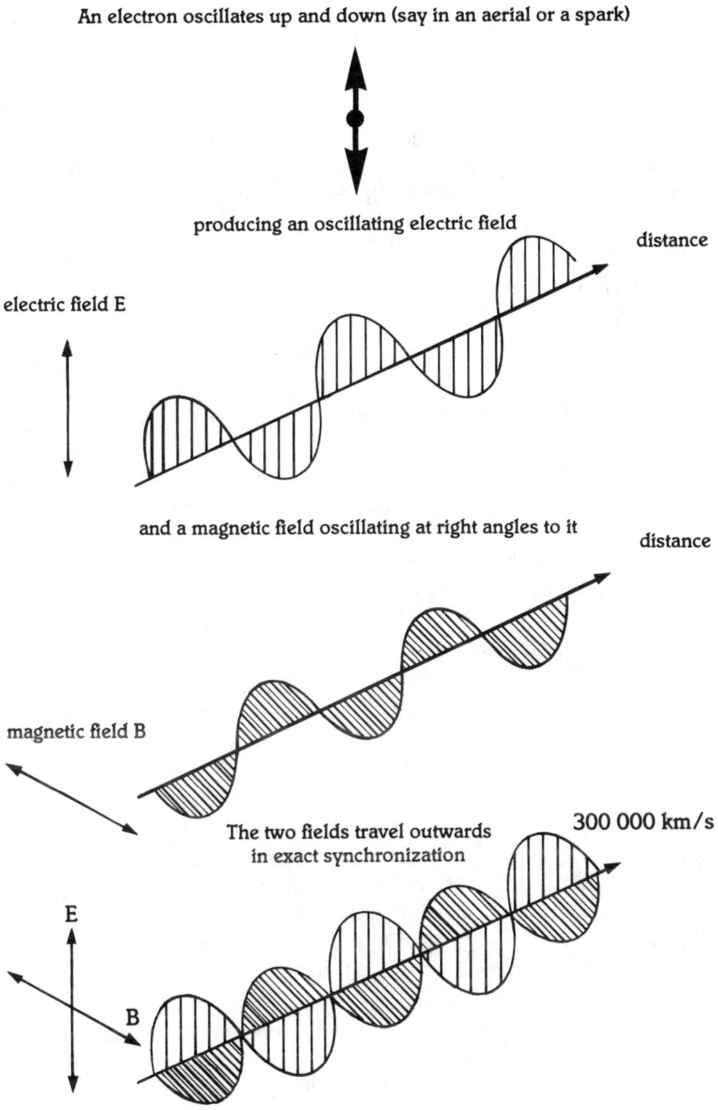

An electron oscillates up and down (say in an aerial or a spark)

producing an oscillating electric field
distance

electric field E

and a magnetic field oscillating at right angles to it
distance

magnetic field B

The two fields travel outwards
in exact synchronization
300 000 km/s

E

B

Figure 3.2: Propagation of an electromagnetic wave

worked out the case of such a transverse wave initiated by a magnetic rather than an electric disturbance, making due acknowledgement to Faraday:

The conception of the propagation of transverse magnetic disturbances ... is distinctly set forth by Professor Faraday in his Thoughts on Ray Vibrations. The electromagnetic theory of light, as proposed by him, is the same in substance as that which I have begun to develop in this paper, except that in 1846 there were no data to calculate the velocity of propagation.

(Hurd and Kipling, *The Origins and Growth of Physical Science*, II, p. 253)

Theory of *light* . . . ? Whatever has this electromagnetic wave propagation got to do with light? At first sight, nothing. But Maxwell proceeded to calculate the speed with which electromagnetic waves travelled. He was able to do this calculation because, as he said, the necessary data were now known. They had already been determined with considerable accuracy because of their importance to the rapidly growing electrical industry. Maxwell obtained a correspondingly accurate value for the speed of propagation of electromagnetic waves through space: close to 300 000 kilometres per second. This sounded a fantastic speed. Perhaps too fantastic to be credible, were it not that just three years previously the French physicist Jean Foucault had used his rotating-mirror method to measure the speed of light in air with an accuracy of better than 0.2 per cent and the value he had obtained was 298 000 kilometres per second. Could that possibly be a coincidence? Maxwell thought not. Light, he decided, is not just *related* to electricity and magnetism: it is *identical* with them — a bundle of electric and magnetic transverse vibrations travelling through space together at that tremendous velocity. 'This velocity', he wrote, 'is so nearly that of light, that it seems we have strong reason to conclude that light itself (including radiant heat, and other radiations, if any) is an electromagnetic disturbance in the form of waves'. Thus at one swoop Maxwell had not only achieved the unification of electricity, magnetism and light, he had also opened the door to the possible existence of other forms of electromagnetic radiation, forms which could be thought of as 'invisible light' because they cannot be seen by the human eye. These 'other radiations' would be found to include ultraviolet light, as well as hitherto undiscovered forms such as radio waves and X-rays.

But how could there be any 'other radiations' if they are all simply electromagnetic waves travelling at the same speed? The colours in the visible spectrum differ by having differing wavelengths; as Young found, they range from about 400 nanometres for violet light to 700 nanometres for the red. Perhaps there could be radiations with wavelengths outside this range? It was already supposed that heat radiation had wavelengths greater than 700 nanometres because a thermometer bulb placed just *beyond* the red end of the spectrum thrown by a prism showed a rise in temperature. That alone was not enough: scientists demanded experimental proof that these unseen radiations existed; they must be generated and be shown to have the same sorts of properties as light. Such experimental proof was not readily forthcoming. Faraday died in 1867 and Maxwell in 1879, but still the theory of electromagnetic waves was regarded as a rather dubious though fascinating hypothesis. Not until 1887 was the required experimental evidence provided. The young German physicist, Heinrich Hertz, conclusively demonstrated the existence of electromagnetic waves. He showed how to produce such waves with wavelengths much greater than those of the visible spectrum, and thereby opened the door into the world of radio and television.

Hertz used an induction coil, similar to the coil on a motor car but having a vibrating spring as a contact breaker, to generate electric sparks. The coil was connected to two brass balls which formed a spark gap as shown in Figure 3.3a. The balls were fixed to long brass rods which were intended to act as aerials. To detect whether any electromagnetic waves were emitted from this primitive spark-transmitter, Hertz used a secondary spark gap with its own aerial as shown in Figure 3.3b. As any received signals would be very weak, he made the secondary gap small and adjustable.

One end of the wire carried a polished brass sphere a few millimetres in diameter; the other end was pointed, and could be brought up, by means of a fine screw insulated from the wire, to within an exceedingly short distance from the brass sphere. As will be readily understood, we have here to deal only with minute sparks of a few hundredths of a millimetre in length; and after a little practice one judges more according to the brilliancy than the length of the sparks.

(Hurd and Kipling, *The Origins and Growth of Physical Science*, II, p. 253)

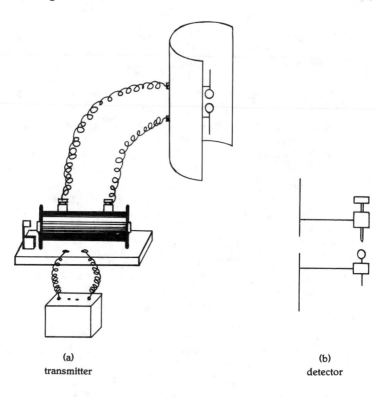

(a)   (b)
transmitter   detector

Figure 3.3: Hertz' apparatus for generating and receiving radio waves (1888)

The experiments were an immediate success. Hertz observed sparks in the secondary gap at distances of several metres from the transmitter. Enhancing the effect by using parabolic 'mirrors' made from zinc sheet enabled him to detect the waves at a much greater distance — even in the next room. The waves could be blocked by metal sheets or by human bodies, but not by insulating materials:

If a screen of sheet zinc 2 metres high and 1 metre broad is placed on the straight line joining both mirrors, and at right angles to the direction of the ray, the secondary sparks disappear completely. An equally com-

plete shadow is thrown by a screen of tinfoil or gold-paper. If an assistant walks across the path of the ray, the secondary spark-gap becomes
dark as soon as he intercepts the ray, and again lights up when he leaves
the path clear. Insulators do not stop the ray – it passes right through
a wooden partition or door; and it is not without astonishment that one
sees the sparks appear inside a closed room.

(Hurd and Kipling, *The Origins and
Growth of Physical Science*, II, p. 260)

Hertz proceeded to complete the identification of his electromagnetic
rays as an invisible form of light by demonstrating that they displayed
the phenomena of polarisation; of reflection from plane and curved surfaces; and even, using a huge prism of pitch weighing over half a tonne,
of refraction. By setting up an interference experiment, he showed that
the wavelength of the waves received by his detector was 66 centimetres, a million times the wavelength of red light.

Unbeknown to Hertz, his work had been anticipated seven years
earlier in England by David Hughes, who had used a primitive form of
microphone to detect signals from a spark transmitter at a distance of
800 metres. He maintained that the signals were transmitted through
the intervening space by means of electric waves. Unfortunately for him,
the group of eminent scientists attending the demonstration, including
the Chief Electrician of the Post Office and the President of the Royal
Society, took the view that the reception of signals even from 800 metres
away could be explained by ordinary electrical theory, and therefore did
not prove that the hypothetical electric waves actually existed.

Hertz' experiments were much more comprehensive, showing not
merely transmission but also the other wave-like phenomena – reflection, refraction, polarisation and interference – and were much harder
to dismiss. They were repeated successfully by workers in Italy and in
England, and the claims he made were accepted even before his death
in 1894 at the age of thirty-six.

We have applied the term rays of electric force to the phenomena which
we have investigated. We may perhaps further designate them as rays
of light of very great wavelength. The experiments described seem to
me, at any rate, eminently adapted to remove any doubt as to the identity of light, radiant heat, and electro-magnetic wave-motion. I believe
that from now on we shall have greater confidence in making use of

the advantages which this identity enables us to derive both in the study of optics and of electricity.

(Hurd and Kipling, *The Origins and Growth of Physical Science*, II, p. 266)

The great benefit flowing from this work was the recognition of a way of sending signals from one place to another without the use of wires. The idea of using the 'Hertzian waves' for this wire-less transmission, also known as radio, came to the Russian physicist Alexander Popov and to the Italian electrical engineer Guglielmo Marconi. As so often happens, the military applications of science were to the forefront, and in 1897 both Russian and Italian warships were using experimental radio systems for signalling over distances of several kilometres. But Popov, the physicist, was more interested in using the detection of electromagnetic waves to study the physics of thunderstorms. It was left to Marconi, the engineer, to pursue the domestic and commercial applications of radio. His successes began in 1898 when one aged British physicist, Lord Kelvin, paid for the first radio-telegram ('Marconigram') to be sent to an even older British physicist, Sir George Stokes. Telegraphy at that time was of immense social importance, but even it was dwarfed by Marconi's main achievements which lay in the field of broadcasting.

I'll put a girdle round the earth in forty minutes
I'll put it much quicker than that — G. Marconi, 10th Jan. 1911

Weekly Dispatch

109TH YEAR · SUNDAY JULY 31, 1910. · SUNDAY SPECIAL EDITION. · ONE PENNY.

CRIPPEN'S LIFE AT SEA DESCRIBED BY 'WIRELESS.'

CRIPPEN'S LIFE AT SEA DAY BY DAY.

DESCRIBED BY CAPTAIN KENDALL OF THE MONTROSE.

FULL EXCLUSIVE "WIRELESS" TO "THE DAILY MAIL."

THE BOOKS CRIPPEN READS AND THE SONG HE LIKED.

WHY HE FAILED TO ANSWER THE NAME "ROBINSON."

Marconi repeatedly hit the headlines with dramatic rescues from ships wrecked at sea following radioed SOS calls. The survivors from the *Titanic* disaster in 1912 owed their lives to the distress calls that were picked up by other ships within range. And a blaze of publicity surrounded the arrest of Dr Crippen in 1910, following a wireless message to Scotland Yard from the captain of the *SS Montrose* who had identified the suspected murderer among his passengers. Marconi's first ambition – to break through the isolation of those at sea – was thus amply fulfilled, and he turned his mind next towards the formation of a world-wide network of wireless communication.

The 11th of December 1901 is generally taken as the birthday of radio. On that day Marconi successfully transmitted signals across the Atlantic, from Poldhu in Cornwall to St John's in Newfoundland. No respectable theoretical physicist would ever have planned this fantastic experiment. Electromagnetic waves, like light, travel more or less in straight lines, their path being modified in certain situations by diffraction. But even at the wavelengths of several thousand metres that Marconi was using, the diffraction would be far too small to bend the waves round from Cornwall to Newfoundland. Marconi believed from his preliminary experiments that some unknown effect would enable the signals to reach their destination, and it turned out that he was right. Layers of charged particles in the upper atmosphere acted like the zinc sheets in the experiments of Hertz and reflected the upward-travelling waves down towards earth again.

The next twenty years witnessed many technical developments, especially the use of electronic valves for amplification, and the gradual emergence of 'the wireless'. A major advance was Fessenden's introduction of amplitude modulation. A continuous signal was broadcast at a convenient high frequency, but its power was 'modulated' — that is made to increase or decrease as the intensities of the sound waves reaching the microphone increased or decreased. At the receiving station the signal was 'demodulated'; the variations were sorted out from the high frequency 'carrier' signal and used to energise headphones or a loudspeaker which reproduced (more or less!) the original sounds in the studio. In 1920, with a real radio system available at last, the Marconi Company began broadcasting from Chelmsford in England, and a commercial American radio station opened in Pittsburgh.

The infant radio had to struggle for several years against strong opposition before attaining its position — which it now shares with television

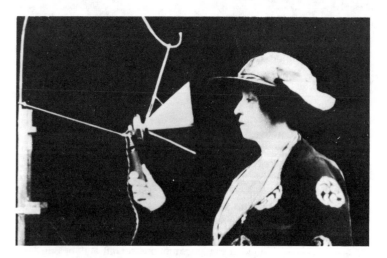

Dame Nellie Melba broadcasting a song recital, 15 June 1920

— as a major cultural force in a developed nation. Politicians and business people were almost as slow to realise its potential as the scientists had been to appreciate Maxwell's equations. But right from the beginning it captured the imagination of the public. In June of 1920, Dame Nellie Melba swept into the little Marconi studio in Chelmsford and produced one of her magical trills for the benefit of the sound engineers. She then sang a number of arias to the microphone, which went out over the single aerial rigged up on high poles and were heard by listeners not only in London and Paris, but even in places as far away as Italy and Newfoundland.

Melba at the microphone hit the headlines and from then on wireless was news. Celebrities queued up to follow Melba. Lauritz Melchior, for example, the leading Wagnerian tenor, believed that the louder he sang, the more people would be able to hear him. It is alleged that for his performance the microphone was placed in the corridor and the studio door was left open. Telephone exchanges in Scandinavian towns were connected to receiving stations so that subscribers without wireless sets could hear Melchior on their telephones.

In the 1930s, though, radio became fully professional and by the Second World War it was arguably the most important medium of news and entertainment for the people; television was available only to a small, affluent minority. In some countries — Britain and the U.S.S.R., for example — the importance of radio was recognised from the start and it was placed under the control of a single authority funded from tax revenue. In the U.S.A., in contrast, broadcasting was developed by private enterprise and hundreds of competing commercial stations soon appeared. Chaos ensued as listeners found that they could hear two or sometimes three stations at once. Regulation of the power and wavelengths of broadcasting stations was clearly essential and it was achieved after a series of conferences called by Herbert Hoover, then Secretary of Commerce. At the 1924 conference broadcasting in the United States was limited to wavelengths between 200 and 545 metres. The wavelengths of the invisible light of radio are thus up to a thousand million times greater than those of visible light. As radio waves travel at a speed of 300 000 000 metres per second, their frequencies are easily calculable from the relationship:

$$\text{frequency} = \frac{300\ 000\ 000}{\text{wavelength in metres}}$$

A station operating on 300 metres, for instance, sends out electro-magnetic waves with a wavelength of 300 metres and at a frequency of one million vibrations per second – that is, one million hertz or one megahertz (1 MHz), the unit of one vibration per second being named the *hertz*, after the discoverer of the wireless waves. The 1924 conference expressed the allowable broadcasting band as the frequency range 550 kHz to 1.5 MHz and limited each station to a narrow band of 10 kHz around its fixed operating frequency. But apart from these necessary technicalities, the social significance of the blossoming industry was made clear by Hoover in his opening address:

Radio has passed from the field of adventure to that of a public utility. We have, in fact, established an entirely new communication system, national in scope. At the end of four years, 530 stations are in operation, making radio available to every home in the country. The sales of radio apparatus have increased from a million dollars a year to a million dollars a day. It is estimated that over 200 000 men are now employed in the industry and the radio audience probably exceeds 20 millions of people.

(*Encyclopaedia Britannica*, 1958, vol. 4, p. 213)

On the other side of the Atlantic the British Broadcasting Company – soon to become a Commission, but still the B.B.C. – was occupied with questions of social ethics, and with repelling the attacks of the newspaper proprietors who saw it as a threat to their monopoly of news. An early broadcaster, Derek Parker, recalls some of the opposition that broadcasting in Britain aroused:

Radio would close all the theatres, keep people out of the cinemas, all social intercourse would cease, bridge parties would be disturbed, good conversation would be a thing of the past, and the Vicar would no longer get an audience for the Church Concert. People would stop thinking for themselves and only think what 'the wireless' told them to think; they would lose their regional accents and all talk alike . . .

(Parker, *Radio, the Great Years*, p. 15)

The opposition was met head on by the driving force of the B.B.C., a young and highly moral Scotsman, John Reith. After replying to a newspaper advertisement for a general manager of the B.B.C., Reith had been interviewed and offered the job at £1750 a year. Accepting, he wrote in his diary, 'I am profoundly thankful to God for His goodness in this manner. It is all His doing.' He countered the critics through the pages of the weekly B.B.C. journal, the *Radio Times*, asserting that radio would keep families together in the evenings, bring music to those who could not go to concerts, and catch news flashes ahead of the most rapidly circulated newspaper. Minds would be opened and horizons enlarged.

Reith with his moral and religious fervour built for the B.B.C. an unrivalled reputation of fairness and reliability, tempered by a tendency to be too staid and even dull. There were, of course, occasional lapses, such as an entry in the *Radio Times* for the late-night religious program, 'The Epilogue':

10.30 pm. The Epilogue.
The Commandments.
'Thou shalt not commit Adultery'
(For details see page 140)

While Hoover was lauding the American radio industry for its dynamic progress, Reith was more concerned with the quality of the programs and their social function. Part of the policy of the B.B.C., he said, must be to provide relaxation: 'Mitigation of the strain of a high-pressure life, such as the last generation scarcely knew, is a primary necessity, and that necessity must be satisfied.'

At the time of the General Strike in 1926, though, the B.B.C. had not yet acquired the sturdy independence that it enjoys today. Under government direction it broadcast false news of large-scale returns to work which, in the complete absence of newspapers, had a demoralising effect upon strikers all over the country. Thus was born a technique that would be brought to perfection seven years later by Josef Goebbels.

For it was in 1933, the year that Adolf Hitler became Chancellor of the German Reich, that the Nazis became masters in every sense of the German radio. They also took their opportunity to extinguish the German trade unions. At the same time, in the United States, that land of rugged individualism across the Atlantic where unionism had been slower in developing, an equally grim economic crisis was bringing almost the opposite result. With fifteen million unemployed, and the financial system collapsing, Franklin Delano Roosevelt became President just one month after the election of Hitler. He immediately closed the banks and went to the microphone. In a speech which would ring through the years he attacked the leaders of uncontrolled free enterprise who had brought about the crisis, and he lifted the morale of the entire country by presenting his New Deal, which would bring back prosperity:

The only thing we have to fear is fear itself – nameless, unreasoning, unjustified terror ... This great nation will endure as it has endured, will revive and will prosper ... The people of the United States have never failed ... it is the rulers of the exchange of mankind's goods who have failed, through their own stubbornness and their own incompetence ... Their efforts have been cast in the pattern of an outworn tradition ... They have no vision, and where there is no vision the people perish ...

Roosevelt rapidly backed up his fine words with fine actions. He reopened the banks and stock exchanges under reformed legislation. To help the unemployed he introduced great schemes of public works. An Act was passed setting minimum wages and maximum hours of work and introducing tight controls over child labour. It also gave workers 'the right to organize and bargain collectively through representatives of their own choosing ... free from the interference, restraint, or coercion of employers of labor.' The Congress of Industrial Organizations, led by John L. Lewis, set up independent unions in the big industries – steel, rubber and automobiles – replacing the unions previously set up by the employers. The C.I.O. was less successful with smaller firms and in other industries, notably the optical industry.

But probably the dramatic pinnacle of radio's impact on society came on an October night in 1938 from an American radio station. Orson Welles and his Mercury Theatre on the Air were broadcasting an adaptation of H. G. Wells' science-fiction story *The War of the Worlds*. The Martians arrived to take over the Earth, and the imaginative talents of Welles had them landing not in Wimbledon but in a field in New Jersey. The program opened with the news in brief, including an odd remark about an unusual weather disturbance near Nova Scotia; there was an announcement from the Observatory that small explosions had been seen on the surface of Mars, and that jets of hydrogen seemed to be travelling toward the Earth at an incredibly high velocity. The program then moved to the ballroom of the Hotel Park Plaza in downtown New York for a session of dance music. Just as the band was playing the popular melody 'Stardust', the music faded for a news flash: a meteorite had crashed at Grover's Mill in New Jersey; a reporter was on the way there, and listeners would be kept informed. The meteorite turned out to be a large metal cylinder. An agitated reporter described how the end of the cylinder was starting to unscrew itself; how a strange reptilian creature was emerging holding aloft a tube; how it pointed the tube at the excited crowd that was milling about near the fallen cylinder; and how a bright beam had suddenly shot from the tube. Flames leapt up from wherever it touched, the terrified crowd was screaming; and then the line went dead . . .

The tension was maintained throughout the program, although during commercial breaks the announcer pointed out, just in case anyone should be getting alarmed, that it was simply a play. At the very end, after the apparently invincible Martians had been conquered by the common cold, Welles himself came on to say that the Mercury Theatre had that night annihilated the world and destroyed the Columbia Broadcasting System. But he added that listeners might be relieved to know that it wasn't really true, and that both institutions were alive and open for business. After all, it *was* the night of Hallowe'en!

The warnings came too late. Right from the first breathless interruption by the reporter, New Yorkers had been thrown into a state of panic. By the end of the broadcast, which saw New York police milling around the studio, tens of thousands of citizens had gone to their cellars, collected their families together in prayer, or simply set off with a few belongings for the country by whatever means they could muster. Such was the power of radio in its heyday.

In the hands of the military, radio had been developing a more deadly form of power. European navies had taken up radio from the start and the armies and air forces had not been slow to follow. By January 1915 the throbbing of the bomb-laden Zeppelins as they droned over England at 100 kilometres an hour brought in another dimension. The Zeppelins came at night. Fingers of light stabbed at them from searchlights, huge parabolic mirrors with a carbon arc blazing at the focus. Fighter planes and anti-aircraft gunners could easily pick out the cigar shapes of the slow-moving airships, silvery bright in the searchlight beams, and that phase of the war in the air came to an end with the defeat of the Zeppelins.

In 1940 England again lay under the threat of death from the air. The bomber fleets of Hitler and Göring, battle tested in Spain, had blitzed their way through Poland and now they were gathering in France for the final attack. Could the conventional defence of fighters, searchlights and anti-aircraft guns, resist these fast, manoeuvrable, heavier-than-air machines? The Battle for Britain, however, was not fought out solely by conventional means. In *Their Finest Hour*, Churchill explained the failure of the Nazis' three main attempts to conquer Britain after the fall of France:

The first was the decisive defeat of the German Air Force during July, August and September . . . our second victory followed from our first. The German failure to gain command of the air prevented the cross-Channel invasion . . . The third ordeal was the indiscriminate night bombing of our cities in mass attacks. This was overcome and broken by the continued skill and devotion of our fighter pilots and by the fortitude and endurance of the mass of the people . . . But these noble efforts in the high air and in the flaming streets would have been in vain if British science and British brains had not played the ever-memorable and decisive part which this chapter records.

Science was needed to produce or to counter the beams of invisible light that were either guiding the bombers across Europe to their targets or locating them for the benefit of the avenging fighter planes. Even in 1939, the Nazi bombers had been guided to the heart of Warsaw by narrow, short-wave radio beams sent out from large aerials just inside the German borders. And in that critical summer and autumn period of 1940, the Battle of Britain turned into the Battle of the Beams. Just in time it was discovered that two narrow radio beams were directed from Germany to intersect above the Midland town of Derby (Figure 3.4).

Night bombers were to fly towards Derby along one beam and release their load when they heard the signals from the second beam. The intersection point was calculated precisely, even allowing for the non-spherical shape of the earth, so that the bombs would descend on the *Luftwaffe*'s primary target, the Rolls-Royce factory where the Merlin engines were being made for the Spitfires and Hurricanes that were England's aerial defence.

In those first few hectic days the beams were jammed by commandeering the radiotherapy apparatus from every hospital in the vicinity and switching them all on at once. More sophisticated counter-measures were introduced, but the Germans continued to instal more beam transmitters right round the arc of occupied northern Europe. Further counter-measures were met by changes in the frequency and form of the transmissions, followed by additional counter-measures, and so forth. Despite grievous losses in such industrial centres as Coventry and Southampton, the counter-measures became more effective,

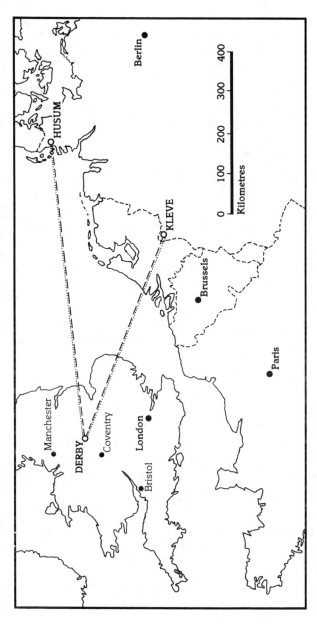

Figure 3.4: How to bomb Rolls-Royce

German radio beams intersecting over Rolls-Royce aero engine factory at Derby, detected on 21 June 1940. Each beam was only 500 metres wide. The 31.5 megahertz beam from Husum was modulated to carry dots on its northern side and dashes on the southern. This pattern was reversed for the 30.0 megahertz beam from Kleve, to assist bomber navigators.

and the urgent problem became the contest between bomber and night-fighter. How could a defending fighter locate an attacking bomber, too fast for the searchlights and invisible in the dark or in cloud? The answer again lay with beams of invisible light, but light of what wavelength?

Behind the scenes a struggle had been going on for several years between the advocates of infra-red detection and the advocates of radar. The infra-red method simply involved picking up the heat radiated by the engines and the exhaust gases of the target aircraft. Because radiation of these wavelengths was absorbed by water vapour the method was useless in cloud and even in clear conditions it needed a very sensitive infra-red detector. As a schoolboy, oblivious of the feverish activity that had been going on secretly in this area, I worked out a system and took my calculations, together with some sketches showing a Heinkel 111 bomber, to the Air Ministry. I left them on a table for a few minutes in a file but when I returned it had disappeared. I sometimes wonder what the recipients made of my calculations and my drawings of the Heinkel . . .

By 1940, though, both sides had realised the superiority of radar. If only an airborne radar set could be developed, it would provide the night-fighter with the range, and not just the direction, of the enemy bombers. Infra-red was used instead by the Germans in other ways, such as in the anti-tank gunsight which operated at night and delayed the Russian capture of Warsaw in the closing stages of the war. It also was the basis of a German attempt in 1942 to set up a huge 'burglar alarm' with infra-red 'searchlights' beaming across the Strait of Gibraltar. Detectors 16 km away on the Spanish coast were to record the passage of ships into the Mediterranean. They would thus reveal the build-up of Allied troops in north-west Africa, the troops who would cut off the rear of the Afrika Corps as it was driven back from El Alamein in the east. But the German scientific activity at the intended infra-red receiving station in Algeciras was itself detected by Kim Philby of the British secret service and intense diplomatic pressures persuaded the Spanish government to have the whole operation closed down.

Radar was altogether a more potent application of invisible light to warfare. The idea of using radio waves to locate metallic objects, such as enemy tanks or ships, had occurred repeatedly to the pioneers of radio ever since Hertz had shown how well they were reflected by his zinc sheets. The principle was the same as that of using a torch on a dark night — shining it around to locate objects by the light that is reflected from them. A similar system using ultrasonic rather than radio waves has been operating naturally for millions of years: bats, porpoises and whales navigate in total darkness by using this 'echolocation' or bio-logical sonar. Over that long period the moths preyed on by bats have evolved a counter-measure: a two-celled ear which responds to these ultrasonic frequencies, too high for the human ear to detect, and warns them of the approach of the bats.

The possible use of radio in direction finding was stated quite explicitly by Marconi in 1922:

It seems to me that it should be possible to design apparatus by means of which a ship could radiate or project a divergent beam of these rays in any desired direction; which rays, if coming across a metallic object, such as another steamer or ship, would be reflected back to a receiver screened from the local transmitter on the sending ship, and thereby immediately reveal the presence and bearing of the other ship in fog or thick weather.

(*Encyclopaedia Britannica*, 1958, vol. 18, p. 873)

Moreover, by the 1930s, advances in electronics enabled not only the direction but also the distance of a ship (or aeroplane or railway station or . . .) to be determined. (These waves travel three hundred million metres in one second, or 300 metres in each microsecond (one-millionth of a second).) Equipment could be built to time a pulse of waves from its transmission to its reception after being reflected from a ship, with an accuracy of one microsecond. The round trip to the ship and back could thus be estimated with an accuracy of 300 metres, so that the position of the ship could be pinpointed within 150 metres.

Marconi demonstrated a working radar system in 1935, two years before he died. The news of his death was carried to all parts of the world by radio and it produced a remarkable tribute. Every radio station in the world closed down for two minutes. For the last time the ether became as quiet as it had been sixty-three years earlier when Marconi was born.

In 1937, with appropriate fanfare, the French luxury liner *Normandie* was equipped with a system of Radio Detection And Ranging, known for short as radar, to avert collisions with other vessels or with icebergs on the North Atlantic run. The equipment was unsuitable for use in a small aircraft, but in the crisis of 1940 the problem of airborne radar had to be solved. Success came through the introduction of a new form of magnetron, a very high-frequency electronic valve, enabling compact radar sets to be operated with narrow pencils of very short radio waves. These *microwaves* are only a few centimetres in wavelength. They have found widespread application, for instance in microwave ovens, plastics sealing equipment, communications, satellites, and in treating certain forms of cancer. Together with radar — the most important aid to navigation and safety in modern transport — these aspects of our present-day society illustrate some of the benefits flowing from the nineteenth-century revolution in optics, especially from the wave theory of light.

Yet let us not run away with the idea that this sort of progress is always automatic and beneficent. Microwaves and radar systems also govern the operation of the guided atomic bombs that imperil half the citizens of the world. This century of brilliant scientific achievement has produced such marvels as the Cruise missile, essentially a pilotless aeroplane which can be flown from its base with such precision that it could be exploded between the goal-posts on any chosen football field, thousands of kilometres deep into enemy territory. It may carry as its warhead a neutron bomb which inflicts a slow and horrible death on its victims.

The enormous power of science can be harnessed to humanitarian ends but only with public awareness and firm political control. Technology has become too important to leave to the technologists, who too easily become obsessed with the technical challenge to the exclusion of other values. In Arthur Clarke's book, *The Coming of the Space Age*, there is a chilling example of such an attitude. It is an account by Walter Dornberger of the launching, under his direction, of the first V2 rocket. The place is Peenemünde on the Baltic Coast of Germany and the date, 3 October 1942. Dornberger's prose has a cold beauty about it as he describes the scene under that clear north German sky as the launching time approaches. The camouflaged production sheds nestling in the dense pine woods, the light blue contours of the oxygen plant, the elegant shape of the rocket, the six chimneys of the power station behind and on the hills in the distance the tower of Wolgast Cathedral. The technicians, busy and excited at their batteries of recorders, gauges, control panels and signal lamps; the television crew making final focus adjustments; and the nasal tones of loudspeakers in the background.

With Werner von Braun beside him, Dornberger starts the countdown: 3 minutes to go. He describes the tense scene up to the moment, 60 seconds after blast off, when the rocket is seen streaking away precisely on its planned course at 5000 kilometres an hour. 'I couldn't speak for a moment, my emotion was too great ... And then we yelled and embraced each other like excited boys. Everyone was shouting, laughing, leaping, dancing and shaking hands.' But then he had to call for quiet, for the experiment wasn't yet over. Soon the rocket would re-enter the earth's atmosphere at well over 5000 kilometres an hour. Would it withstand re-entry or would it be torn to pieces long before it reached the ground? After 296 seconds had elapsed from the moment of take off, the rocket's transmitter stopped abruptly and they knew that their experiment had been successful. In the midst of the renewed excitement Dornberger joyfully announced that the rocket had struck the earth with an impact energy equal to that of fifty express engines each weighing 100 tonnes and racing along at 100 kilometres an hour.

Two years later I was in Blackheath, in South London, on a Saturday morning when one of Dornberger's beautifully shaped rockets carrying an explosive warhead landed on Woolworths. Among the dust and the debris I watched the rescue squads sorting out the bits of the prams and the babies. I wonder how his 'excited boys' would have reacted had they been there with me.

4

The Last Word...?

Light as particles

4

Dear Franz,

Congratulations on your diploma. You shouldn't have any difficulty in finding a job now!

I'm still working hard without getting much encouragement. Only yesterday we were in the dark room testing our spark gaps when I noticed that the tiny sparks in my detector seemed to grow brighter whenever the light from the big sparking machine fell upon it. I told Professor Hertz and he said it was very interesting but we must get on with our main experiments and not be diverted by all these strange things we keep finding. He is absolutely set upon proving that his electrical waves really exist.

Soon we must meet and celebrate your success!

With friendly greetings,

Rudi

Karlsruhe, 1888

Although this letter is purely an invention, one of Hertz' assistants actually did notice the enhancement of one spark by the light from another, though it would be wrong to blame Hertz for not immediately appreciating the significance of this observation. At that time he was steering his way through a tangle of experimental results to arrive at the first demonstration of radio waves, and a letter to his parents shows his state of mind:

. . . For the moment, I am blundering without precise method. I repeat old experiments in this field and demonstrate others which pass

through my head ... I hope that, among the hundred remarkable phenomena which I come across, some light will shine from one or another.

(cited in Taton, *Reason and Chance in Scientific Discovery*, p. 41)

Whether or not that was a subconscious pun, the phenomenon observed by his assistant proved to be as remarkable as the radio waves themselves. The phenomenon, later to be called *photoelectricity*, provided the last big clue to the nature of light.

What was happening to make the detector sparks grow brighter? It would subsequently be realised that when the ultraviolet light from the big sparks fell on to the metal points of the detector spark gap, it knocked electrons out of the metal atoms, causing the resistance of the air gap to be lowered. The faint, tiny sparks of the detector then seemed to burst into a brighter activity. When the existence of this photoelectric effect became widely recognised it was eagerly investigated in more controlled experiments. The spark gap was replaced by metal electrodes in a vacuum tube so that the changes in electric current passing through the tube could be measured while different lights were shone upon the electrodes. The strength of this photoelectic current indicated how many electrons were being knocked out of the metal per second. It was soon discovered that the current depended directly upon the intensity of the light. If the intensity was doubled the current also doubled; that was hardly surprising. But then it was found that the frequency of light — its *colour* — affected the current in a strange way indeed: each metal tested had its own 'threshold frequency' of light below which there was no photoelectric effect at all! Ultraviolet light was more effective than blue light, and later on it was discovered that X-rays were more effective still. Above the threshold, the current always increased as the frequency of the light increased (see Figure 4.1).

And that threshold was an absolutely invincible barrier. A current might be produced with a certain metal, sodium for example, by a faint violet light, but a yellow light even a million times brighter had no effect whatsoever.

Wave theory would have had a hard enough time cooking up an explanation for this odd behaviour, but there was one result which stumped it altogether. Suppose you shine a blue light onto the bright surface of a piece of sodium the size of a small coin. Electrons are shot out and immediately there is a photoelectric current. When the intensity of the blue light is reduced, by using filters, the current is also reduced.

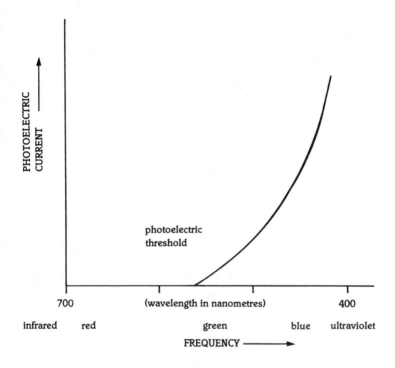

Figure 4.1: Photoelectric response to visible light showing the sharp threshold
At lower frequencies (higher wavelengths) there is no photoelectric effect however bright the light. Different metals have different threshold wavelengths.

The intensity can be cut down so far that it would take a whole year to build up enough energy on each atom to start knocking out electrons. For if light were simply a wave, the energy of this very faint light would be spread thinly and equally over all the sodium atoms in the surface. But instead of a year's delay, what happens? As soon as this faintest possible light strikes the metal, *the photoelectric current starts up instantaneously!*

The only way out of this puzzle was to suppose that as each 'wave' of light reaches the surface, it must concentrate all of its energy on a single atom — on an area less than one-million millionth of the sodium surface. Could such a thing be possible? It would be far less surprising

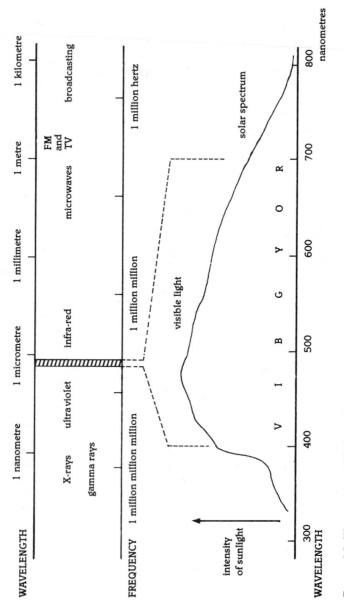

Figure 4.2: The position of light in the spectrum of electromagnetic radiation
Sunlight ('white' light) has a maximum intensity at about 475 nm.

if an ocean wave the full width of the Pacific Ocean broke on the coastline and all of its energy was concentrated on a single hair on one
bather's head. Wave theory was completely baffled by this instantaneous action of the photoelectric effect. It had succeeded with large-
scale optical phenomena like interference, but on the scale where the
interaction of light with one atom at a time was concerned, it failed. Evidently an entirely new concept was needed — and in 1905 it was supplied by a young clerk in the Swiss Patent Office called Albert Einstein.

Since 1900 there had already been one devastatingly new concept in
the air — Max Planck's idea of the *quantum* of energy, which would
dominate physical science throughout the twentieth century. Conventional physics had run into a brick wall trying to explain the nature of
the radiation from a heated object. A warm poker emits infra-red light
and cannot be seen in the dark; as it is heated it becomes red, orange
and finally white hot. The even hotter sun emits white light and a considerable proportion of its energy goes into the even higher frequencies,
into the ultraviolet and X-ray regions of the radiation spectrum (see Figure 4.2). Conventional physics, so successful in other respects, gave the
ridiculous answer that at any temperature a body would give out an infinite amount of energy at the highest frequencies.

Max Planck had obtained a complete solution to this problem by proposing that an atom vibrating in the hot body could only absorb or emit
energy in definite chunks. No such restriction had ever been dreamed
of before and even Planck himself only regarded it as a temporary fiddle
to produce the right answer. The crucial feature that made the theory
successful was that the size of each chunk of energy was directly dependent upon its frequency. The relationship is expressed by the formula

$E = h\nu$. The Greek letter ν stands for frequency, so the formula says,
in words, that

Energy = h multiplied by Frequency

where the symbol h, known as Planck's constant, is a very, very small
quantity indeed. Expressed as energy divided by frequency (which is the
same as energy multiplied by time), it has the value

h = 0.000 000 000 000 000 000 000 000 000 000 000 66 joule second.

Even at a frequency of six hundred million million oscillations per second, the frequency of blue light, the quantum of energy radiated by a
single atom is still very small. It would take three million million million
such quanta to make one joule, the amount of energy needed to lift a
cup of coffee to your lips.

No wonder these small changes in energy which are vital to a single atom are unnoticeable in everyday life, where we perceive only the averaged effect of countless millions of atoms. And no wonder the human race existed right up to the year 1900 before it became aware of the quantum of energy.

In the early years of the twentieth century, though, how could anyone possibly find out just what was happening at the level of a single atom? Einstein tackled the problem with his characteristic simplicity. He imagined himself in the position of an atom in the surface of the metal. Light did not now appear to him as a succession of waves washing over him as if he were a pebble on the seashore, but it seemed (and felt!) more like a hail of bullets. Each bullet carried just one quantum of energy; the higher the frequency of light, the more the energy in the quantum ($E = h\nu$), so a bullet of blue light had almost twice the energy of a bullet of red light. When a bullet made a direct hit on an atom this energy was used to eject an electron. All of the mysterious experimental observations, including the instantaneous emission and the dependence upon frequency, could now be explained.

Einstein was at pains to point out that his theory of light as quantum bullets — *photons* as they came to be called — did not conflict with the use of wave theory for optical behaviour on a much larger scale: 'The wave theory of light', he wrote, '. . . has worked well in the representation of purely optical phenomena and will probably never be replaced by another theory'. But where interactions of light with matter were concerned, only the photon theory could be used, the theory in which

. . . the energy of a light ray spreading out from a point is not continuously distributed over an increasing space, but consists of a finite number of energy quanta which are localised at points in space, which move without dividing, and which can only be produced and absorbed as complete units.

(Arons, *Development of Concepts of Physics*, p. 839)

Einstein thus saw light as essentially *granular* in structure, rather than smooth and infinitely divisible. It was composed of photons in much the same way that matter was composed of atoms and an electric current was composed of electrons. As all of these basic components were very small on everyday scales, the granularity of light, matter or electricity only became important when dealing with the behaviour of one or a few atoms at a time.

'We appeal, as human beings to human beings:
Remember your humanity and forget the rest.'
   Manifesto on Nuclear Weapons, 9 July 1955, drafted by Bertrand Russell and
   signed by Albert Einstein just before he died.

The photon theory not only explained previously unexplained observations but also made predictions that were soon confirmed by experiments. Wouldn't you expect that it would be hailed with enthusiasm by the scientists who had been struggling to understand these phenomena? It didn't work out like that. In 1910 the scientific world was still suspicious of Planck's theory, and Planck himself was suspicious of Einstein's: 'If the photon concept were accepted', wrote Planck in 1910, 'the theory of light would be thrown back by centuries . . . for the sake of a few still rather dubious speculations'. And in 1913, eight years after Einstein's paper was published, four eminent German physicists, proposing Einstein for membership of the Prussian Academy of Science, found it necessary to apologise for his 'hypothesis of light quanta'. They praised his contributions to nearly all of the great problems of modern physics, but pointed out that no one could introduce fundamentally new ideas without taking risks. Missing the target in his speculations on photons, they said, 'cannot be really held too much against him'. Fortunately it was not. After another eight years Einstein was awarded the Nobel Prize, not for his work on relativity but specifically for his photon theory explaining the photoelectric effect.

If this were a Sherlock Holmes story, Dr Watson would by now be spluttering with rage. Damnit, he would say, we went to all that trouble to show that light is some sort of wave and now you say that it *is* a wave as far as ordinary optics is concerned but really, at the scale of atoms, it is a particle after all. What about that so-called crucial experiment of Thomas Young, the one with light shining through two pinholes? Wasn't the interference pattern of stripes that it produced supposed to be incontrovertible proof of the wave nature of light?

It was indeed. But so was the photoelectric effect incontrovertible proof of the particle nature of light! Here, in the very year that Conan Doyle published *The Return of Sherlock Holmes*, was a pretty puzzle that Watson might well have put to the great detective. The joke is that it wasn't really a puzzle at all. Light is light; a photon is a photon, having both wave-like *and* particle-like properties, but being neither a wave nor a particle in the everyday sense of those words. The joke is really on us for the way in which we misuse analogies and become the prisoners of our own language.

'It's really quite elementary', you can hear Holmes saying to Watson, 'if you consider the strange behaviour of a photon taking part in Dr Young's interference experiment. The photon leaves the light source,

encounters the card with the two pinholes in it, and finishes up somewhere on the final screen. Just **how** it gets past the pinholes we cannot
tell; nor can we tell just **where** it will strike the screen! All that we know,
from observing the result of millions upon millions of photons, is that
there is a very high probability that it will strike an atom in one of the
bright stripes of the interference pattern, and a decreasing probability
of a hit as we move further away into the dark stripes.

'But I can see from the look in your face, my dear Watson, that you
find this explanation unacceptable.'

'Oh, not at all Holmes, I was simply thinking what an ingenious piece
of speculation the idea was.'

'Speculation, Watson? Ah, my good friend, I see that your return to
private practice has dulled your awareness of what is going on in the
world around you. Had you', continued Holmes, indicating with a wave
of his hand a pile of magazines on the coffee table, 'kept up with your
reading of the **Proceedings of the Cambridge Philosophical Society**,
you would have assuredly discovered that the matter is no longer one
of speculation but a simple case of experimental fact.

'You would have learned of the demonstration carried out by a young
Cambridge physicist by the name of Geoffrey Taylor; an experiment performed, I may say, with the most commendable style. Taylor set up an
interference experiment in a box inside a dark room. He placed smoked
glass filters in front of the light source so that almost no light at all
entered the system. A calculation showed that only about one million
photons per second were reaching the photographic film set up to record any pattern of the photons' activity.

'A million photons may not strike you as a very small number, Watson. However, as you will doubtless recollect, they are travelling with
the speed of 300 000 kilometres per second. They were, therefore, sep-
arated by an average distance of one-millionth of 300 000 kilometres,
or 300 metres. As the experimental box itself was only about one metre
long, this means, you see Watson, that **there was never more than one
photon in the box at any one time.**'

'Really, Holmes, I just can't see what you're driving at. If you've only
got one photon you can't possibly get any interference. If this chap Taylor has a card with two pinholes in it, then the photon must go through
one or the other – it can't go through both, can it? – and then where's
his interference pattern going to be?'

'On the photographic film, Watson. And young Taylor was so confident of the result that, having set up his experiment, he just left it going
for three months while he went away for a sailing holiday. Incidentally,

I'm pleased to say, he took the opportunity during that cruise to work out the theory of the tides in the Irish Sea. And when he came back, all bronzed and healthy, he took out the photographic plate, developed it, and there in black and white was the interference pattern he had expected.

'But your puzzlement is not surprising; after all most of those learned fellows up at the Royal Society are just as puzzled as you are. What you must fix your mind upon is this: that **a photon can behave as a wave or as a particle depending upon the circumstances**.

'If you confront it with a card containing two pinholes, its wave nature produces an interference pattern which determines not precisely **where** any particular photon will hit the photographic film but the **probability** that it will hit any particular point. And when it does reach the film its particle nature ensures that it delivers all of its energy at the point where it happens to hit. That releases an atom of free silver which contributes to the blackening of the plate in that region. The striped pattern that Taylor found on his return was actually the smoothed-out result of the ten million million photons that had hit his film at points in accordance with the predictions of wave theory.

'So you see, my dear Watson, if you put preconceived ideas out of your mind, the explanation is indeed quite elementary.'

So light is a particle with wave-like properties. And is this really the last word in the story of discovering the nature of light? For all ordinary intents and purposes it probably is. There will always be more to learn about the fundamentals of the universe, so the natural philosophers will be happily busy for ever. The natural philosophers can continue to interpret light in their various ways; the point, however, is to use it. The wave and photon theories already enable us to deal with almost any situation or application that can be of the remotest concern to ordinary people. But whether we are thinking of such Baconian benefits to humanity as better lighting or correcting failing eyesight, of the profitability of some new communications device, or of the increased deadliness of weapons of war, it is clear that the way ahead needs little refinement in our understanding of the physical nature of light.

Although the Nobel committee had considered Einstein's introduction of the photon more significant than his theory of relativity there was, in fact, a link between the two. The important feature they had in common was the finite speed of light. Three centuries earlier it had been an open question whether light could be said to have a speed at all. Light was a strange, God-like phenomenon, and it was quite credible that it should travel from place to place instantaneously. But on 7 December 1676, the French scientific magazine, the *Journal des Scavans*, published a paper entitled 'Proof of the movement of light by M. Rømer of the Académie Royale des Sciences'. Ole Rømer was a young Danish astronomer living in Paris, and this was the only scientific paper he ever published. Though only a page and a half long it brought him an immortal place in the history of science.

Rømer's achievement was to show that light is not propagated *instantaneously*, but that it moves with an enormously high, though *finite*, speed. Over a long period he had been observing the rotation of the moons of Jupiter and timing their eclipses, as they passed round that huge planet, with the care and accuracy already shown by his countryman Tycho Brahe. He found that the moons seemed to slow down or speed up depending on whether Jupiter was moving away from the Earth or coming closer to it. This effect, he said, was simply due to the extra time that the light took to cover the distance between the planets when they were further apart:

I have been observing the first satellite of Jupiter over eight years. The satellite is eclipsed during each orbit of the planet on entering its vast shadow. I have observed that the intervals between the eclipses vary. They are the shortest when the Earth moves towards Jupiter and longest when it moves far away from it. This can only mean that light takes time for transmission through space . . .

The speed must be so great that the light coming to us from Jupiter takes 22 minutes longer to reach us at the farthest end of our orbit round the Sun, than at the other end of the orbit when we are nearest Jupiter. That is to say, light takes about 10 minutes to travel from the sun to the Earth; it does not travel instantaneously as alleged by M Descartes.

Nowadays Rømer is held up for our admiration as 'the first person to measure the velocity of light'. He certainly measured the time it took for light to travel from the sun to the earth, and as he was working in the Paris Observatory where the size of the earth's orbit was first determined, he presumably knew the distance from the sun to the earth. But I have found no evidence that he ever troubled to divide that distance by that time to discover the speed of light. His whole interest lay in finding whether it was infinite, as the leading philosophical system of the time, that of Descartes, maintained, or whether it had some finite value, the exact speed being unimportant. The very title of his paper, 'Proof of the Movement of Light . . .', emphasises the vast distinction between the attitudes to science in the seventeenth and the twentieth centuries. A present-day scientist would have been pre-occupied with the actual numerical value of the speed. He or she would have carried out the simple division and called the paper 'Determination of the velocity of light . . .' What will be the reasons for doing science in the twenty-first century . . .?'

A year or two later, it was Christian Huygens who, with full acknowledgement to Rømer, put the distance and time together, arriving at a speed of about 200 000 kilometres per second. This speed was almost unimaginable, and it is hardly surprising that it took about fifty years for Rømer's demonstration to gain full acceptance. From then on, however, increasingly accurate measurements of the speed of light were obtained from ingenious experiments, so that by the time Maxwell put forward his electromagnetic theory a measured speed of close to 300 000 kilometres per second was available to provide its crucial, ultimate confirmation. And this information, as we have seen, led directly to the creation of radio and television.

On a different ethereal plane, the speed of light now has a fundamental role in modern physics. Einstein built the special theory of relativity by denying any meaning to the concept of absolute rest, and then adding the postulate that 'light in empty space always travels with a definite speed which is quite independent of the movement of the source'. And this led him to the stupendous realisation that mass and energy are interchangeable. His famous equation, $E = mc^2$, simply states that one unit of mass can be converted into an amount of energy equal to the square of the speed of light. The enormous amount of energy streaming from the sun, for example, is produced by the disappearance of several million tonnes of the sun's mass every second.

Although Einstein's relativity theories aroused much popular excitement, they did not have the profound and lasting impact of Darwin's Origin of the Species. It was amusing to toy with the idea of flying to the stars and returning to find the world a hundred years older though you had only been away a year; or to come to terms with the conclusion that nothing could ever travel faster than light. But there were skeptics even then. The novelist Rider Haggard noting in his diary that a German, Einstein, had come up with a new Theory of the Universe, showed less than wild enthusiasm: 'If light does bend or space does "warp", I cannot see that it matters much to us who for so long have remained ignorant of the fact without inconvenience.' Even when Eddington in 1919 confirmed that light does bend as it travels near to the sun, the result was a great surge of enthusiasm for Einstein rather than any deep change in attitudes, beliefs, or understanding. The theory of evolution, in contrast, profoundly disturbed religious thinking in the nineteenth century, and is still reverberating through the environmentalist movements today.

Relativity gave a shot in the arm to the popular appreciation of astronomy. It was exciting to find that the universe was expanding, that the distant galaxies were moving away from us so rapidly that even the colour of the light from them was changed, and that these distant objects were so far away already that we might be looking at the light from a star that had in fact blown up a million years before. But the repetition of huge, 'astronomical' numbers became oppressive, and when Eddington observed that we were just a middle-class planet revolving round a middle-class star, not even at the centre of our middle-class galaxy, it all seemed to be only an echo from three centuries earlier when Galileo displaced the Earth from its supposed position at the centre of the universe.

Then it was realised that looking at the sky through an optical telescope was not the only way of finding out what the universe was like. The heavenly bodies are giving out all kinds of electromagnetic radiations, not merely visible light, so that ultraviolet light, X-rays, and, especially, radio waves could also be used. Following the electronic techniques developed during the Second World War the science of radio astronomy forged ahead, making revelations that rivalled or surpassed science fiction. Giant radio telescopes picked up radiations from objects too far and faint to be resolved by any optical telescope, quasi-stellar objects known as *quasars*. The most distant quasar observed is alleged to be already about ten thousand million light-years away, and to be departing from us at over 90 per cent of the speed of light. The biggest is six million light-years across, and the power that these strange objects are radiating out in the farther reaches of the universe is probably too great for even an astronomer to grasp.

In 1967 another class of strange objects was discovered under circumstances which are probably more revealing than the objects themselves. Jocelyn Bell, a research student at Cambridge, noticed a very regular pulsation, about once a second, on a recording she was making of the intensity of the radio waves coming from a faint star. After considering the possibility (seriously!) that the pulsations were signals from beings in outer space, Bell and her colleague Hewish announced that they had discovered the first *pulsar*, a star made largely of neutrons and so dense that a teaspoonful would weigh a thousand million tonnes. Quite unimaginable, of course, but the joke was on another laboratory where an even larger radio telescope had been feeding its observations into a computer. *After* Jocelyn Bell had spotted the pulses on her recorder chart the scientists in that other laboratory hurriedly examined their computer tapes and found that they contained a beautiful record of a pulsar taken two years earlier. The computer had not reported a regular pulsation once a second simply because nobody had asked for it.

And in this mysterious universe of the astrophysicists there is an even more mysterious kind of star than either the quasars or the pulsars — the *black hole*. At the end of the eighteenth century Pierre Laplace proposed the existence of stars so massive that not even light could escape from the pull of their gravitation. In recent decades intense theoretical work and X-ray observation has convinced most astronomers that such black holes do exist. They even think that they have found one — Cygnus X-1 they call it — probably only a few kilometres across, but already with more than three times the mass of the sun and growing all the time. It is growing because black holes are sucking in matter from the surrounding universe; a hundredth of 1 per cent matter from the universe may have gone that way already and the rest might follow. But there is an escape route: the 'back' of a black hole is a white hole out of which spew great torrents of energy — perhaps into another space and time in our universe or perhaps even into some other universe altogether.

These findings and theories are all very absorbing for the astrophysicists and cosmologists. For the rest of us, though they provide entertaining television programs from time to time, there are better things to do than to concern ourselves overly with events ten thousand light-years away in space or a hundred million years in time. We may wish to explore the down-to-earth benefits to be obtained from optics; or, even perhaps, if more artistically inclined or just overpowered with the deluge of astronomical numbers, to follow the example of the great nineteenth-century American poet, Walt Whitman:

When I heard the learn'd astronomer,
When the proofs, the figures, were ranged in columns before me,
When I was shown the charts and diagrams, to add, divide, and measure
  them,
When I sitting heard the astronomer where he lectured with much
  applause in the lecture-room,
How soon unaccountable I became tired and sick,
Till rising and gliding out I wander'd off by myself,
In the mystical moist night-air, and from time to time,
Look'd up in perfect silence at the stars.

5

The Human Camera

The superb optical system of the eye

'All life on this planet runs on sunlight'

George Wald

The Tax Collectors

5

It is fashionable among those astrophysicists who study the evolution of the universe to calculate its history in reverse, going back to a time about twelve thousand million years ago when an explosive event took place which they call the Big Bang. The singularity of the Big Bang precludes them from saying anything about what happened before, but they can be astonishingly precise about what happened immediately afterwards.

The calculations of this dramatic event – a drama without an audience – show that for the first few hectic minutes the universe was a seething, unimaginably hot sea of matter and radiation. After three minutes the temperature had fallen to a thousand million degrees Celsius. The universe which went on expanding and cooling was dominated by radiation for nearly a million years; not only by visible light but also by radio waves, infra-red, ultraviolet, X-rays and gamma rays. The temperature had by then dropped to only (!) about 3000°C and the balance began to swing from radiation towards matter. The residue of material particles still remaining after that holocaust of the first three minutes formed itself into clouds of hydrogen and helium which condensed under the influence of gravity into the galaxies and stars that we see shining at night.

One star that was formed, together with its attendant planets and asteroids, about five thousand million years ago, is of particular interest to us: our sun. Bathing the spinning earth with its heat and its light, it brought gales, violent electrical storms and discharges of lightning. The fierce ultraviolet rays of the sunlight passed easily through the primitive atmosphere, smashing the molecules in the oceans into fragments and continually re-arranging them into more and more complicated forms.

Some were the long molecules – made mainly out of the abundant elements, hydrogen, oxygen, carbon and nitrogen — of fats and sugars, proteins, and the nucleic acids RNA and DNA. And out of this collection of molecules still more complex structures evolved, things such as bacteria and primitive plants that could move and reproduce themselves and were, by any definition, alive.

The struggle by which this living world had emerged had been long and slow, but evolution now took a sudden leap forward, precipitating an environmental crisis so great that most forms of life on earth were extinguished in the process. The key to this catastrophe was the light from the sun. Green plants, particularly the blue-green algae in the oceans, led the revolution by using their green pigment, chlorophyll, to capture and store the energy in sunlight. In this process of photosynthesis, hydrogen is taken from water and combined with carbon dioxide to make carbohydrate. The oxygen of the water is simply released into the atmosphere, but to the primitive organisms floating around two thousand million years ago oxygen was deadly. They were used to an atmosphere that was not the sweet, pure air of today, but a collection of gases that we should find decidedly unpleasant, indeed lethal: methane, ammonia and carbon dioxide, for example. A world-wide struggle for existence ensued, with the green plants and certain bacteria that adapted to oxygen coming out on top. As the tide of battle turned, vast quantities of oxygen were produced and the carbon dioxide in the atmosphere was used up. From then on the ultraviolet light from the sun was almost entirely cut off by the new atmosphere and the conditions under which life originated would not occur again. The world now belonged to the oxygen-breathers.

As more complex organisms evolved, the simple light-or-dark responses of the primitive single-celled creatures were replaced by increasingly sophisticated organs of sight. Within the last hundred thousand years a species emerged that could see fine details and distinguish a full rainbow of colours. This species, *Homo sapiens*, had also a brain that would wonder at, and later come to understand both light and sight. Perhaps even more marvellous, this new arrival on the evolutionary scene would be able to laugh at its own understanding. Kuzma Prutkov, a delightful character in Slavonic fiction, was asked:

'Which is more useful, the Sun or the Moon?'

'The Moon', he replied, 'because it shines at night, when it is dark, while the Sun shines only in the daytime'.

Today green plants are maintaining life on earth by harnessing solar energy to make sugar and cellulose out of carbon dioxide and water. They make these carbohydrates, on which all living things ultimately

SPECIAL OFFER!

STEREOSCOPIC MOVIE CAMERAS!

Now available! Movie camera of advanced design. Developed over 500 million years.

Automatic focusing from close-up to infinity.

Automatic cleaning mechanism operates intermittently during use. Lens cover closes automatically during rest.

Automatic iris enables operation over a 100 000-fold range of brightness.

HIGH SENSITIVITY. CAN DETECT A CANDLE FLAME AT A DISTANCE OF 20 KILOMETRES.

Digital electric output, matched to the cortex of the brain.

Waterproof. White ring goes red to indicate over-exposure or excessive alcohol concentration.

Accessory lenses available.

COMES COMPLETE WITH COLOUR FILM TO LAST UP TO 100 YEARS!

Choice of colours – BLUE or BROWN. Other shades sometimes available.

ONE PAIR FREE PER CUSTOMER!

depend for their supply of food, at a rate of about 6000 tonnes a second.

As green plants are our lifeline, it was worth quite a prodigious effort to find out just how they harness the energy of sunlight. And the mechanism turned out to be very complicated ideed, at least in terms of our still rather elementary understanding of science. The key substance in the process is the chlorophyll that gives the green colour to plants. Each chlorophyll molecule acts as a tiny aerial. It captures its quota of sunlight and passes it on along a chain of molecules, transferring energy and electrons from one molecule to another.

Thousands of research-worker years have gone into discovering how many photons of sunlight are needed to convert one molecule of carbon dioxide into carbohydrate. Theoretically three should suffice, but experiments have indicated numbers from four up to twelve. Bitter arguments about the exact efficiency of the process have raged for years.

More significant than these academic disputes, however, is the possibility of imitating natural photosynthesis to obtain energy. The electron transfer process splits a molecule of water into oxygen and hydrogen and in laboratories such as those of Melvin Calvin at the University of California and George Porter at the Royal Institution, artificial membranes or semiconductors are being designed to achieve the same result and to provide a cheap way of storing solar energy in the form of hydrogen. Here the physics becomes merged with the chemistry, biochemistry becomes an aspect of electronics, in a concerted attempt to harness science to solve a major need of society.

A more apparent form of interaction between light and life is the *phototropism* of plants, their tendency to bend towards the light. In the good old days of the early nineteenth century, when science was conducted with style, a research worker showed that phototropism is caused by rays from the blue-green regions of the spectrum and not the red. He placed a flask of port wine between a growing plant and the window, and the plant grew just as well as before, but no longer bent towards the light. Is the plant 'seeing' the light? Does a sunflower 'see' where the sun is as it turns during the day? The questions take on a deeper meaning if we ask, instead, what molecules are used to detect the light? They are *not* those of the green pigment, chlorophyll, which strongly absorbs and reacts to red light, but rather are of a yellow pigment called a *carotene*. When animals eat plants they modify the carotene slightly to produce a molecule called *retinal* which is the basis of the light-sensitive pigments in every form of animal vision. As plants turn to face the sun, they use similar light-sensitive molecules, so it is perhaps not too far-fetched to talk of them also as seeing the light.

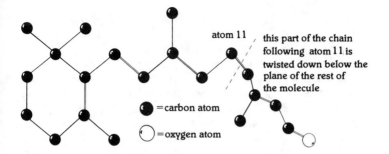

(a) 11 – cis retinal ($C_{20}H_{28}O$).

For clarity the 20 carbon atoms and the oxygen atom are reduced in size, and the 28 hydrogen atoms, attached to the carbons, are not shown at all. In a more accurate model the atoms would all be jostling together and the who' molecule would look like a twisted, lumpy sausage.

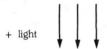

+ light

molecule twists about carbon atom 11 and straightens up into

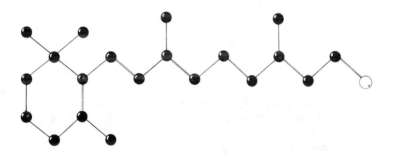

(b) all trans-retinal

Figure 5.1: The photochemical act of vision

A molecule of RETINAL is normally bound to a protein in its kinked form (a). When struck by light it straightens out into the form (b) and a nerve signal passes to the brain contributing to the sensation of light.

How does retinal manage to provide the vision for such widely differing structures as the eyes of a fly, an octopus or a human being? It is essentially a trigger, causing the energy stored in the protein molecule to which it is normally bound to be released, thereby sending a nervous signal to the brain. Retinal is a molecule of 49 atoms, with the composition $C_{20}H_{28}O$. Six of the carbon atoms form a ring which carries the crucial portion, a side-chain of nine carbon atoms. In its normal resting position in the dark there is a sharp bend in this side-chain which is formed by its twisting around the fifth carbon atom (see Figure 5.1a). In 1959 it was discovered that in the act of vision an incoming photon causes the bent chain to straighten (see Figure 5.1b). The retinal molecule then separates from its protein molecule, the protein molecule changes shape, the optic nerve responds by sending an electrical impulse to the brain, and there is a perception of light; all of these events are consequences of the reaction of a retinal molecule to the arrival of a photon.

The idea of a single molecule changing from one shape to another may not seem very odd to us today in the era of the long-chain molecules of plastics and textiles. It was very odd indeed in 1874 when a young Dutch Ph.D. student, Jacobus Henricus van't Hoff, wrote a paper on the *spatial* structure of organic molecules. So odd did it seem, in fact, to chemists who had still not fully accepted the fact that atoms existed, that one of the most eminent among them, Hermann Kolbe, made a scathing denunciation of the very idea:

Not long ago I expressed the view that the lack of general education and of thorough training in chemistry of quite a few professors of chemistry was one of the causes of the deterioration of chemical research in Germany . . .

Will anyone to whom my worries may seem exaggerated please read, if he can, a recent memoir by a Herr van't Hoff on 'The Arrangements of Atoms in Space', a document crammed to the hilt with the outpourings of a childish fantasy.

This Dr J. H. van't Hoff, employed by the Veterinary College at Utrecht, has, so it seems, no taste for accurate chemical research. He finds it more convenient to mount his Pegasus (evidently taken from the stables of the Veterinary College) and to announce how, on his daring flight to Mount Parnassus, he saw the atoms arranged in space.

(cited in Hubbard and Kropf, 'Molecular isomers in vision',
Scientific American, 216, 1967, p. 64)

Fortunately van't Hoff's reputation survived this blast: in 1901, the year of the first Nobel Prizes, van't Hoff was awarded the chemistry prize while the physics prize went to Roentgen for his discovery of X-rays.

Van't Hoff's 'childish fantasy' turned out to be the basis of the act of vision. Several quite different kinds of image-forming eyes have evolved independently, yet in every case it is the sudden change in the 'Arrangement of the Atoms in Space' of the retinal molecule when it is hit by a photon that is the essential mechanism of sight. The retinal molecule has been the common factor throughout the entire development of eyes, just as silver has been the active ingredient in the plates and films used by the earliest brass and wooden cameras right up to the electronic movie cameras of today. A third of the world's silver production now goes into photographic film emulsions.

Retinal belongs to the important family of chain-like molecules built up from units of *isoprene* (C_5H_8) — the member of this family with the longest chains is natural rubber. Retinal itself is almost identical to the molecule of vitamin A ($C_{20}H_{30}O$). It was, in fact, George Wald's discovery in 1933 of vitamin A in the eye that revealed the role of retinal in vision. Wald was then a post-doctoral fellow working in Berlin where Adolf Hitler had just been installed as Chancellor of the Reich. Vitamin A soon became recognised as a crucial factor in vision. A moderate deficiency in this vitamin led to 'night blindness', but gross deficiency produces xerophthalmia, a condition that catastrophically reduces the vision of thousands of Third World children today; eventually the lens of the eye disintegrates and total blindness often results.

Vitamin A and similar molecules of the isoprene family are present in tomatoes and carrots, giving them their familiar red and yellow colouring. The popular belief in the value of vitamin A was exploited by the British in a campaign during the Second World War urging citizens to eat more carrots in order to improve their vision in the blacked-out streets at night. As an encouragement, the rumour was put about that R.A.F. pilots engaged in night operations were not only eating carrots but were being given high doses of vitamin A. The idea was to divert German attention away from the sudden increase in the success rate of the night-fighters, which had secretly been equipped with airborne radar.

Over the millennia, as the light-sensitive retina evolved, so did the organs of sight, the eyes which focused an image of the outside world upon it. The eyes of the arthropods — insects, crabs or spiders — are probably the most ancient. Fossilised eyes of trilobites more than five hundred million years old have even been found. Their complicated structures may include hundreds or thousands of lenses, each lens having its own light-detecting element behind it. Unlike 'ordinary' glass lenses, which are homogeneous and derive their refracting power from the curvature of the surface, these lenses function by being denser in the middle than the edges. These 'compound eyes' present a point-by-point field of view to the brain. They are highly efficient detectors of movement, as demonstrated, for instance, by the swift and accurate dart of a dragon fly to snap up its prey.

The human eye is much simpler than the arthropod eyes, even though the human brain is far more complex. Typical of vertebrate eyes, it has only a single lens which throws its image upon its retina, a network of millions of individual light-detecting cells (see Figure 5.2). This cellular network is connected by nerves directly to the cortex of the brain and is really an extension of the brain itself. The eye is often compared (sometimes unfavourably!) to a simple camera. Perhaps a closer analogy would be to a television camera. The job of an ordinary camera is simply to produce a two-dimensional replica of the view to which it is exposed; television cameras and eyes also make an image of the view, but go on to translate that image into electrical signals, either for broadcasting or for sending to the brain. The purely optical function of forming the image is governed by the wave theory of light, but the point-by-point trans-lation of the image into electrical signals is produced by the action of individual photons. It is still amazing that twenty grams or so of salty, watery jelly enclosed in a membrane and containing soft, fibrous tissues, can perform such a wonderful range of functions.

The basic physiology of the human eye has been known for centuries. In 1637 Descartes published a picture showing the cornea, the iris, and the lens focusing light from an object to produce an inverted image on the retina at the back of the eyeball (see Figure 5.3). A striking exper-iment had in fact, already been performed to demonstrate this function. A section was cut out from the back of an eye taken from an ox and replaced by a piece of thin paper. In a darkened room the eye was held with its cornea against a hole in the shutters and an inverted image of the sunlit scene outside appeared upon the paper!

The production of the image upon the retina can be understood with-out, at first, considering the lens at all. A primitive mollusc, *Nautilus*, which flourishes in the deep seas around Fiji and the Philippines, has no lens; it simply has a tiny hole in the front of its eye. The *Nautilus* eye is thus a pinhole camera − a camera without a lens − its sensitive retina being washed continuously by the sea water in which it lives. Our salty tears are an ancestral recollection of such primitive life forms.

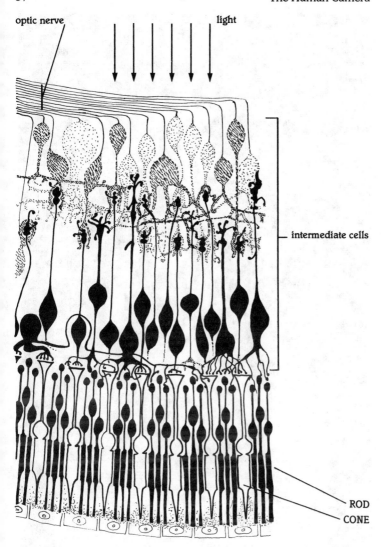

Figure 5.2: Section of human retina
(schematic after Gregory, *Eye and Brain*)

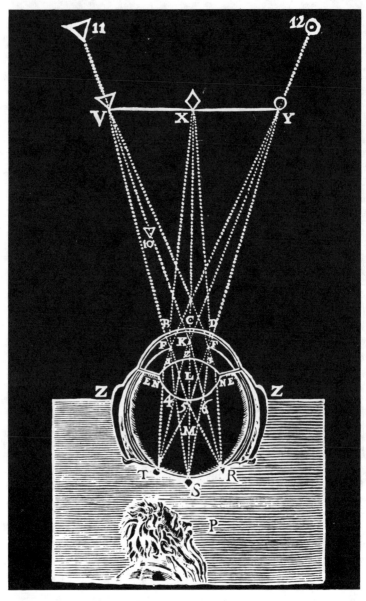

Figure 5.3: Descartes' explanation of vision

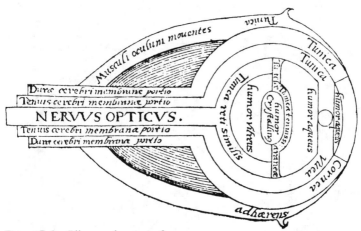

Figure 5.4a: Alhazen drawing of eye

A pinhole camera is an insensitive light detector simply because the amount of light entering it is so small. Refraction is needed to concentrate the light collected from a larger area, and in a camera this function is performed by the lens. There *is* a lens in the human eye, but most of the refraction takes place at the shiny front surface of the eye, the cornea (see Figure 5.4b). To convince yourself of the surprisingly important role of the cornea, try reading even quite large letters on a card with your eyes open under water, in a swimming pool for instance. The refracting power of the cornea is greatly reduced, because the refractive index for light going from water is much less than when going from air. Consequently it is impossible to obtain a sharp focus — or perhaps even to see that there are any letters there at all!

The main function of the lens in the eye is not for collecting light but for fine focusing. A camera is focused by moving its lens nearer to or farther from the film. In the eye, the fine adjustments needed to focus on near or distant objects make use of the soft, elastic quality of the lens. The ciliary muscles around the edge of the lens, controlled by signals from the brain, contract causing the lens to change its shape. This alteration in the curvature of its surface in turn changes the power of refraction just sufficiently to bring the image of the required object into sharp focus on the retina (see Figure 5.5).

Throughout life, however, the lens is steadily hardening. The cells in the middle are dying through oxygen starvation and although new cells

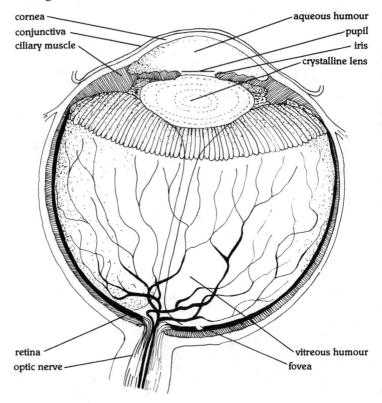

cornea
conjunctiva
ciliary muscle

aqueous humour
pupil
iris
crystalline lens

retina
optic nerve

vitreous humour
fovea

Figure 5.4b: Contemporary drawing of eye .
(schematic after Gregory, *Eye and Brain*)

are continually being added from the outside they cannot prevent the stiffness from increasing. The ability of the muscles to change the shape of the lens, and thereby to focus over a wide range of distances, is gradually lost. The loss of this 'power of accommodation' is a sad but common characteristic of middle age. Until about 1500 A.D., this deterioration could be disastrous for craft workers and scholars wanting to look closely at fine detail; thereafter the invention of spectacles brought them a new degree of freedom.

It is noteworthy that an additional five hundred years of progress, including the wave and photon theories of light, have brought only minor technical improvements to the original invention – now there are contact lenses or lenses with varying curvature. The significant advances

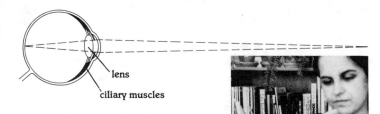

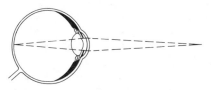

(a) normal distant vision

normal close-up vision; the lens is fattened

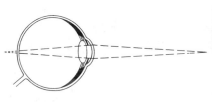

(b) in middle-age the lens hardens and the ciliary muscles may fail to change its shape sufficiently to obtain sharp focus of near objects

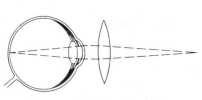

(c) spectacle lens supplements eye lens to obtain sharp close-up focus

Figure 5.5: The miracle of spectacles: how lenses enable millions to read and see fine detail

have been in design, production, and marketing, so that the benefits of spectacles are now brought to millions of people instead of to just a few wealthy people. It is, perhaps, not surprising that one such person should have been the Tax Collector, shown in the portrait Marinus van Roymerswaele painted in about 1550.

In normal vision the eye refracts incoming light at the cornea, bending it through the system − aqueous humour, lens, and vitreous humour − to form a focus on the retina (see Figures 5.3 and 5.4b). But how does it get through all these liquids, jellies and fibrous tissues, and still form a sharp image? After all, camera manufacturers go to enormous trouble to make their lenses homogeneous and transparent. They try to keep irregularities on the scale of atomic structure, say below 10 nm, and to avoid inclusions − bubbles or grit − as large as a wavelength of light, around 500 nm, which would scatter the light and spoil the quality of the image.

The focusing components of the eye, the cornea and the lens, are built up from protein fibres to the required shape and strength. Layers of parallel collagen fibres form the cornea, while the lens is made from other protein fibres layered like an onion. These two natural optical components can thus be considered as elastic glasses, capable of defor-mation without damage. You might expect that a tissue of fine fibres set in a watery jelly would appear milky or opaque because of the scat-tering of light by the individual fibres, or in any case, by the bundles and layers of fibres. A calculation using wave theory, however, shows that, on the contrary, the light scattered from any small region is cancelled out by interference in every direction except the forward direction of the beam. Hence that glorious transparency of the cornea and brightness of the eye that we daily observe and that moves poets to ecstasy:

> Two of the fairest stars in all the heaven,
> Having some business, do entreat her eyes
> To twinkle in their spheres till they return.
> What if her eyes were there, they in her head?
> The brightness of her cheek would shame those stars
> As daylight doth a lamp; her eyes in heaven
> Would through the airy region stream so bright
> That birds would sing and think it were not night.
>
> (Shakespeare, *Romeo and Juliet*;
> Romeo, beneath Juliet's balcony)

The eye is certainly a superbly evolved miniature movie camera, but only after the image has been formed on its retina does the action really begin. The retina is an exquisitely fine structure lying like a mat round the inside of the eyeball. Figure 5.2 shows some of its salient features, particularly the two types of light-sensitive element, the *rods* and the *cones*, which contain retinal.

One striking aspect of the retina is that it seems the wrong way round! The light-sensitive cells are at the *back* of the retina and not, as you might expect, at the front. Light converging from the lens thus has to pass through all of that jungle of cells and optic nerve fibres before it forms the final image. It is like finding that the camera has been loaded with the film back to front. However, the arrangement works extremely well; when we look at the sensitivity of the eye and the sharpness of its images we may decide that perhaps the arrangement is not so stupid after all.

Another puzzle is why there should be two quite different types of light-sensitive cells, the rods and the cones. A little arithmetic will set the problem in perspective. In an average human retina there are something like one hundred and twenty million rods and eight million cones. There are, however, only one million nerve fibres leading back to the brain. A complex system of cells converts the information about the picture received on the retina into nerve signals, and each nerve fibre has to process information from many individual receptors. When you are looking at something, the detail you are concentrating on falls on a very special part of the retina, only about a half a millimetre across, called the *fovea centralis*. When you are looking at the full moon, for example, the tiny moon-like image on your fovea fills about half its diameter. The special quality of the fovea is that it contains about ten thousand cones and no rods at all. It appears then that the cones are the really important photo-receptors and one wonders what function the rods could possibly have.

Over a century ago the anatomist Max Schultze put forward his *Duplicity Theory of Vision* which explained the existence of both cones and rods. The cones are for colour vision in normal lighting conditions; the rods are very sensitive and therefore come into action in dim lighting, but they cannot resolve very fine detail nor can they respond to different colours. Schultze's evidence for this theory was only indirect; he discovered, for instance, that day birds had retinas composed mainly of cones, whereas a night owl had mainly rods. But he had, of course, had the common experience of being in the garden in the late afternoon as the sun was going down. In the sunlight, the garden is bright, colourful and in sharp detail. As twilight descends the colours become more subdued;

at dusk, or in moonlight, only broad outlines are visible in their dark greyish tones; all semblance of fine detail is lost. We are now seeing with our most sensitive vision — according to Schultze, the rods — and we are touched by a chill of emptiness as the greyness spreads around.

> **Do not go gentle into that good night,**
> **Old age should burn and rave at close of day;**
> **Rage, rage against the dying of the light.**

The cones can distinguish different colours, but their absolute sensitivity is much smaller than that of the rods. At low intensities they do not respond at all; in dim light we see only by using the rods. It has been found that the rods are connected together in quite large groups. Each group sends the same electrical signal to the brain no matter which of its rods is illuminated, and that is why they cannot resolve the fine detail that can be seen with the normal foveal cone vision in bright daylight.

Vision in a faint light was studied in an elegant series of experiments pioneered by Maurice Pirenne and his co-workers and described by him in *Vision and the Eye*. An observer sits in a pitch-dark room for half an hour to bring his or her vision into a standard, 'dark-adapted' state. A big, triangular-shaped block sits on a table so that the observer is looking directly at one edge, with one matt, white face on each side. When the observer is ready, the left-hand face of the block is illuminated with a faint light of a particular colour. The observer controls the illumination of the right-hand face and can select any colour and then adjust the intensity until both faces look equally bright. Matching lights of different colour is not tricky, as might be expected, because, at these low levels of illumination, there is no perception of colour at all! If the left face is lit with faint blue light and the observer has chosen yellow for the right, both faces appear pale grey, and it is simply a matter of turning the intensity knob until the division between the two patches of light disappears. Both areas look the same to the observer, but it turns out that the yellow light actually has a much higher physical intensity than the blue. Vision in weak lighting is evidently much less sensitive to yellow light than to blue. A complete experiment demonstrated the wide variation of sensitivity with colour shown in Figure 5.6. The sensitivity rises to a maximum for green light and falls to a level a thousand times smaller for red. This tallies with the gradual disappearance of the 'warm' colours from the landscape as darkness falls.

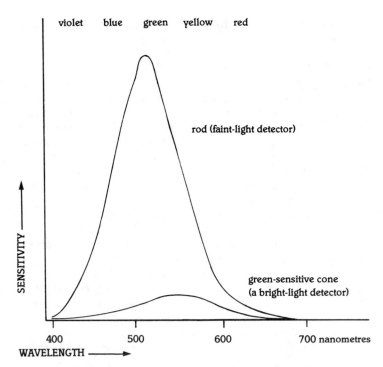

Figure 5.6: Relative colour sensitivities of the two types of light detectors in the retina

How could qualitative observations of birds and gardens be connected with the properties of the tiny rods in the retina? The purple colouring of the rods gave a clue. A pigment – *visual purple* – was extracted from the rods and made into a pink-coloured solution which turned colourless when it was exposed to light. That gave a strong hint that visual purple was the light-sensitive ingredient in the rods. To test this hypothesis, light beams of different colours were shone through the solution and the amount of energy absorbed from each colour was measured. The absorption varied with the colour in just the same way as the sensitivity of vision in a faint light had been found to vary. It was concluded that our most sensitive vision does indeed depend upon the purple pigment of the rods in the retina, a substance known as *rhodopsin*. Each molecule of rhodopsin is a compound in which one molecule of a protein, *opsin*, is bound to one molecule of the substance *retinal*.

The rod and cone model of the retina gives the basis for understanding how the eye works and what the limits to our vision are. Can you see the smile on the face of a mosquito? If not, why not? The limiting factor turns out to be the coarseness of the structure of the retina. Cone vision in bright light gives us our sharpest resolution as the cones are spaced very closely together, at intervals of only about two microns (1000 microns = 1 millimetre). If you examine a small object in bright light at a comfortably close distance, two neighbouring cones will be receiving light from two points on the object which are about one-fiftieth of a millimetre apart. You should thus be able to resolve two or even three distinct markings inside a distance equal to the width of a human hair. In dim lighting conditions, of course, the fovea does not respond and the discrimination is limited by the much coarser groupings of the rods.

This power of resolution is exceptionally high. A honey bee, for instance, has only a hundredth of our sharpness of vision. Looking across a room it wouldn't be able to see that there were any books on a bookshelf, let alone what the titles were.

I once read in an old science book that the eye is so sensitive that it can detect a candle flame at a distance of seventeen miles. Whether that was the result of an experiment, and whether the candle flame would have been invisible at eighteen miles was not made clear. But the sensitivity of the eye to light is indeed astonishingly high, approaching the ultimate where it is limited by the photon nature of light and not by any quality of the eye itself.

Precise experiments have been made to determine the smallest amount of energy needed to produce a sensation of light. Subjects were conditioned to the dark for half an hour before being presented with faint flashes of light of different intensities. With very short flashes it was found that the eye responded only to the total energy in the flash. A flash of a certain intensity lasting for a tenth of a second could not be distinguished from a flash ten times as bright lasting for only a tenth of that time.

It was convenient to work with flashes of one-thousandth of a second, and by varying the intensities it was found that the minimum energy required to fall upon an eye and give the impression of light was about 4×10^{-17} joules, that is about forty million million millionths of a joule (in case you have forgotten, a joule is about the amount of energy needed to lift a cup of coffee to your lips). How can we possibly form any sensible idea of what this sort of number means? From Planck's formula ($E = h\nu$) we find that the energy of one photon of yellow light is about one-hundredth of this minimum energy, so for a flash of

light to be visible, about one hundred photons need to strike the cornea.
That is really a very small amount of energy, and it emphasises the
extreme sensitivity of the eye. Pirenne uses an amusing analogy to illustrate this point: the energy of a pea dropped from a height of a few centimetres onto a table is enough, if converted into luminous energy, to give
a faint flash of light to every person who has ever lived.

Yet the sensitivity of the retina itself is even more striking and significant. Of those hundred photons arriving at the cornea, at least ninety
are effectively wasted – by reflection, scattering or absorption in the cornea, the lens, or the liquids in the eyeball, or else by passing right
through the retina without being captured by the photosensitive pigment
in the rods. Not more than ten photons are actually captured by the
rhodopsin molecules, but that is enough to produce a sensation of light.

More refined experiments showed that the faintest flash of light that
could be seen required the incidence of more than one, but still only
a small number of photons on the retina. In other words, several rods
have to be excited within a short space of time if any visual effect is to
be produced. This requirement is perhaps an evolutionary safeguard. If
a single rod were sufficient, rods all over the retina would continually
be indicating flashes of light because of their normal, spontaneous electrical activity. We should never be able to rest in peaceful darkness with
our eyes closed.

A last and most sophisticated question – how does the eye produce
a sense of colour? – has been answered in part by exquisitely delicate
experiments in which the optical absorption of a single cone was
measured. The results from these techniques would certainly have
pleased our old friend, the phenomenal Thomas Young, for they showed
that his 'trichromatic theory' of colour vision was essentially correct.
Young deduced that the retina must contain three different kinds of light-
sensitive pigment, having their maximum sensitivities in three different
regions of the spectrum. In his own words:

... as it is almost impossible to conceive each sensitive point of the retina to contain an infinite number of particles, each capable of vibrating
in perfect unison with every possible undulation, it becomes necessary
to suppose the number is limited; for instance to the three principal colours red, yellow and blue ...

(cited in Gregory, *Eye and Brain*, p. 118)

Later on he changed his 'principal colours' to red, green, and violet, but he stuck to his view that the three kinds of pigment particles detected three different colours and sent their information on to the brain: '. . . and each sensitive filament of the nerve may consist of three portions, one for each principal colour . . .'

These ideas may seem commonplace today, although many people still are under the impression, originally shared by Young, that the 'primary colours' are red, yellow and blue. They may be when mixing paints, but mixing coloured lights to produce a particular sensation of colour is an entirely different problem. The magnitude of Young's contribution was, however, fully appreciated in the nineteenth century by Clerk Maxwell:

It seems a truism to say that colour is a sensation; and yet Young, by honestly recognising this elementary truth, established the first consistent theory of colour. So far as I know, Thomas Young was the first who, starting from the well-known fact that there are three primary colours, sought for the explanation of this fact, not in the nature of light but in the constitution of man.

(cited in Gregory, *Eye and Brain*, p. 118)

The trichromatic theory received its strongest support from experiments which measured the spectral absorption of one single cone at a time. Three different types of cone were found in the human retina, each with its own distinct type of response to light of different colours (see Figure 5.7). And, sure enough, three different pigments were extracted from the three types of cone, each being a combination of retinal with its own protein. These pigments have been designated as:

cyanolabe: the *blue* detector, with maximum absorption at 447 nm.
chlorolabe: the *green* detector, with maximum absorption at 540 nm.
erythrolabe: the *red* detector, with maximum absorption at 577 nm.

Calling erythrolabe the 'red' pigment may seem odd, because 577 nm corresponds to a brilliant yellow! The other pigments, however, are almost completely inactive in the red end of the spectrum, so a pure red light is detected *only* by the cones containing erythrolabe. In the middle regions of the spectrum the responses of the three pigments overlap (see Figure 5.7), and any single colour (except pure red) may generate some response in each of the three types of cone.

Evidently Thomas Young had a profound insight into the physics of the way the retina deals with coloured images. More recent research

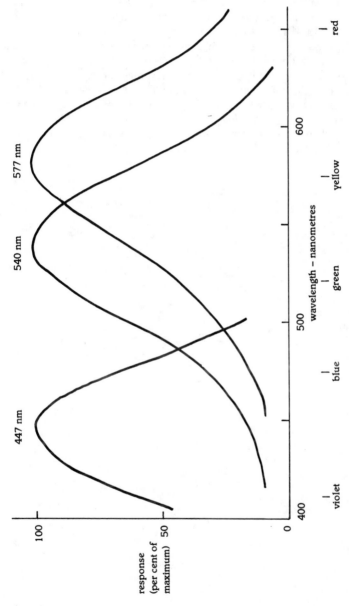

Figure 5.7: Response of the three types of cones to different colours

indicates that he was not quite right in believing that each of the three cone systems sends its own information through independently to the main part of the brain. It seems that data processing begins already at the retina: the three-colour information can be encoded at a sort of relay station into on-off electrical signals which then proceed along a single channel to the brain. The story here becomes part of the unfathomed and possibly unfathomable working of the higher levels of the brain. Is it then perhaps one of those esoteric matters that will only ever be of concern to neurophysiologists and, maybe, psychologists? Perhaps it is. But when we look later at some of the remarkable achievements of Edwin Land, we may think differently.

The Magic Shadow Show

The long path to the vital discovery — the lens

EDMUND·J·SULLIVAN

6

Somewhere in his reminiscences Maxim Gorky relates 'I saw Chekhov sitting in the garden catching sunbeams in his hat and trying in vain to tip them on his head.' In ancient times, though, it would not have done at all to joke about the sun. It was not only the Egyptians who wondered at the light from the heavenly bodies and worshipped them. The hunting people living ten thousand years ago in the last Ice Age would have been even more keenly aware than we are of the vital importance of the sun, the bringer of light and heat. It seems a fair guess that they took it seriously, even to the point of worshipping it.

The earliest records come from the Sumerians of Mesopotamia, the inventors of the wheel, because they were the first to develop the art of writing, but the sun was worshipped in all of those early civilisations that grew up five thousand years ago along the great river valleys of Mesopotamia and Egypt, the Tigris, the Euphrates, and the Nile. It is a far cry from there to finding out how photons stimulate your eye, or building a huge telescope to look at stars beyond the reach of human vision. Yet there is a three-stranded rope of ideas about the nature of light stretching back continuously over those thousands of years. There is the mystical strand, much weaker today, although astrology is flourishing and the United States is said to have ten times more astrologers than astronomers. There is the strand of scientific understanding, very thin in Ikhnaton's time but now fully formed. Then there is the strand of technological development − how to use light to improve human affairs − immensely strong today, though far from negligible even in the dim mists of ancient times. Any of these strands may dominate at any of the different stages in the evolution of optical ideas and practices.

Well over three thousand years ago, the civilised world had not only its mystical view of sun gods and omens in the sky, but also an accurate astronomy which was applied to such down-to-earth problems as the construction of the pyramids or the calendar. For the practical purposes of navigation the stars had been grouped into constellations: long before Ikhnaton was born, ships were setting their courses by Aquarius the water-carrier, Orion the mighty hunter, the Great Bear, and all the other people and animals immortalised in the night sky.

There are today about a hundred recognised constellations: forty in the northern hemisphere and fifty in the southern, together with the twelve constellations of the zodiac. Some of the southern constellations, it is true, were named comparatively recently. Only in 1679, for example, did Augustine Royer introduce Crux australis, the Southern Cross. But many constellations appear under their present-day names in books going right back to Hipparchus in Rhodes around 130 B.C. Hipparchus himself, the greatest astronomer of the ancient world, made a critical attack on the famous book written by the Greek astronomer, Eudoxus in 350 B.C. The King of Macedonia had commissioned the Greek poet Aratus to set Eudoxus' book into verse and the resulting poem, published in 270 B.C., was an instant success. It was compulsory in Greek schools to learn passages from it by heart; St Paul quoted from it in his address to the Athenians; and during the idle days between campaigns Germanicus Caesar spent his time translating it into elegant Latin hexameters. The poem gives Eudoxus' precise statements about the positions of the stars at different times, information clearly intended as an aid to navigation. Yet when Hipparchus examined the poem he discovered that many of the statements were wrong! For example:

Eudoxus displays ignorance about the North Pole in the following Passage: 'There is a star which remains always motionless. This star is the pole of the world'. In fact there is no star at the pole but an empty space close to which lie three stars which, taken together with the point at the pole, make a rough quadrangle, as Pytheas of Marseille tells us.

Evidently Eudoxus had written the treatise on his globe without bothering to go out and look at the night sky − not, perhaps, uncommon behaviour for a theoretical scientist. But these discrepancies alerted Hipparchus to what was actually going on. He deduced that the earth's axis is slowly rotating round its average direction, rather like the slow wobble of a child's spinning top. This so-called 'precession of the equinoxes' is caused by the attraction of the sun and the moon on the bulge round the middle of the earth. Hipparchus calculated that each complete wobble takes almost twenty-six thousand years, and the best modern measurements differ from his value only by 0.2 per cent. Hipparchus then realised what Eudoxus' problem had been: it wasn't that he was a bad astronomer, but simply that he was working with a globe that was a long time out of date. At some time in the past, when the earth's axis was pointing in a different direction, there *would* have been a North Polar star, and Eudoxus' other statements would also have been correct.

Michael Ovendon and Archie Roy, two astronomers at Glasgow University, seized on the challenge of discovering just where and when the globe of Eudoxus was made. They programmed a planetarium to display the starry skies as they would have appeared at different times and places in the past. As they moved back through the centuries, with the axis of the earth slowly turning, more and more of Eudoxus' statements started to fit. In about 2000 B.C. and at a latitude of 36°N every statement was correct.

And on the island of Crete, latitude 36°N, around 2000 B.C. were flourishing the Minoans, the leading sea-power of the Mediterranean and the first great European civilisation. Here, it seems, were made the celestial globes for the Cretan navigators, one of which may have been given to Eudoxus by Egyptian priests in 350 B.C. Roy speculated about the way in which the globe came into the possession of the Egyptians over a thousand years before.

A Minoan merchant ship is crossing the Mediterranean one night on course for its home port of Amnissos in Crete. It has been a successful journey, trading timber, pottery and ornaments for gold and jewellery. The navigator is sitting in his cabin with his globe and his flickering oil lamp. From time to time he gets up to check on the positions of the stars and to talk to the steersman about whether the prolonged rumbles of thunder they have been hearing in the distance are the forerunners of a storm. As they talk the thunder grows louder. Suddenly they are nearly deafened by the mightiest roaring they have ever heard and the ship rolls alarmingly in the heaving ocean. Throughout the night the sailors fight for survival. Torn by the driving, grit-filled winds they steer blindly; the stars have long since disappeared from sight.

The night seems endless. With no means of telling the time they pray for the dawn. But dawn there was not. The sky was filled with the suffocating powder that covered the ship, choked their lungs and let only a dull glow through from the sun at its noon-day height. As the ship drives southward the days begin to lighten but the food and the water are gone. The few survivors are just able to guide the ship when the coastline of the Nile Delta is sighted and to make landfall before collapsing. As the ship and its contents are being dealt with by port officials, the globe is taken by the priests to a place of honour in the archives where it will rest for over a thousand years.

The story is fanciful, but it is not fancy that the biggest explosion in history occurred in about 1450 B.C. when the Aegean island of Thera was split by a volcanic eruption. There was a similar event when the volcano, Krakatoa, in the Sunda Strait just off Java, erupted in 1883. Then day turned to night over a radius of 150 kilometres; the terrible noise was heard across Australia, thousands of kilometres away. A mountain twenty square kilometres in area was blown out of the sea, whole new islands of pumice were formed; volcanic ash was deposited as far away as Europe. The worst calamity was a series of huge tidal waves which spread out over the neighbouring islands, killing 36 000 people in a single night.

The explosion on the island of Thera, often called Santorini, was ten times more powerful. In 1500 B.C. Thera was a 'normal' Aegean island, with its people living happily within the Minoan culture of its large neighbour, Crete. The volcano rose on its west coast to a height of over eighteen hundred metres. After the explosion the west coast was no more. Today a twelve-kilometre bay flanked by stark perpendicular cliffs makes the island look as if some giant had taken a bite out of its side, right down, indeed, to a depth of 400 metres below the sea. Calculations show that the resulting tidal wave (the Tsunami) must have rushed out from Thera at about 400 kilometres an hour. On the open sea this wave would simply have lifted a ship, as on a giant swell; but as the wave approached Crete it would have piled up, as the shallower waters were approached, until it became an onrushing battering ram of water forty metres high to smash that unhappy land. All of the low-lying cities, the houses and the palaces were destroyed. So may have ended the great civilisation of the legendary King Minos, the home of Daedalus and Icarus, of Ariadne and the Minotaur — the bull that in Minoan legend lived beneath the ground and whose roaring produced the earthquakes had bellowed once too often.

A thousand years later Solon, the enlightened law-giver of Athens, visited Egypt seeking the wisdom of that ancient civilisation. The Egyptian priests taught him much about geometry and astronomy, the sciences that would set the Greeks on to the study of the behaviour and nature of light. And they told him of an earlier civilisation in a golden age, a mighty civilisation that had grown too big for its boots and that was punished by the gods for the sin of hubris, of excessive and vainglorious pride. In a single night this civilisation was destroyed by fire and flood. It sank beneath the waves and became, according to Plato who reported this discussion in his *Timaeus*, the Lost Land of Atlantis.

Minoan Crete was the superpower of its day, yet it was cultured and unwarlike: even its sports with the bulls were completely unarmed, essentially athletic contests. Today's superpowers stand bristling with nuclear weapons and pursue such lunatic strategies as Mutually Assured Destruction (known, naturally, as M.A.D.). Until they can be persuaded to divert the enormous cost of this escalating suicide-power towards the real needs of humanity, let us hope that at least their early warning systems are proof against the unsuspected eruption of another volcano like Thera or Krakatoa.

When Roy lectured on the origin of the constellations to an enthralled audience of physicists, he may have had some such thoughts in mind when he concluded by saying 'As scientists it is our duty to tell our fellow men how they may destroy the Earth. I hope that we won't be like the Minoans — our little day in the sun to be followed by night and disaster.'

The Minoans had harnessed the light from the stars for their navigation but a thousand years would elapse before the Greeks began the attempt to understand and to harness light here on earth.

The most influential of the ancient Greeks was an Athenian aristocrat named Aristocles. Because of his powerful physique he was given the nickname by which he is now known, Plato, meaning broad. Plato's interest in science lay in ideals, in absolute values preferably uncontaminated by reality. Following the spirit of Pythagoras, pure mathematics was one of his ideals. Over the door of the Academy where he taught his philosophy he mounted the inscription

ΜΗΔΕΙΩ ΑΓΕΩΜΕΤΡΗΟΣ ΕΙΩΙΤΩ

saying, in effect, if you don't have a credit in mathematics, keep out. He supported the idea of astronomy, but he warned astronomers of the dangers of actually looking at the stars themselves: better to sit back and work out the ideal scheme of what they really ought to be like. He wanted to study *astrology*, a word he coined meaning the reasoning about stars, rather than *astronomy*, the mere naming of stars. Unfortunately his successors went on to invent the horoscope, based on the concept that the positions of the stars at one's birth (or conception) are a key to one's character and fate. Astrology came into disrepute and the old word 'astronomy' was brought back.

Today, although we proclaim our belief in astronomy rather than astrology, readers of newspapers and magazines are treated to regular columns advising what the stars have in store for them. Of course they don't really believe it, but perhaps . . .? It seems rather like Niels Bohr's favourite story of the physicist who had a horseshoe nailed to his door: 'Of course I don't believe in it', he said, 'but they say that it brings you luck even if you don't believe in it'.

Plato's contribution to the nature of light was to propose a modification of the astonishing theory of ocular beams, the beams of light that were supposed to shine out of the eyes like tentacles to touch the objects that were being seen. The obvious question challenging the ocular beam theorists was: if the illumination comes out of your eyes, why can't you see at night? Plato's answer was that the inner light which streams out through the eyes only works when it mixes with a kindred light, the light from the sun.

But despite Plato, and contrary to the beliefs espoused by textbook writers, the Greek scientists were not content to be merely armchair thinkers, and based their studies of light soundly upon experiment. Indeed, the Greeks brought into being the first state-supported scientific research institute in the world – the Museum at Alexandria.

The port of Alexandria on the Egyptian shores of the Mediterranean was founded in 332 B.C. by Alexander the Great. It grew rapidly into one of the most important cities of its age, described by one writer as 'a beautiful place with . . . 4000 palaces, 4000 baths, 12 000 gardeners, 40 000 Jews who paid tribute, and 400 theatres and other places of amusement'. In it stood the most famous library of all, destroyed by fire when Julius Caesar gave the order to burn the Egyptian fleet at anchor in the harbour. Here Archimedes studied, and here Euclid wrote the *Elements of Geometry*. The Museum was set up by Ptolemy I, one of Alexander the Great's chief generals, who had become King of Egypt after the death of Alexander. Setting out to rule a vast empire, Ptolemy and his successors recognised the connections between science, technology and government. They founded the research institute and maintained it over the following centuries with the primary aim of providing for the training of engineers, doctors, astronomers, mathematicians and geographers.

The research program did not always follow the lines envisaged. As research directors the world over are still learning, it is next to impossible to keep a tight rein on the activities of research scientists. So it was with the Museum. Experimental physics forged ahead in unexpected areas such as pneumatics, mechanics and optics. The work of Hero and of Claudius Ptolemy in particular brought the science of optics up to a pitch that would not be reached again until the dramatic developments of the seventeenth century A.D.

Hero of Alexandria is perhaps more famous as an inventor than as a physicist. He built elaborate devices mostly designed to deceive worshippers into believing that a divine agency was at work, devices such as a mechanical singing bird, a sacrificial vessel which flowed wine or water when money was put into it, and a machine enabling temple doors to be opened by a fire on the altar. He also understood the reflection of light, from plane or from curved mirrors, as is shown in his textbook on that subject, *Catoptrics:*

Catoptrics is clearly a science worthy of study and at the same time produces spectacles which excite wonder in the observer. For with the aid of this science, mirrors are constructed which show the right side as right side, and similarly the left side, whereas ordinary mirrors by their nature have the contrary property and show the opposite sides.

(cited in Gamow, *Biography of Physics*, p. 18)

Hero is dealing with the problem Alice had in describing her Looking-Glass House: 'the books are something like our books, only the words go the wrong way: I know that because I've held up one of our books to the glass, and then they hold up one in the other room'. He solves it by using two mirrors set up edge-to-edge and at right angles. He goes on to explain some of the other clever tricks you can do with mirrors, plane or curved:

It is possible with the aid of mirrors to see our own backs and to see ourselves inverted, standing on our heads, with three eyes and two noses, the features distorted as in intense grief . . .
Who will not deem it very useful that we should be able to observe, on occasion, while remaining inside our own house, how many people there are on the street and what they are doing?

(cited in Gamow, *Biography of Physics*, p. 18)

The Alexandrian astronomer Claudius Ptolemy adopted Hipparchus' model of the solar system with Earth at the centre, and elaborated his ideas in a huge book, *Megale mathematike syntaxis*, 'the great mathematician composition'. The Earth-centred system became known as the Ptolemaic System. Ptolemy's book became the bible of astronomy and was popularly referred to as *Megiste*, meaning greatest. After the fall of the Roman Empire it was taken up enthusiastically by the Arabs who called it *Almagest*, meaning 'the greatest', an expression used by Islamic boxers even today.

Ptolemy also wrote a book on optics in which he went beyond the work of Hero to deal with the behaviour of light in passing through transparent media.

Visual rays may be altered in two ways: by reflection, that is the rebound from objects called mirrors, which do not permit penetration, and by refraction, that is by bending, in the case of 'transparent materials' for the reason that the visual ray penetrates them.

(cited in Gamow, *Biography of Physics*, p. 20)

One typical experiment of Ptolemy's looks rather like a children's party trick: put a coin at the bottom of a bowl and then stand so that you can't quite see it. How can you see the coin without moving either your head or the bowl? Hero would presumably have cheated by using a mirror, but the proper answer is to pour some water into the bowl, whereupon the coin comes into view. Ptolemy converted this harmless trick into a crucial scientific experiment, using a graduated copper disk vertically in the water. He carried out another series of experiments on the refraction of light in glass (even harder to do!), but he could see no systematic relationship governing the amount of bending in either case.

Ptolemy's work stopped just short of discovering the law of refraction, and there was no one left to follow it through at the Museum. The whole Graeco-Roman world was sliding into decay. Successive Roman emperors succeeded for a time in protecting the vestiges of Greek culture against the rising power of the Christian church. But after the death in 415 A.D. of Emperor Julian there was no holding it back. With a bitter irony the only noted woman scholar of the times, Hypatia, was attacked and torn to pieces by the Christian mobs. The rioters went on to destroy the libraries of Alexandria so that most of the works that had been accumulated since the great fire were lost.

But what of the nature of light itself? How far had the Greeks gone in speculating on this profound challenging theme? Leaving aside the strange concept of ocular beams, there were two main schools of thought, two apparently incompatible ideologies which would clash repeatedly in the future, with a strange but powerful synthesis of the two being attained in the twentieth century.

The first view was that light is a disturbance of a thin, invisible and intangible medium which fills space. This elusive medium, known as the ether, was introduced as the quintessential element (earth, air, fire and water being the first four) by Aristotle, the star pupil of Plato and in turn the tutor of Alexander the Great. Aristotle's views on the branch of science that he named *physics* were, to say the least, unfortunate. He believed that applied science had already completed its task because, as he put it, 'nearly all the requisites of comfort and social refinement have been secured'. The object of his physics was to find the *nature* of everything: the nature of a stone is to fall to the ground; the nature of men is to be either masters or slaves. His view of light as a sort of perturbation or wave in the ether was accepted along with the rest of his natural philosophy, and it dominated physical thinking for the next two thousand years.

The alternative point of view — that light is really a stream of tiny particles — emerged from the school of Greek atomists, scientists who believed that matter was built up from tiny, elementary particles which they called *atoms*. Atomism was strongly opposed by Plato and Aristotle, and it remained an eccentric, minority movement until it was resuscitated in the seventeenth century. The materialistic philosophy of the movement was expounded with great style by one of its later admirers, the Roman poet Lucretius. It was a time when serious ideas were often put forward in verse and Lucretius published his great work, *De Rerum Natura*, On the Nature of Things, in the form of an epic poem, written in 55 B.C. while Julius Caesar was busy landing in Britain. The poem was never finished, but its breathtaking scope is shown by the titles of the sections that he did complete: Matter and Space; Movement and Shapes of Atoms; Life and Mind; Sensation and Sex; Cosmology and Sociology; Meteorology and Geology.

All of these complex things Lucretius relates to the behaviour of atoms. What is really solid and durable he asks? Even hard gold is softened and melted by heat. Yet 'there exist certain bodies that are absolutely solid and indestructible, namely those atoms which, according to our teaching, are the seeds or prime units of things from which the whole universe is built up'. Explaining light in similar atomistic terms, Lucretius describes the formation of optical images as the result of objects 'spraying particles from their surfaces'. And reflections, he notes, have the same appearance as actual objects. They must therefore be composed of films given off by those objects. There exist, therefore, flimsy but accurate replicas of objects, individually invisible but such that, when flung back in a rapid succession of recoils from the flat surface of mirrors they produce a visible image.

(Lucretius, *On the Nature of the Universe*, p. 133)

A narrow-minded technocrat looking at the thousand years of civilisation after the decline of Alexandria might simply say that the only thing of importance that happened to optics in that time was the discovery of the lens. The reality is, of course, more subtle than that and more interesting.

Certainly the lens was a great advance. It seems to have emerged from the studies of Islamic scholars, many of whom were practising doctors. Eye diseases were widespread in the Arab countries and in the process of developing their surgery the doctors would have learned the inner physiology of the eye and realised the action of its lens. It was only a short step then to artificial lenses, made at first out of crystal and later from glass. The focusing of light by lenses was explained in one of the world's foremost scientific books, the *Optical Thesaurus*, published in 1040 A.D., shortly before the Norman conquest of England. The author of this book, known today as Alhazen, made his own spherical and parabolic mirrors and also constructed a pinhole camera.

Alhazen's work is remarkable in part for the difficulties under which he carried it out. He obtained a job working for the Caliph of Egypt by making the outrageous claim that he could devise a machine for controlling the flooding of the Nile. Unfortunately the Caliph was a power-mad dictator who promised to have Alhazen put very slowly to death if the machine was not rapidly forthcoming. Alhazen's only way out was to feign insanity, and his work had to be carried on in secret until the death of the Caliph in 1021.

But the road forward for optical science was not simply the story of overly clever physicists trying to discover the new laws in the teeth of opposition by potentates, politicians or priests. The astronomer Omar Khayyám, who lived in Iran at about the same time as Alhazen, used his astronomy to make a major reform of the Muslim calendar, comparable in importance to the Gregorian reform of the European calendar five centuries later. Even this achievement did not save him from feelings about the purposelessness of life, and the sterility of medieval science in particular. His verses show a boredom with the contentious academics even while he hints at the sun-centred theory of the solar system, also five centuries into the future:

> But leave the Wise to wrangle, and with me
> The Quarrel of the Universe let be:
>   And, in some corner of the Hubbub coucht,
> Make Game of that which makes as much of Thee.
>
> For in and out, above, about, below,
> 'Tis nothing but a Magic Shadow-show,
>   Play'd in a Box whose Candle is the Sun,
> Round which we Phantom Figures come and go.

Those Islamic scientists who chose not to opt out of the struggle pursued their optical work in the great observatories of Baghdad, Cairo and Samarkand. They built huge protractors and quadrants to increase the accuracy of their observations which were initially aimed solely at improving the calendar. After all, Mohammed had laid down in the Koran that 'Allah has placed the Sun for daylight, the Moon for night light and also as an instrument for reckoning time and counting the years.' Science was now, and for centuries would essentially remain, the handmaiden of religion.

In medieval Christian Europe the Church had set its face against astrology, holding that it was incompatible with God's omnipotence and human free will. Astronomy was close enough to astrology to come under the same ban, and at one time astronomical competence had sunk so low that the Pope had to send an envoy to Spain to find out from the Arabs the correct date for Easter. As Christianity spread northwards a stream of translations from Arabic, including the classics of ancient Greece, poured into Europe. The astrology came in all mixed up with the astronomy and percolated right through the Church. In 1514, Pope Leo X founded a professorship of astrology at the University of Rome and subsequent Popes employed astrologers to fix the dates of coronations and consistories.

But it was the work of Roger Bacon that really started to sharpen the focus on optics. Bacon was a thirteenth-century Franciscan friar who advanced the theory of refraction beyond the ideas of Ptolemy and Alhazen. He gave constructions for tracing the paths of light rays through lenses and showed how to use a lens as a magnifying glass.

If a man looks at letters and other minute objects through the medium of a crystal or a glass . . . placed upon the letters, and this is the smaller part of a sphere whose convexity is towards the eye, and the eye is in the air, he will see the letters much better and they will appear larger to him.

Bacon spent vast sums of money on his experiments in alchemy and optics, regarding them as part of the divine revelation. He sought the support of his friend Pope Clement IV for a grandiose scheme to unify the study of the sciences, but after the death of Clement in 1268 he lost favour with his order and was sent to prison.

The explanations for his imprisonment range from 'suspected novelties in his teaching' to conspiring with the devil in the invention of spectacles. It seems possible, however, that his aggressive big-headedness, an occupational hazard for theoretical physicists through the ages, was at least partly responsible for his undoing. He also aroused opposition by his brilliant conception of the *experimentum crucis*, the idea of designing a crucial experiment to give an unequivocal answer about the truth of a proposition rather than submitting it to the usual process of long and scholarly debate. In his later years his reputation was somewhat restored. He became known as *Doctor Admirabilis* and his last theological works show him looking beyond science for the glory of God to a science for the service also of humanity. He wrote of the creation of steamships, motor cars and aeroplanes, of telescopes and microscopes, and even of a form of chemistry that would 'teach how to discover such things as are capable of prolonging human life'.

It was a Golden Age for the non-specialist: art, science, technique, craftmanship, were all at the disposal of a single individual. Typical of such all-rounders was Leone Battista Alberti, illegitimate son of a nobleman politically exiled from Florence to Genoa. Alberti was architect, poet, lawyer, painter, surveyor and town-planner. He advocated Brunelleschi's formal theory of perspective and characteristically brought all of his relevant knowledge to bear on the problem, employing not only his artistic experience and his aesthetic judgement, but also co-ordinate geometry and optical devices such as the camera obscura, a large-scale form of pinhole camera.

Another notable Renaissance figure who saw science as an integral part of the full life of a person, also an illegitimate son of a gentleman of Florence, was the engineer, sculptor, architect, scientist, prophetic inventor and painter, Leonardo da Vinci. Leonardo went beyond the

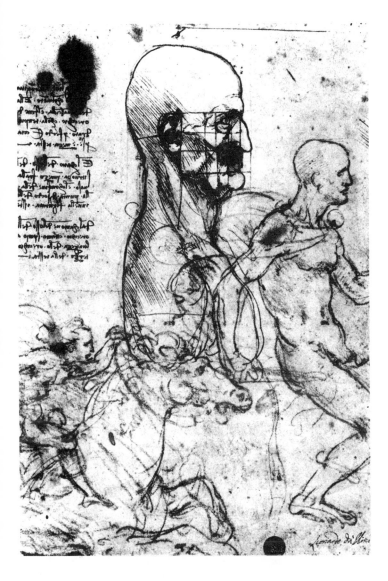

Profile of a man squared for proportion. 'From the eyebrow to the junction of
the lip with the chin, the angle of the jaw, and the angle where the ear joins the
temple will be a perfect square . . .'

static realism of the perspective painting that was in vogue at the end of the fifteenth century, adding dynamics and anatomy to produce pictures with unrivalled grace and movement. He insisted that painting was a noble form of applied science, writing in his treatise

The science of painting deals with all the colours of the surfaces of bodies and with the shapes of the bodies thus enclosed; with their relative nearness and distance; with the degrees of diminutions required as distances gradually increase; moreover, this science is the mother of perspective, that is, of the science of visual rays.

Leonardo's achievements enabled him to get away with this bold assertion. Apprenticed to Verocchio he added the figure of a kneeling angel to a painting of the Baptism of Christ with such brilliance and depth that the master is reputed to have laid down his brush for ever. Despite a reputation for indolence, unreliability and homosexuality, the golden-bearded Leonardo in his rose-coloured cloak rapidly became one of Florence's favourite painters. Moving to Milan he served the Duke, Ludovico the Moor, as a combination of architect, engineer, scientist, painter, entertainer and master of ceremonies to the court.

It was the Duke who enabled Leonardo to put his ideas of light and perspective to the test by commissioning his masterpiece, *The Last Supper*. Leonardo spent four years on this stupendous picture in the church of Saint Maria delle Grazie, completing it in 1498. The picture, about nine metres wide and five high, occupies the rear wall of the convent refectory. It is hard to believe that the soft light streaming across the table where Christ sits with his disciples does not come from the blue sky and the bright countryside that shines through the windows; but that the whole thing, windows included, is simply paint on a very solid wall.

Slowly Leonardo began to realise that he was not going to see his great ambitions fulfilled. Neither the Florentines nor the Milanese were going to create the garden city he had dreamed of and planned in such detail: wide, spacious streets; light and airy houses with efficient plumbing; industry set well away from the city and using the automatic machines he had designed for working wood or metal. The ferocious machines of war that he designed for Duke Ludovico remained unbuilt, though this did not, perhaps, distress him; they fitted strangely with the character of a man who used to buy caged birds in the market so that he could release them, and who refused to divulge details of his submarine because it might be used by men with evil intentions.

One deep frustration came from his failure to make progress with the theory of lenses. His theory was based on the functioning of the human eye, but unfortunately he had dismissed the retina as unimportant because the image on it was upside down. He was therefore led into the incorrect assumption that the light sensitive detector in the eye was the lens itself.

Leaving Milan for the last time, he took with him just a few precious things — Salai, his curly-headed model, and a portrait he had worked on devotedly for over four years, showing a middle-aged Neapolitan woman, known today as the *Mona Lisa*. He took with him also the knowledge that *The Last Supper* was already starting to decay because of errors in his material techniques. He had painted it in tempera, binding the paint pigments with eggs and priming the wall with a glue and chalk mixture, and it was already showing cracks and stains from the high humidity. He could not foresee that despite invasions, world wars and the covetousness of kings and emperors seeking to remove it, *The Last Supper* would be the object of devoted and largely successful restoration throughout the centuries to come.

He could however, and probably did, foresee that his other brain-children — the aeroplane, the submarine, the automatic machine and the motor car — would one day be built and come to change the world. In the fifteenth century there was neither the economic incentive nor the necessary scientific knowledge to implement the dreams of a Roger Bacon or a Leonardo. These would soon come: incentives from the great expansion of trading, colonisation and navigation and laws of mechanics from the astronomers who were trying to account for the movements of the planets. And another piece of the jigsaw to be fitted in was the law describing the refraction of light. In almost one and a half thousand years the science of light still had not advanced much beyond the achievements of Claudius Ptolemy. But Europe was changing. Social pressures were developing which would soon put a premium upon astronomy and the use of the telescope. Applied optics was coming into its own, and dominating the earlier part of the seventeenth century would be the problem of the planets.

7

From Myths to Microbes

The lens extends vision
up to the stars and down
to living cells

7

By the year 1600 the cultural excitement of the Renaissance had spread up from Italy and was sweeping through Northern Europe. In France the works of Rabelais were bringing literature to the common people. In England, Shakespeare was working on his new play, *Hamlet*, while *Julius Caesar* was playing to full houses at the Globe.

Yet the greatest excitement of all lay out on the high seas: on the Spanish Main where the treasure-laden galleons were the targets for Dutch, English and French warships and buccaneers; across the wide oceans where the navies sailed in search of new colonies and trade; and even in the English Channel where Francis Drake and his fleet had defeated the Spanish Armada for being so rash as to launch an invasion during the rigours of an English summer. The note was struck clearly by Jean Fernel:

This age of ours sees art and science gloriously re-risen, after twelve centuries of swoon . . . Our age today is doing things of which antiquity did not dream . . . Ocean has been crossed by the prowess of our navigators, and new islands found . . . In all this, and in what pertains to astronomy, Plato, Aristotle and the old philosophers made progress, and Ptolemy added a great deal more. Yet, were one of them to return today, he would find geography changed beyond recognition. A new globe has been given to us by the navigators of our time.
(Sherrington, *The Endeavours of Jean Fernel*, p. 17)

The navigators of that time, however, were in very serious trouble. When the Earl of Cumberland's fleet sailed home into the English Channel there was nothing unusual about the heated argument that broke out as to whether they were approaching the coast of England or France. Luckily they decided it was England and changed course just in time to avoid destruction on the Ushant rocks. A telescope could have helped them to identify the distant coastline, but this simple optical instrument had, surprisingly, not yet been invented. But why were they so far off course anyway? Their problem was the inadequacy of the star charts and astronomical tables they used for navigation. Because of the needs of the navigators, astronomy became for a time the most important of the sciences. It did not lose that privileged position until the end of the eighteenth century, when steering by the stars was largely supplanted by navigation based upon timing, using new and accurate chronometers carried on board ship.

In the 1600s, the pursuit of astronomy, especially the motions of the planets, was justified both by the navigational needs and by the consequent discovery of the laws of mechanics, which had far-reaching and practical applications. Brecht, in his play, *The Life of Galileo*, has Galileo explain his position clearly. Galileo argues with a monk who excuses himself for giving up astronomy because it may upset the belief that God has put the Earth at the centre of the universe. And that belief, he says, is the only thing that can keep the peasants feeling secure and contented. Galileo makes no attempt to justify his science for its own sake. He agrees with the monk's humane concern but angrily proclaims that the well-being of the peasants is the very reason why the science needs to be pursued. The peasants desperately need irrigation for their fields, but we can't invent machinery for pumping water from the river, he thunders, unless we first study 'the greatest machinery that lies before our eyes, the machinery of the stars'.

The sun-centred system that so worried the monk had been revived from an ancient Greek theory by the Polish canon Nicholas Copernicus fifty years earlier. Although Copernicus seems to have been no better an astronomer than Columbus was a navigator, his imperfect model of the solar system nevertheless had as big an effect on science as Columbus' discovery of America had upon Europe. Yet his success was achieved as much by the old mystical way of thinking as by the cool rationality claimed for modern science. After describing his system, Copernicus tosses in the revolutionary thought that the stars must be at immense distances away from us; he then gives a simple and rational explanation of the hitherto baffling motion of the planets, which appear to pass through the sky in gigantic loops, but his triumphant conclusion reveals the way his mind is really working:

In the middle of all sits Sun enthroned. In this most beautiful temple
could we place this luminary in any better position from which he can
illuminate the whole at once? He is rightly called the Lamp, the Mind,
the Ruler of the Universe; Hermes Trismegistus names him the visible
God, Sophocles' Electra calls him the All-seeing. So the Sun sits as upon
a royal throne ruling his children, the planets which circle round him.
The Earth has the Moon at her service. As Aristotle says, in his **de
Animalibus**, the Moon has the closest relationship with the Earth. Meanwhile the Earth conceives by the Sun, and becomes pregnant with an
annual rebirth.

> (Royal Astronomical Society, 'Nicolaus Copernicus,
> De Revolutionibus, Preface and Book I',
> *Occasional Notes*, No. 10 [May 1947])

The tension between the old and the new ways of thought reached
its climax — and its resolution in favour of the new — in the brilliant,
mixed-up mind of the German scientist Johannes Kepler. It was Kepler
who corrected the main errors of Copernicus and set a straight course
for the future of physical science; it was Kepler whose analysis of the
functions of lenses in telescopes founded the science of optical instruments; yet it was also Kepler who announced that there are only six
planets because the Creator had to fit their orbits between and around
the Five Perfect Solids. It was Kepler, moreover, who spent half of his
professional life in casting horoscopes. True, he seems gradually to have
lost faith with the predictions from the stars, saying that 'God provides
for every animal his means of sustenance — for astronomers He has provided astrology'.

Kepler is, indeed, one of the principal figures in the story of how the
mystery of the planetary motions was solved. This tale is usually told
around a sequence of great men — Copernicus, Tycho, Galileo, Kepler
and Newton. In the hands of a writer like Koestler, as in his book *The
Sleepwalkers*, the interplay of these strange characters can become high
drama. But somehow one never seems to read about people such as
Erasmus Habermel or Jost Bürgi. Yet it was these Bohemians and their
Danish counterparts who constructed the astronomical instruments
with the superb precision that was essential to the enterprise. History
would look very different without their contributions.

Consider, for instance, the achievement of Tycho Brahe. He and the
Greek Hipparchus are generally considered to be the greatest of the
naked-eye astronomers; each has one of the most impressive craters of
the moon named after him. Tycho was a Danish nobleman, a member

of the haughty Junker class, who wore a silver nose in place of his original nose, which had been sliced off in a duel. In his youth he was obsessed with the problems of building bigger and bigger sighting instruments — sextants and quadrants — to improve the accuracy of fixing star positions. When the King appointed him Court Astrologer and gave him the island of Hven, lying between Elsinore and Copenhagen, Tycho promptly set about building himself the palace of Uraniborg, the first great observatory in the West.

Tycho's success was dependent on the abilities of his instrument makers, who made him a quadrant with a radius of six metres and a two-metre celestial globe. He introduced the idea of repeating every measurement many times and then quoting an estimate of its accuracy. In this way, over fourteen years, he amassed a new star catalogue giving the positions of 777 stars, the exact framework on which future astronomy would be built. The accuracy of these positions was within two minutes of arc (0.03 degrees) and could hardly be bettered without the aid of lenses because of the limitations of the human eye in resolving fine detail (see Chapter 5). Ptolemy's observations had been accurate to only about ten minutes of arc. The increase in accuracy from within ten minutes to within two minutes may not seem earth-shaking, but when Kepler came to do his calculations, it turned out to be just that.

When Kepler and Tycho Brahe met in Prague in 1600, Tycho had less than two years left to live. And in that brief time Kepler had to extract the starry observations from the master and also to carry out the assignment that Tycho had set him: to determine the orbit of Mars. The first of these tasks was hard enough; the second had hitherto proved impossible. The wily old Dane intended to keep his measurements to himself until he had proved his own version of the Copernican solar system; only as he grew near to death did he start to put his hope into Kepler as his true successor, and in his last night he kept repeating in his delirium 'let me not seem to have lived in vain'. Kepler's copious diary — kept so carefully in order to check his astrological predictions — shows his appreciation of the difficulties in dealing with Tycho even before they had met. He determined to obtain, somehow, the exact details of the ten positions of Mars recorded by Tycho with his supreme accuracy when that planet stood in opposition to the sun. Tycho did not part with these secrets during his lifetime and upon his death his data and his priceless instruments were appropriated by his heirs with the intention of selling them to the Emperor Rudolph II. The sale never materialised and the instruments decayed and were later lost altogether during the chaos of the Thirty Years War. But Kepler was too quick for the avaricious Junkers,

and the Martian measurements were safe. He coolly wrote to a correspondent: 'I confess that when Tycho died, I quickly took advantage of
the absence, or lack of circumspection, of the heirs, by taking the observations under my care, or perhaps usurping them . . .' (Koestler, *The
Sleepwalkers*, p. 350).

These observations supplemented the measurements Kepler had
already made with Tycho in Prague to give him just what he needed.
When he had arrived with his family in 1600, they had taken up resi-
dence in a small house in an alleyway in the old quarter of the city. Each
day he would walk through the quiet, narrow streets and cross the river
to the elegant buildings of the Belvedere Castle. The Belvedere sported
a fine verandah where he and Tycho used to set up their equipment —
some of the great old pieces from Hven and some newly made in
Prague. Outstanding among the new instruments was an exquisitely
beautiful sextant, one of the works of art produced by that master crafts-
man Erasmus Habermel. The original instruments from Uraniborg are
all lost and though it is possible to see the copies of them that were taken
by the Jesuits to Peking, this original gem of Habermel's is still on display
in the National Technical Museum in Prague.

When the raw young Kepler had been assigned the problem of the
orbit of Mars because it had proved too difficult for anyone else, he had
boasted that he would solve it in eight days. It was actually eight years
and several abandoned theories later that he reached his goal. He published his astonishing result in 1609, seven years after Tycho's death.
Koestler's translation of the title of this great work reads:

A NEW ASTRONOMY Based on Causation
or A PHYSICS OF THE SKY
derived from Investigations of the
MOTIONS OF THE STAR MARS
Founded on Observations of THE NOBLE TYCHO BRAHE
(Koestler, *The Sleepwalkers*, p. 317)

And why had it taken him so long? Mainly because the orbit turned out
to be different from the expected classical form of a circle. The difference
was slight, very slight: it was only eight minutes of arc, about a tenth
of a degree, but it was enough for Kepler to abandon his hard-won
theories and start all over again, an act of scientific integrity that was
perhaps unprecedented. He later wrote

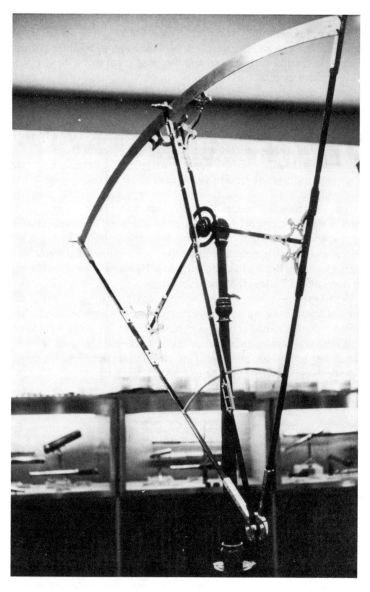

Habermel's sextant, used by Kepler and Tycho

For if I had believed that we could ignore these eight minutes I would
have patched up my hypothesis accordingly. But since it was not per-
missible to ignore them, those eight minutes point the road to a complete reformation of astronomy: they have become the building material
for a large part of this work . . .

(Koestler, *The Sleepwalkers*, pp. 326-7)

Starting again with Tycho's observations, Kepler calculated and theor-
ised, trying desperately to discover the true shape of the Martian orbit.
Day after day he tramped up to the Belvedere and back. In Charles
Street, just a few hundred metres from his house, he passed by a modern and very elegant chapel, built to an unusual design: its walls curved
smoothly round and its ground plan had the form of an ellipse.

After six years of intense calculation, of many trials and many errors,
Kepler suddenly realised what his equations had been trying to tell him:
the orbit of Mars is an ellipse. 'Ah, what a foolish bird I have been', he
cried, looking back on the tortuous path he had followed. Imagine the
weary Kepler trudging home one evening down Charles Street, puzzling
as usual over the shape of the orbit, and suddenly awakening from his
reverie to find himself staring as if for the first time at the shape of that
elliptical chapel.

Kepler went on to show that the other planets also move in ellipses,
and he produced an extremely accurate law relating the size of each
orbit to the time the planet takes to go right round it. Exactly the same
relationship applied to all of the known planets, suggesting that there
is some general law explaining *why* the planets move like this, not just
a description that they do. And it was this insight that marked Kepler
out as a modern thinker, despite his mysticism and his astrology. He
was seeking the *physical* reasons underlying his results. To him the solar
system was a kind of great machine up in the sky, and he wanted to
understand how it worked:

My aim is to show that the heavenly machine is not a kind of divine,
live being, but a kind of clockwork . . . insofar as nearly all the manifold
motions are caused by a most simple, magnetic, and material force, just
as all the motions of the clock are caused by a simple weight. And I also
show how these physical causes are to be given numerical and geometrical expression.

(Koestler, *The Sleepwalkers*, pp. 327)

But the dead hand of Aristotle still lay too heavily upon Kepler for him to reach the final revelation of just what that 'simple force' was and how it acted, and the final synthesis of all these ideas and observations had to wait half a century for Isaac Newton.

In 1665 Newton graduated at Cambridge just before the university was closed as a precaution against the Great Plague which was devastating London. He retired for a year and a half to his mother's farm in Lincolnshire where, according to his own account, he was watching an apple falling from a tree when the thought crossed his mind that perhaps the force that was pulling the apple down was the same force that was pulling on the moon and stopping it from flying off into space. Evidently the Aristotelian tradition had weakened since Kepler had struggled with the problem and scientists were starting to speculate about a force of attraction between the sun and a planet.

The intricate machinery of the stars, more exactly of the solar system, was about to be understood and seen to be not so intricate after all. One Wednesday in January 1684, a heated discussion took place between Robert Hooke the physicist, Edmund Halley the astronomer, and Sir Christopher Wren. Hooke was claiming that he had 'demonstrated all the laws of the celestial motions', but said that he would not tell anyone yet as he wanted others to find out how difficult the problem was before revealing his own solution. Wren took the tension out of the discussion by saying that he was prepared to wait up to two months for a convincing demonstration and offered a prize of a book worth 40s to the first one to produce it. Neither of them claimed the prize, but Halley did not give up. He was an enthusiastic young astronomer who had already set up an observatory at St Helena, produced the first star catalogue of the southern hemisphere, and become a strong supporter and friend of Isaac Newton.

Visiting Cambridge that August, Halley put the question directly to Newton: how would the planets move if they were controlled by a gravitational force from the sun that weakened as the square of the distance? 'In ellipses of course' replied Newton, adding that he had worked that out years ago though he had mislaid his proof. Kepler's elliptical orbits were thus revealed to be the simple consequence of gravitational attraction. The eager Halley badgered Newton, who really wanted to get on with his work on optics, electricity and alchemy, until he reproduced his original proof and published it together with his whole theory of mechanics in his book *Philosophiae Naturalis Principia Mathematica*, the mathematical principles of natural philosophy.

Principia soon became the bible of science in general and of physics in particular. Bernal made the pertinent observation though that, just like the other bible, few people have actually read it. One of those who did try to read it was the eager young Edison. After hours of study he finally abandoned it, saying 'it gave me a distaste for mathematics from which I have never recovered'.

Principia was published by the Royal Society under the imprint of its President, Samuel Pepys, but as the society was short of money Halley had to come to the rescue by financing the publication. Halley's reward came in a pleasant way. He had spotted some similarities in the comets which had appeared in 1456, 1531, 1607 and 1682, and was struck by their spacing at intervals of nearly seventy-six years. He decided that these were all visits from a single comet orbiting on a very long and narrow ellipse, visible only when it came near to the earth. He used the methods of *Principia* to predict that it would return very close to the year 1758. Halley died in 1742 but his comet turned up loyally in 1759 and was duly named Halley's Comet. The calculations predict that it should appear twice in the twentieth century: in 1910 and 1986.

Thus ended the saga of the machinery of the stars. It had confirmed the validity of Newton's system of mechanics and helped to clarify the relations between philosophy, religion and science. In particular it had no direct influence upon the seventeenth-century resurgence in optics. Kepler's laws of planetary motion, Newton's laws of mechanics and the law of gravitation were all based entirely upon observations made with the naked eye. They needed neither lenses nor the law of refraction. Let us leave the planets, then, and go back to one of the big optical problems that were occupying Newton when he was interrupted by Halley's insistence to write the *Principia*, the question of the operation of the telescope.

During the year 1608 many people discovered the telescope. One legend locates the event in the exquisite Dutch town of Delft. A little girl waiting in Hans Lippershey's shop while her mother is being fitted with spectacles idly peers through two lenses that happen to be displayed in the shop window. To her amazement she sees the houses on the other side of the canal brought so close to her that she can almost reach out and touch them. But when Lippershey mounts the lenses in a tube, calls it a telescope and tries to patent the idea he runs into a difficulty: so many others have applied with the same idea that it is not possible to patent it. A phenomenon that must have been casually observed many times before is suddenly being recognised as having commercial potential.

By June 1609 rumours of the new invention had reached Padua, an inland town near Venice, where the professor of mathematics was a

Detail from the Bayeux tapestry showing Halley's Comet (Battle of Hastings, 1066) which will be visible again in 1986

man with a very sharp eye for a commercial opportunity, Galileo Galilei. It didn't take Galileo long to make himself a small low-power telescope, which could magnify about three times, and then to improve on this until by August he was able to demonstrate a telescope with a power of nine to the Senators of Venice on the top of the tower of St Mark. From this vantage point they could see 'sails and shipping that were so far off that it was two hours before they were seen with the naked eye, steering full-sail into the harbour'. Such information was invaluable to the warlords and merchants of Venice. The appreciative Senate rewarded Galileo by doubling his salary and making his appointment permanent.

Then Galileo turned his telescope on the skies. His reports of the moons of Jupiter and the craters of the Moon, and, particularly, his championship of the Copernican sun-centred system, caused a furore and brought him into his well-known conflict with the Church. Up to the north in Prague his strongest supporter, Kepler, was wildly excited and wrote begging for one of Galileo's powerful telescopes so that he could study the new wonders for himself.

Although Galileo let him down, Kepler was fortunately able to borrow a telescope from a visiting duke for a month in the summer of 1610. Harbouring no resentment he immediately published an enthusiastic confirmation of Galileo's observations of the moons of Jupiter. Carried away by the beauties of uncharted space he wrote rapturously of the future joys of space travel, then got down to finding out just how a telescope works. In six weeks he had worked out the theory of light rays and lenses – geometrical optics – and put it all into a classic book which he called *Dioptrice*. The theory showed how optical instruments could be designed, and as an example Kepler described a new kind of telescope in which the eyepiece – the lens nearer to the eye – was convex instead of concave as it was in the little girl's experiment in the shop and in the Galilean instruments.

Kepler's theory of geometrical optics showed how to design spectacles which corrected for short-sight or for long-sight, and this prepared him well for his later work with the telescope. His theory also encompassed the popular camera obscura and thus anticipated the development of photography. He went far beyond Leonardo in recognising not only that the light-sensitive region of the eye was the retina, but also that the lens and the cornea combined in throwing an inverted image upon it.

If the speed with which Kepler founded the science of optics makes it all seem easy, we should recall some of the difficulties, both physical and mental, facing a scientist of those times. Civil war and religious per-

secution were rife. Transport and communications were slow and un-
reliable. Physical conditions were usually primitive: Galileo ends one of
his few letters to Kepler by saying that he has to stop 'because it is getting
dark'. Hygiene and sanitation were almost non-existent. If you had children, disease could usually be relied upon to carry off at least one of
them. In 1611 Kepler lost his first wife through a fever and his favourite
child from smallpox. He had promised his wife that he would remarry
to provide a mother for the children and for two years he searched systematically through a field of eleven possible candidates to select
another wife. And as if all that weren't enough, he spent the best part
of six years defending his mother against the charge of witchcraft. The
case against her was prepared in meticulous detail, even down to the
accusation that she had failed to shed tears when admonished with texts
from Holy Scripture; to this she had replied that she had wept so many
tears in her life that she had none left to shed. Kepler put the final case
for the defence but his own Law Faculty found that the accused should
be subject to questioning under the threat of torture. Perhaps owing to
the old woman's toughness she was set free after her interrogation, just
six months before her death.

In the middle of these proceedings Kepler's daughter died, the disas-

Witch's balance. A woman accused of witchcraft could be weighed against a
sheet of paper. If she was heavier (true witches are weightless), she was given a
certificate which saved her from burning at the stake.

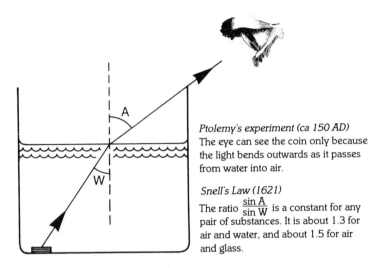

Ptolemy's experiment (ca 150 AD)
The eye can see the coin only because
the light bends outwards as it passes
from water into air.

Snell's Law (1621)
The ratio $\frac{\sin A}{\sin W}$ is a constant for any
pair of substances. It is about 1.3 for
air and water, and about 1.5 for air
and glass.

Figure 7.1: Snell's law of refraction

trous Thirty Years War began in Prague and his book announcing the
third of his planetary laws was published. It says something about the
temper of his mind that he was able to call it *The Harmony of the World*.

Kepler had discovered the movements of the planets and explained
the science of optics without even knowing the basic law of the refraction of light. For it was only in 1621, the year of Frau Kepler's trial, that
this law was at last discovered by the Dutch mathematician and astronomer Willebrord Snell (see Figure 7.1). It was apparently not thought
to be of tremendous interest and did not appear in print until 1638 when
it was published, without acknowledgement, by the French philosopher
and mathematician, René Descartes.

The constant in Snell's equation, the *refractive index*, is a number
which depends on the particular media involved, both the one the light
is at first travelling in and the one it is refracted into. Later it was discovered that this refractive index is the ratio of the speeds with which light
moves through the two media; but in the 1600s nothing whatever was
known about the speed of light.

The story of optics now gathers a tremendous speed and maintains
it throughout the second half of the seventeenth century.

So far the telescope had stolen all the glory. True, Kepler's great work
on optics had shown that two lenses can be arranged not only to make

distant objects seem near, but also to make small nearby objects seem large. But the resulting 'small-seeing instrument' – the *microscope* – appeared at first to be little more than a toy. Galileo had pointed his telescope at the skies and his observations of craters on the moon and of the moons of Jupiter had undermined the world view of two thousand years' standing. The early microscopists merely saw magnified views of commonplace objects – a flower petal, an insect, or the fibres in a piece of cloth. But this impression was deceptive. The astronomical telescope had, in Galileo's hands, already made its big contribution to the progress of humanity. The microscope, in contrast, was just starting to open new doors to the understanding of materials of all kinds, and it was about to revolutionise the fields of biology and medicine.

In 1660 Marcello Malpighi, an Italian physiologist, showed the kind of insight that the microscope could give. Malpighi was studying sections of the lungs of frogs. He discovered the fine hair-like blood vessels that are now called *capillaries* and he was able to see that they form the connections between the smallest visible arteries and the smallest visible veins. He thereby provided the evidence needed for Harvey's theory that the blood is pumped by the heart and circulates round the various organs of the body before returning to it. This was a huge step forward for medical science.

And that was only the beginning. Further advances followed rapidly, notably from the Dutch amateur scientist Anton van Leeuwenhoek and the English physicist Robert Hooke. Leeuwenhoek kept a draper's shop in Delft and supplemented his income by taking a job as a caretaker at the Town Hall. His almost obsessional hobby was exploring the microscopic world of life and showing that the tiniest of creatures also multiplied by reproductive processes; contrary to popular belief, he claimed, life did *not* grow spontaneously out of dewdrops or dust. He constructed several hundred microscopes of a quality that would not be even approached by anyone else for over a century. Each instrument had a tiny, fixed lens, often no bigger than a pinhead, and the object being examined was moved up and down until it was in exact and sharp focus. Some people say that the secret was in the way that he ground these tiny lenses; others that he didn't grind the lenses at all but made hundreds of them by melting a glass rod in a fierce gas jet, collecting the little blobs of glass that were thrown off and simply selecting the best ones. Still others say that his secret lay not in his lenses but in his methods of illumination – methods which he never revealed to anyone even though he gave many of his microscopes away.

Whatever the secret, his results were astounding. He studied the tissues of our bodies — hair, skin, muscle and bone. He followed the development from the egg of weevils and fleas and the propagation of shellfish. His study of the flea showed that it was as perfectly constructed as the larger animals, and he even found little parasites living on the flea, inspiring the well-known doggerel

> **Big fleas have little fleas**
> **Upon their backs to bite 'em;**
> **And little fleas have littler fleas**
> **And so ad infinitum.**

Leeuwenhoek found an unsuspected world living in ponds or stagnant pools and made nonsense of the phrase 'as dull as ditch-water'. Ditch-water, he showed, was full of all kinds of exciting little beasts, 'animalcules' as he called them:

We can easily conceive that in all rain water which is collected from gutters in cisterns, and in all waters exposed to the air, animalcules may be found; for they may be carried thither by the particles of dust blown about by the winds.

His discoveries, including the existence of spermatozoa, made him so famous that a steady stream of eminent people came to see him at work, including the Queen of England and the Tsar of Russia, Peter the Great. After some initial hesitation the Royal Society published several hundred of his papers with their beautiful drawings of hitherto unseen creatures. As photography had not yet been invented, the Society at first required that all of his observations be attested by a public notary before they would accept the drawings, which must have appeared to them like science fiction. In 1683 Leeuwenhoek made perhaps his greatest discovery — bacteria. These observations were at the limit of resolution of even his microscopes; he alone saw them and it was over a hundred years before anyone would see them again.

The microscopes of Robert Hooke were more conventional. They used one lens (the objective) to produce a magnified image of the object, followed by a second lens (the eyepiece) to give a further stage of magnification. Although they never reached the quality of Leeuwenhoek's strange instruments, they enabled Hooke, with the help of his friend Sir Christopher Wren, to produce some of the most beautiful and accurately

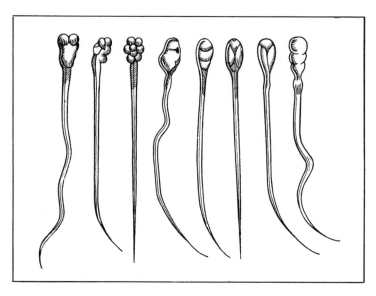

Leeuwenhoek's drawings of spermatozoa, 1678

detailed drawings ever made of insects or of tissues such as feathers or fish scales. His most famous discovery was the structure of cork; he showed that cork, and therefore the original growing tree bark, was built up from tiny compartments which he called *cells*, thereby introducing into biology its equivalent to the atom.

One of the main defects of these early microscopes was that their images, even of black and white objects, were surrounded with fuzzy coloured bands making it impossible to resolve the finest detail. The same limitation was confronting the astronomers with their lens-telescopes. Colours and lenses somehow seemed to be inseparable. Isaac Newton's investigation of the nature of colour led him to a practical solution of the telescope problem: he designed a reflector telescope that used a concave mirror instead of a lens. But it was still not enough. The simple ray-optics of Kepler sufficed to make a telescope or a microscope that worked, but to get maximum performance from the instrument a designer needed to understand exactly what the optical system was doing to the light. Only after another two hundred years would that understanding be achieved, with the re-emergence of wave theory and its translation into practice by the creative genius of Ernst Abbe in Germany.

Hooke's compound microscope, using three lenses. The microscope magnified up to 470X. Hooke often used sunlight from a hole in the window-shutters (following Newton), but for a more reliable source employed a glass bulb filled with water and aqua vitae to focus the light from an oil lamp.

8

The Phoenix from the Ashes

The microscope is perfected and
an industry is humanised

8

On 21 July 1801, Thomas Young was expounding the wave theory of light in London, Napoleon was preparing for the invasion of England, and an event of apparently much smaller significance was taking place in a village just outside Munich. A glazier's workshop had suddenly collapsed bringing down the whole building on top of it. The glazier's assistant, Joseph von Fraunhofer, had been buried under the great pile of bricks, beams and glass, but as if by a miracle the debris had formed itself into a sort of arch from which young Joseph had finally been extricated, dusty but unhurt.

The Duke of Bavaria happened to be driving by in his carriage and saw the commotion going on. Sending for Joseph, the Duke found him to be a bright, intelligent boy who had learned about glass from his father, but little else. He had never been to school and he was discouraged from study, even being forbidden to read books on his free Sundays. Greatly impressed by the young Fraunhofer, the Duke presented him with a bag of money. Joseph promptly used it to buy himself a glass-working machine, some books on optics, and a release from his apprenticeship. During the rest of his short life of thirty-nine years, he made outstanding advances in glass-working, in the construction of optical instruments, and in the wave theory of light. With a prism and telescope of his own manufacture he discovered hundreds of fine black lines crossing the spectrum of sunlight thrown by a prism, lines that Newton had missed completely in his experiments. He made great use of these lines as wavelength markers when he was developing his new lenses. Later on they would be recognised as 'optical fingerprints', identifying individual elements whose atoms absorbed only certain wavelengths from the light of the sun.

Fraunhofer himself did not follow up his spectral observations any

further. But he soon became one of the world's outstanding scientific instrument makers, wresting the leadership in optical instruments from the opticians of London. His aim was always to achieve a perfect marriage between science and craftsmanship, and the three principles he followed so successfully to achieve this goal were:
1. the improvement of technical manufacturing methods,
2. research and development of basic theories, and
3. the improvement of raw materials.
Each was important in its own right, but only a combined attack on all three enabled Fraunhofer to progress beyond the old methods of trial and error. When he died in 1826 the German scientific instrument industry went into a decline. The powerful thrust of Fraunhofer's approach was lost and not regained until the optical team of Carl Zeiss and Ernest Abbe went into collaboration with Otto Schott, the glass-maker, in 1882.

Carl Zeiss, son of a German toy-maker who was also Cabinet Maker and Carver of Portraits in Ivory at the Grand Duke's court in Jena, had one ambition: to become a great instrument maker. After leaving high school in 1834, he spent twelve years of apprenticeship, studying and working in various scientific workshops until he felt qualified to set up his own instrument workshop. In those days you couldn't just put your name over the door: a stiff examination was required. But with his practical and theoretical background he had no trouble in passing, and the Office of the Grand Duke's Superintendent of Works duly awarded him 'a licence, as requested, to manufacture and sell mechanical and optical instruments and to establish a mechanical workshop'. So in November 1846, Carl Zeiss went into business as an instrument maker in the little university town of Jena. Jakob Schleiden, a founder of modern botany and a professor at the University of Jena, guided him gently into the manufacture of microscopes and in 1857 wrote a testimonial to Zeiss' success:

Herr Zeiss has asked me to recommend his work, and I must confess, I do not quite know why. My recommendation can only be of value as regards his optical work, and this surely, stands in no need of a word from me. Herr Zeiss describes his microscopes as no more than first attempts, and this modesty does him as much credit as his skill and art. As regards the optical portion these first attempts may well range themselves at the side of the work of old masters, and they justify the expectation that Herr Zeiss will not fail to reach the standard of the best existing microscopes and that he will probably surpass them.

(cited in Auerbach, *The Zeiss Works and The Carl Zeiss Foundation in Jena*, p. 6)

Although Zeiss was doing well by the standards of the day, he was increasingly unhappy. His microscopes were, like all others, being produced by trial-and-error methods — 'hundreds of lenses to produce one good objective', he complained. Moreover, the future looked bleak. How could this little workshop compete with the huge British and French concerns, whose accumulated experience gave them a great advantage in trial-and-error productions?

In 1866 the little company celebrated its twentieth birthday by turning out its thousandth microscope. The staff had increased from three to twenty, all now working an 11¾-hour day, with a quarter of an hour's break in the morning and an hour for lunch. Yet Zeiss could not be satisfied until he had replaced the old hit-or-miss methods with a true scientific understanding of the microscope. He spent long nights on the problem; he enlisted the help of the mathematician Barfuss, who worked on it until his death. All to no avail. In Paris a superb microscope with a water-immersion lens had just come on to the market, and Zeiss began to feel that he would never be able to compete at the top level. Finally, he managed to arouse the interest of one of his university customers with whom he had already developed a friendship, the young physics lecturer Ernst Abbe.

How nice if one could say that the brilliant young physicist came to the rescue, solved all the theoretical problems, and set the Zeiss workshop on the road to success and fame. Unfortunately the road at first was hard and unpromising. Abbe made a wide-ranging search of the available optical literature, but found nothing of any help. He visited the workshop repeatedly and came to the conclusion that the main fault with existing microscopes was that the rays of light passing through the outer parts of the lens came to a focus at a slightly different point from the rays passing through the middle, thereby spoiling the sharpness of the image. He worked out theoretical ways of removing this weakness and obtained an exact specification for the shapes, sizes and positions of the lenses. Absolutely nothing would be left to the judgement of the instrument maker.

With the enthusiastic support of Zeiss, a dozen microscopes were duly built in accordance with Abbe's scientific determinations. One by one they were taken to the testing room until the hopes that had been riding so high had all been dashed to the ground. Every one of the twelve was inferior to the standard trial-and-error instruments they had been producing. It was now 1868 and Zeiss could see they were set on a road leading downhill to ruin.

What a remarkable man was this Carl Zeiss! Practical men are notoriously suspicious of academic scientists but Zeiss never wavered in his faith. He urged Abbe to try again and stayed closely with him while he spent the next two years working in the shops, studying the techniques, and designing the measuring and testing equipment that would be needed *if* a satisfactory theory could be found. And slowly he came to realise just what that theory had to be: it all came down to the wave theory of light. The objects being examined under the microscope were so finely structured that the light from each tiny detail did not go simply in a straight line but was diffracted into a pattern of light and dark bands, just as in the early experiments with small pinholes or slits. To obtain a true image of that detail, it was necessary to collect *all* of the light diffracted from it and to reassemble it with the system of lenses.

Abbe then calculated the precise geometry of the lens system using the wave theory of light. The microscopes made to his new specification were good, but still not good enough. With the little workshop now facing bankruptcy, he recalculated the system to ensure that points a little way off the direct axis were brought into the same sharp focus as points in the direct line of sight. The 'Abbe Sine Condition' that he devised to meet this requirement is still a key feature in modern microscope design. At last, success! The new 'theoretical' microscopes were at least as good as the best English and French instruments, and, as each was made to a reproducible specification, the firm of Zeiss had a decided edge over their rivals who still had to make repeated trials and errors with every instrument.

Abbe used the old ray theory of light to obtain his sine condition and the wave theory to ensure that the microscope collected enough light from the object to resolve the finest possible detail. It must have been a great delight for him, when he examined a number of the best microscopes available, to find that they all fulfilled the Abbe Sine Condition! The old craftsmen had successfully corrected their lens systems for off-axis focusing without knowing just how they were achieving their results.

Abbe now ran into an apparently insurmountable hurdle, the deceptively simple problem of how to get the right kind of glass. At that time a lens designer had only two distinct types of glass to choose from: *crown glass*, made of silica, soda and potash, and *flint glass*, the same mixture made heavier by the addition of oxide of lead. Flint glass refracted light more strongly, and it also showed a much greater difference between its refraction of the different colours. The 'achromatic' microscope lenses being produced combined a crown glass lens with a flint glass lens in such a way that two chosen colours were brought to a focus at the same point. This went some way to eliminating the confusing multi-coloured images which had limited the performance of the earlier microscopes. Fraunhofer's work, which was interrupted by his untimely death, had shown that a complete solution to the colour problem was theoretically possible, and Abbe succeeded in finding this solution, only to meet with frustration because it was impossible to obtain glass with the required optical properties. Now he brought in the third of Fraunhofer's principles. Surveying the problem of colour correction, he wrote

This discussion then leads to the conclusion that the deficiencies of present-day microscope objectives . . . are caused by the optical properties of the presently available raw materials. Therefore, perfection of the optical quality of the microscope seems to depend primarily on the progress in the art of glass-making . . .

(Abbe, *Gesammelte Abhandlungen*, vol. 1, p. 159)

Abbe and Zeiss pondered the problem and conceded that this time they were beaten. They had neither the experience nor the resources to get into the complex business of glass-making themselves, nor were the big glass-makers interested in an application which might, even if it worked, produce a demand for glass equal to that of a few hundred bottles or windows. Abbe was driven to making hollow lenses which he filled with suitable liquids to prove that his theory was right. The hollow lenses did the trick, producing sharp, colourless images, but only under carefully controlled laboratory conditions; they were neither a practical nor a commercial proposition. Looking back wryly on their struggles with the glass problem, Abbe later wrote

For many years we were engaged, not only in real optics, but also in a sort of utopian optics, in which we played with designs incorporating hypothetical non-existent glass. We discussed new developments which would become reality if we could only interest the glass manufacturers in the varied possibilities of application of optics. We knew, however, that they would not budge.

(Abbe, *Gesammelte Abhandlungen*, vol. 3, p. 71)

Then, one memorable day in 1879, salvation arrived out of the blue in a large parcel addressed to Dr Ernst Abbe of Jena. Inside it were some carefully wrapped pieces of glass and a letter explaining that these were samples of new types of glass made by substituting lithium for the sodium or potassium in ordinary glass. Would Dr Abbe be prepared to measure the optical characteristics of these new materials? The letter was signed, Otto Schott.

Dr Abbe was indeed prepared to make these measurements! The optical properties differed from those of the conventional glasses, though unfortunately not in the way required for Abbe's achromatic lens design. Nevertheless Abbe's hopes were revived by the very existence of such an enterprising glass-maker, particularly one who evidently appreciated the importance of producing a number of small batches of glass with systematically varying composition. He wrote enthusiastically to Schott:

I consider it a great success that you were able to obtain test melts in small crucibles of such quality which permit a complete optical analysis of the product. Feil in Paris, who is a well-known, experienced glass-maker, has not provided me with any test melts from which I could have made even approximate determinations of the average dispersion, let alone a reliable determination of partial dispersion, such as I obtained from one of your samples.

(cited in Volkmann, 'Ernst Abbe and his work')

By the term *dispersion*, Abbe is referring to the way that the refractive power of a glass changes as the colour of the light is changed; partial dispersion is simply a measure of the difference in the degree of refraction of two particular colours. Abbe needed a very precise form of dispersion for his lenses and he stated emphatically to Schott that there was only one way of finding it:

It seems to me that the most important requirement for progress in optical glass production is the ability to produce test melts suitable for optical measurements, because only in this manner can methodical experimentation be undertaken. As long as it is necessary to produce all samples in quantities of 60 to 80 pounds, only to obtain a usable prism for laboratory tests, it is impossible even to consider systematic testing of new combinations.

(cited in Volkmann, 'Ernst Abbe and his work')

Otto Schott turned out to be a young chemist whose father owned a plate glass works in Westphalia. But although young Otto had written his graduation thesis on the manufacture of window glass, he was less interested in making windows – or in making money – than in using his basic chemical knowledge of minerals to discover entirely new kinds of glass. It was as natural for him to join the team of Zeiss and Abbe as it was for Athos to join the Three Musketeers, and within three years he had moved to Jena to operate a small glass-making laboratory which the three set up jointly. In 1884 this became The Technical Glass Laboratory of Schott and Co. Two years later it signalled a new era for optical instruments by issuing a catalogue of forty-four different types of glass – heat-resistant glasses, thermometer glass, borate, phosphate and zinc glasses, as well as the special optical glasses that Abbe needed for his colour-correcting lenses.

The remarkable bond between these three men stood up to some severe testing. The formation of the glass-working company had only been made possible by a large government subsidy which was to be conditional upon the transfer of the works to Berlin. But Schott categorically refused to leave his colleagues: he stayed with his glass-works in Jena and the government withdrew its condition. Another great test came when a leading German bio-physicist at the University of Berlin, Hermann von Helmholtz, heard of Abbe's explanation of image formation in terms of the wave theory of light. Helmholtz had worked on this problem himself without success, and he set off eagerly for Jena to obtain a first-hand account from Abbe. Greatly impressed, he returned to Berlin and wrote to Abbe offering him a professorship at the university, but he was met with the same answer that Schott had given to the German government. Nothing would deter the three partners from pursuing their work together in optical science.

It was in 1889, shortly after the death of Carl Zeiss, that Abbe created his masterpiece. It was a microscope with an oil-immersion objective, Abbe's famous 'condenser', which directed the light upon the specimen, and a newly designed eyepiece; together these three components took the instrument to the ultimate limit of resolving power. Abbe's own theory had shown that no detail finer than about one-half of a wavelength of the illuminating light could ever be resolved. Some microscopists disputed Abbe's conclusion, claiming that they had observed finer details, but they had been deluded by the diffraction fringes that appear round an image when an imperfect microscope is pushed beyond its limit.

And in 1889 achieving the maximum resolving power in a microscope was no mere academic exercise: it was of the utmost importance for the study of micro-organisms in the rapidly growing field of bacteriology. In only the previous year the Pasteur Institute had been founded in Paris, a recognition of Pasteur's successful inoculation of animals against the bacterial diseases of chicken cholera and anthrax, culminating in 1885 with his dramatic, life-saving inoculation against rabies of a boy who had been badly mauled and bitten by a mad dog. Back in 1683 the Dutch pioneer Leeuwenhoek had made the first observations of dental bacteria, using his single lens microscope magnifying perhaps 150 times; Abbe's new instrument could be used with a magnification of 2000 times to resolve detail in bacteria which are only a few wavelengths in size, not only the 'bad' bacteria of diseases but also the far greater number of 'good' bacteria in the soil, in food, or in ourselves. However rabies was caused not by a bacterium but by a virus, and virus particles are much smaller than a wavelength of light and were therefore not resolvable even in the best of Abbe's microscopes. Only with the advent of the electron microscope could detailed pictures of these strange creatures, hovering on the borderline between living and non-living, be obtained.

Reaching a limit of any sort must have been saddening for the visionary little group at the Zeiss works, but it probably saved many other microscope manufacturers from striving after the unattainable. It may also have contributed to the belief that was gaining currency in Europe around 1890, that physical science was largely complete, that all of the major discoveries had already been made. Yet Abbe, though he was the first to realise that an ultimate optical limit was about to be attained, did not share in that belief. With prophetic vision he wrote, in 1878:

Perhaps in some future time the human mind may succeed in finding processes and in conquering natural forces which will open important new ways to overcome in an unforeseeable manner the limitations which now seem unsurmountable to us. This is my firm belief. But I think that the tools which some day will aid mankind in exploring the last elements of matter much more effectively than the microscope, as we now know it, will probably have no more in common with it than its name.

(cited in Volkmann, 'Ernst Abbe and his work')

The belief that physics was really at an end was shattered within a very few years by a succession of unexpected discoveries of the greatest

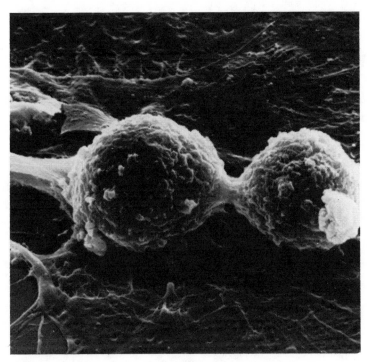

Mouse tumour cell in process of dividing (magnification approximately 3000X)

importance – radioactivity, the electron, and X-rays, as examples. It was Roentgen's discovery of X-rays that opened the way to X-ray diffraction, a most effective tool for 'exploring the last elements of matter'. When the Braggs, father and son, both Nobel laureates in physics, began their far-reaching studies of the structure of crystals, they referred to their work as 'microscopy on the atomic scale'. The wavelength of an X-ray depends upon the voltage applied to the X-ray tube, but it is typically about one-ten thousandth of the wavelength of ordinary light. This is small enough to enable diffraction patterns to be obtained from the regular arrays of atoms in a crystal, so that the *spacing* between the atoms can be deduced even though the individual atoms cannot be 'seen'; in other words, an X-ray diffraction instrument is not truly a 'microscope', even in name.

The instrument that comes nearer to Abbe's speculation is the electron microscope. One of the great surprises of twentieth-century physics was the discovery that matter, just like light, could behave as a particle or as a wave, depending on the circumstances. An electron, in particular, can act as a particle when accelerated from the filament in a television tube to produce a point of light on the screen; it can also act as a wave, with a wavelength similar to that of X-rays. And as a beam of electrons can be focused, using electric or magnetic lenses, the image of a very small object indeed can be greatly magnified and projected as a picture on the screen. The electron microscope is thus a true microscope and it is almost as different from the conventional light microscope as Abbe had envisaged in his far-seeing prediction back in 1878.

But Abbe could not rest content simply with designing superlative microscopes and making far-sighted predictions. He became increasingly preoccupied with an even harder problem: how to ensure the continuing success of the Carl Zeiss enterprise and equally, indeed as a part of the same problem, how to ensure the well-being of its workers. The situation in the 1890s was vastly different from that which had faced the little optical company when it started nearly half a century earlier. An echo of those early times was captured in 1922 during an interview with Herr Löber, a very old employee who had been Zeiss' first foreman:

Since there was not always enough to do in glass work, I had sometimes to take a hand in brass work as well. In 1848 Herr Zeiss was in the citizens' corps, and, as there was little doing in the way of business, old flint locks were converted into percussion locks, locks had to be filed and occasionally also to be hardened . . . Apart from this year of revolution, the business met with set-backs later in the fifties owing to commercial crises and high prices, so much so that the journeyman had to be discharged, with the result that Herr Zeiss and your humble servant constituted the entire staff . . .

From all this it will be seen that the fleshpots of Egypt were none too well filled at times. I remember occasions when Herr Zeiss breakfasted on a ha'pennyworth of black rolls and a small gin. I have not only seen this, but I have even had the good luck to receive a mouthful of gin if I happened to come upon my principal during such a repast . . .

And so it happened not infrequently that I was fetched away from my Sunday occupation (gardening) for the sake of a measly pair of spectacles costing 1/9. You will understand why I never developed obesity.

(cited in Auerbach, *The Zeiss Works and The Carl Zeiss Foundation in Jena*, p. 176)

Zeiss workshop in 1864. August Löber is seated extreme right.

A far cry from the large and flourishing concern of which Abbe had become the sole owner by 1891! Zeiss was dead, and Abbe had bought the remaining share from Zeiss' son, Roderich, who had no taste for his radical schemes for reorganising the company. And radical they were indeed. Even in the young and rapidly growing Germany, where Bismarck had introduced sweeping measures of social reform — pensions, sickness benefits, and workers' compensation — in order to spike the guns of the Social Democrats, Abbe's innovations were breathtaking.

Abbe considered that the common forms of corporate structure, the limited liability company or the co-operative, for example, offered no guarantee that the social responsibility of the concern would not one day be submerged by selfish and profit-oriented motives. He therefore created a new form of organisation, the Carl Zeiss Foundation, drawing up the statutes of the Foundation himself after much legal research which, incidentally, brought him an honorary doctorate of laws from an astonished law faculty. His guiding belief was that the material and scientific success of the Zeiss works did not stem from the activity of only a few individuals, but that it was due to the participation of the entire personnel. It followed that all employees should share in the benefits from the firm's operations and should be entitled to life-long economic security. However, the Zeiss works could fulfil this objective only if its sound financial position were ensured. The statutes therefore contained precise regulations as to the way the income was to be distributed between maintenance, replacement, production and scientific research, in accord with Abbe's considerable experience and judgement. But the regulations that aroused the most controversy were those aimed at safeguarding the rights of the workers. For example:
• an hourly wage or salary, once granted, cannot be reduced;
• all employees of more than five years' standing enjoy job protection;
• hiring of employees must always be irrespective of race, political affiliation or religious belief.
In addition to the statutory provisions, Abbe introduced a nine-hour day, which was reduced in 1900 to eight hours, sickness pay, holiday pay, retirement benefits, health insurance, and a workers' council which, he said, 'shall truly represent them and not be a screen behind which management can hide'. And all of the provisions in the statutes were permanently binding on the employer, so that the personal and economic status of the employees was not a matter of charity but an inalienable legal right.

Abbe established the Carl Zeiss Foundation in 1889, and two years later he transferred to the Foundation his ownership of the optical works and his half-share in the glass-works, together now worth many millions. He thereby gave up his position of owner to become one of the team of four managers who governed the company according to the statutes. He did *not* become managing director: there was no such position and even the use of the word 'director' was forbidden. The four managers were charged with the responsibility for policy decisions, none of which could be acted upon without their unanimous agreement.

It is a tribute to the inspiration of Abbe, as well as to the success of his plan, that twenty years later Otto Schott followed in his footsteps. At the end of the First World War, he presented his share of the glass-works to the Foundation, exchanging his position of owner for that of a manager.

Characteristically, Abbe had taken a giant step in the managerial revolution. The Foundation had no place for the private ownership of capital, but neither did it allow its well-cared-for workers any direct say in the management. Both capitalist and socialist could admire the Foundation without seeking to copy it. In 1947 Dr Alfred Weber of Heidelberg proposed a voluntary socialisation of German industry modelled on the lines of the Carl Zeiss Foundation, but no one seems to have taken up the idea. Nevertheless the social conditions of the workers in the highly successful Foundation affected industrial development in Prussia and later on throughout Europe. Abbe came to be rated as a sociologist as highly as he had been as scientist or technologist. After all, there were many good microscopes, but only one Carl Zeiss Foundation.

Did I say only one Foundation? That is now a matter of some contention. For on 19 March 1945, squadrons of British and American bombers descended on the little town of Jena and departed leaving the Carl Zeiss optical works a blazing ruin. But not all was lost. Within weeks the Russians were at the gates of Berlin; to the south the allied Russian and American armies were meeting near Dresden on the banks of the Elbe, and en route to this rendezvous the U.S. Army had occupied Jena. According to the Allied Agreements at Yalta, Jena was to be in the Soviet zone of occupation, so that the Russians should have been responsible for removing the machinery committed to war production. In the heat and emotion of the last days of the German Reich many things were done which should not have been done. It is hard to recapture that nightmarish atmosphere, but a report by a British war correspondent who visited Jena immediately after seeing the gas ovens of Auschwitz conveys something of the feeling:

The Carl Zeiss works in 1945 – after the bombers

... It is my hope that when, after the war, Cook's or some other travel agency takes people on tours of the historic places of this war, they will swing open those oven doors to general view.

Meeting these Germans and talking to them, as is unavoidable for a war correspondent or an Army officer in an administrative position, one finds it difficult to conceive that it may be they who are responsible directly or indirectly, for these atrocities. They are clean, well-dressed, educated, correct in their conduct, though inclined to be a little condescending if permitted.

The men I have in mind are the managers of the great Carl Zeiss optical lens firm of Jena, captured yesterday afternoon. Four professors ran Zeiss – Paul Henrichs, commercial manager, Heinz Küppenbender, Walther Bauersfeld and Georg Joos, all members of the Nazi Party ...

I was particularly startled when I read this report. Joos' *Theoretical Physics* had been a treasured textbook during my student days, especially valued for its treatment of optics, and the significance of its introduction, written in 1932, now became more apparent. I recognised the lofty tones I had heard before in discussions with young, austere and dedicated members of the British Union of Fascists:

... I wish to voice the hope that this book may contribute its part to the intellectual and material reconstruction of our Fatherland, by revealing to the young generation striving after truth the immutability of the laws of nature – laws which transcend all human strife – and pointing out the only upward path, that of strenuous unremitting effort.

Of the four managers, it was Dr Küppenbender who took the lead in 1947. After the American economic and technical experts had surveyed the wreckage of the optical works, Küppenbender drew up a list of eighty of the leading Zeiss scientists and engineers, the brain of the firm as he described it. 'We take the brain!' was the exclamation attributed to Colonel Sempke of the U.S. Army Headquarters, but whether or not he actually said that, the eighty finished up in the little country town of Oberkochen, in the southern part of the American zone of occupation. There, together with a similar group of forty emigrants from the Schott glass-works, they began with whatever they managed to salvage from Jena to build up a new optical organisation which they regarded not just as a successor to the Carl Zeiss Foundation, but as the genuine article, the Foundation itself.

Meanwhile back in Jena, the phoenix was rising from the ashes. Much of the undamaged heavy equipment that the Russians had taken away under the reparations agreement was brought back when the factory was rebuilt, and once again Carl Zeiss of Jena was in business. Long legal battles ensued between the East and West German companies as to who was the real Carl Zeiss. Who could use the name? Or the famous trademark? A resolution has been achieved and today both companies are flourishing inside their own agreed spheres of influence.

True to the old traditions, though, both companies are right in the forefront of modern technological developments. They are continually turning out new instruments for research and production, new microscopes, telescopes, spectroscopes and precision measuring instruments, backed up by the powers of electronics, computing and automation. The microscope has long been the handmaiden of medical science, but new fields are being opened up in microsurgery with the use of optical fibres and lasers.

Technology could thus be seen to have triumphed over ideology. But the ideology of Ernst Abbe still has a lot to do with the success of both of these very high-class companies. And it is intriguing to see that the Abbe principles still do not sit entirely comfortably in either the East or the West. A completely autonomous, self-determining Foundation may not always be reconcilable with a planned socialist society where the desires of the Foundation may be at odds with the plan; in Western society it is rarely possible to raise large sums of capital from capitalists who are told they can have no say whatsoever in the policies to be followed by the Foundation. Ernest Abbe was not only a long way ahead of his time: in some respects he was a long way ahead of our time as well.

9

Putting Light in the Picture

The invention of photography —
a science for the people

9

The mastery of light was one of those great scientific advances in the nineteenth century that were giving a new cutting edge to the Industrial Revolution. The Utopia predicted by Francis Bacon and other scientific visionaries, however, seemed to be a long time in coming. In the 1860s, sixty years after the foundation of the Royal Institution, the French writer Taine reported from Liverpool:

At six o'clock we made our way back through the poor quarters of the city. What a spectacle! In the neighbourhood of Leeds Street there are fifteen or twenty streets with ropes stretched across them where rags and underwear are stretched out to dry. Every stairway swarms with children, five or six to a step, the eldest nursing the baby; their faces are pale, their hair whitish and tousled, the rags they wear are full of holes, they have neither shoes nor stockings and they are vilely dirty. Their faces and limbs seemed to be encrusted with dust and soot. In one street there must have been about two hundred children sprawling and fighting . . . Livid, bearded old women came out of gin shops: their reeling gait, dismal eyes and fixed, idiot grin are indescribable. They look as if their features had been slowly corroded by vitriol.

Their rags hardly hold together and here and there reveal glimpses of their filthy bodies: and these rags are old fashioned clothes, their hats once ladies' hats . . . Rembrandt's beggars were happier and better off in their picturesque hovels. And I have not seen the Irish quarter!

(cited in Barker, *The Long March of Everyman*, p. 118)

By the end of the century, electric lighting was, along with the other benefits of science, still spread rather thinly. Great country houses and West

End theatres might be ablaze with light, but the new rays did not reach into the houses of the people. Near the end of the century Charlie Chaplin's father died from the drink; the only prospect that society could offer young Charlie was the workhouse:

Mother had now sold most of her belongings. The last thing to go was her trunk of theatrical costumes ... Like sand in an hour-glass our finances ran out, and hard times again pursued us. Mother sought other employment, but there was little to be found. Problems began mounting. Instalment payments were behind; consequently Mother's sewing mach-ine was taken away. And Father's payments of ten shillings a week had completely stopped ... There was no alternative: she was burdened with two children, and in poor health; and so she decided that the three of us should enter the Lambeth workhouse ... there we were made to separate, Mother going in one direction to the women's ward and we to the children's. How well I remember the poignant sadness of that first visiting day: the shock of seeing Mother enter the visiting-room garbed in workhouse clothes. How forlorn and embarrassed she looked. In one week she had aged and grown thin, but her face lit up when she saw us ... She smiled at our cropped heads and stroked them consolingly, telling us that we would soon all be together again. From her apron she produced a bag of coconut candy which she had bought at the work-house store with her earnings from crocheting lace cuffs for one of the nurses ...

(cited in Barker, *The Long March of Everyman*, p. 151)

Yet fate had in store a happy ending just like an early Hollywood movie. For in 1889, the year that Chaplin was born, Edison had invented the motion picture camera. Soon the silent movie would carry Charlie Chaplin far away from the workhouse and right up to the highest pinna-cles of fame. In 1889, though, the comedy came not from Chaplin but from Edison, the great inventor with over two hundred patents on elec-tric lighting already to his credit. Edison evidently did not see much future in motion pictures; he told his lawyer not to lodge a patent appli-cation for the movie camera as it would not be worth the fee of $150.

Chaplin, of course, was not the only person whose life-style was changed by the arrival of the moving pictures. The silent cinema rapidly became a major vehicle of communication and entertainment, and when sound was added in 1928 'the talkies' emerged as the art form of the twentieth century. After the marriage with television, and with the addition of colour as a bonus, the film achieved an influence more universal than that of any other medium except perhaps the book. Here was a real Baconian application of science: not only did it influence the material things of life, but it was capable of touching deep human emotions such as loneliness. In 1932 Arthur Koestler on a visit to Georgia in the south of the U.S.S.R. spent a night in a small town in the Caucasian foothills. He was feeling depressed and decided to go to the pictures. He took refuge, he said, 'in the international sanctuary for the lonely, the cinema', where he saw Harold Lloyd starring in *Safety Last*. After an hour or two watching Lloyd falling out of windows, narrowly missing automobiles, and clinging desperately to the roofs of skyscrapers with one hand, Koestler found that his own anxieties had, at least for the time being, receded.

When television brought the film into people's houses it met a real human need and fulfilled yet another of the dreams of science fiction. Its origin lay in two major optical developments of the nineteenth century, photography and wave theory. Photography was achieved by taking the fairly obvious step of combining the knowledge of lenses with the empirical development of substances that would change colour on exposure to light. The extension of wave theory revealed the wonderland of the invisible spectrum — the radio waves that carried speech, music and pictures round the world and the mysterious X-rays, discovered as the century came to its dramatic close, that led to new medical techniques.

The idea of photography came to one of its early pioneers, William Henry Fox Talbot, while he was on an Italian holiday in 1833. Sitting by the shores of Lake Como he was vainly trying to sketch the glorious view displayed by his camera obscura upon the sheet of paper in front of him. He reflected on 'the inimitable beauty of the pictures of nature's painting which the glass lens of the Camera throws', but despaired when he contemplated his results and found that 'the faithless pencil had left only traces on the paper melancholy to behold'. The pictures had, after all, been only 'fairy pictures, creations of a moment, and destined as rapidly to fade away' Was there no way round this destiny?

It was during these thoughts that the idea occurred to me . . . how charming it would be if it were possible to cause these natural images to imprint themselves durably, and remain fixed upon the paper!

   And why should it not be possible? I asked myself.

                                                            (Talbot, *The Pencil of Nature*)

Six years later he answered his own question in a lecture to the Royal Society which he entitled 'Some Account of the Art of Photogenic Drawing, or the process by which natural objects may be made to delineate themselves without the aid of the artist's pencil':

In the Spring of 1834 I began to put into practice a method which I had devised some time previously, for employing to purposes of utility the very curious property which has long been known to chemists to be possessed by the nitrate of silver; namely its discolouration when exposed to the violet rays of light.

Talbot made his light-sensitive film in a darkened room, soaking sheets of paper first in dilute salt water and then in a solution of silver nitrate. This process produced a film of the highly sensitive silver chloride, which was reduced to metallic silver wherever the light fell upon it in a camera. The image on this exposed 'negative' film was 'fixed' by immersion in a strong salt solution (later, hypo was used to remove the unexposed chloride altogether). The negative was held in contact with a second sheet of sensitive paper so that sunlight could pass through the clear, unexposed areas and darken the paper underneath; this produced a print looking like the original view as seen by the camera. In 1844 Talbot published *The Pencil of Nature*, a collection of beautiful photographs made in this way; one of the pictures was actually made without a camera – Talbot pressed a leaf between a piece of glass and the printing paper and exposed to the sunlight until done. The photographs were so good that Talbot found it necessary to insert a slip into each copy of the book for the benefit of readers who might mistake them for etchings or engravings:

NOTICE TO THE READER
The Plates of the present work are impressed by the agency of Light alone, without any aid whatever from the artist's pencil. They are the sun-pictures themselves, and not, as some persons have imaged, engravings in imitation.

In his lecture Talbot referred to 'this new process which I offer to the lovers of science and nature'. Unfortunately after such a grand statement he proceeded to patent his 'Calotype' process and to spend the next ten years trying to stop anyone else from developing the noble art of photography. Nevertheless, his introduction of the sensitive negative film had cut the exposure time down to much less than a minute so that photographic portraiture now became a reasonably practical proposition.

There still were difficulties, however. Some of these were indicated in 'Hiawatha's Photographing', a poem by one of the geniuses of Victorian photography, the Reverend Charles Lutwidge Dodgson, an Oxford mathematician better known by his *nom de plume* of Lewis Carroll.

> From his shoulder Hiawatha
> Took the camera of rosewood,
> Made of sliding, folding rosewood;
> Neatly put it altogether.
> In its case it lay compactly,
> Folded into nearly nothing;
> But he opened out the hinges,
> Pushed and pulled the joints and hinges,
> Till it looked all squares and oblongs,
> Like a complicated figure
> In the Second Book of Euclid.
>
> This he perched upon a tripod –
> Crouched beneath its dusky cover –
> Stretched his hand, enforcing silence –
> Said 'Be motionless, I beg you!'
> Mystic, awful was the process.
>
> All the family in order
> Sat before him for their pictures:
> Each in turn, as he was taken,
> Volunteered his own suggestions,
> His ingenious suggestions.
>
> First the Governor, the Father:
> He suggested velvet curtains
> Looped about a massy pillar;
> And the corner of the table,
> Of a rosewood dining-table.

He would hold a scroll of something,
Hold it firmly in his left-hand;
He would keep his right-hand buried
(Like Napoleon) in his waistcoat;
He would contemplate the distance
With a look of pensive meaning,
As of ducks that die in tempests.

Grand, heroic was the notion:
Yet the picture failed entirely:
Failed, because he moved a little,
Moved, because he could not help it.

Next, his better half took courage;
She would have her picture taken.
She came dressed beyond description,
Dressed in jewels and in satin
Far too gorgeous for an empress.
Gracefully she sat down sideways,
With a simper scarcely human,
Holding in her hand a bouquet
Rather larger than a cabbage.
All the while that she was sitting,
Still the lady chattered, chattered,
Like a monkey in the forest.
'Am I sitting still?' she asked him.
'Is my face enough in profile?
Shall I hold the bouquet higher?
Will it come into the picture?'
And the picture failed completely . . .

Before long the pictures did not fail so frequently. The application of lens theory produced better cameras, and improvements in photographic chemistry produced faster films, so that it became possible to take pictures without a studio or the elaborate equipment of the professional photographer.

The turning-point came in 1888 with George Eastman's simple box-camera, the Kodak No. 1. This little black box with a fixed lens ensured that everything beyond about two metres away would be reasonably sharp without any need to focus. Its fixed shutter speed of 1/25 second

Alice through the camera's looking-glass. Alice Liddell by the great mid-
Victorian amateur photographer, the Rev. Charles Lutwidge Dodgson (Lewis
Carroll).

HAWK-EYE
DETECTIVE and Combination
CAMERA, Price, $15.

The only real Detective and practical View Camera. Possessing every advantage of the "Kodak" with the addition of greater utility and making pictures more than three times as large: namely, 4 x 5 inches.

☞ THIS IS THE CAMERA SELECTED IN PREFERENCE TO ALL OTHERS BY Thomas Stevens, THE FAMOUS AROUND-THE-WORLD BICYCLER, WHEN FITTING OUT FOR HIS EXPEDITION TO THE DARK CONTINENT IN SEARCH OF STANLEY AND EMIN BEY. Our illustration represents Stevens as he will appear in the act of photographing an African Potentate.

AS A DETECTIVE CAMERA. The Hawk-Eye is unequaled in convenience and rapidity of adjustment for instantaneous photographs of moving objects under varying conditions, the focus and the speed of the shutter being instantly regulated without opening the Camera.

AS A VIEW CAMERA. The Hawk-Eye may be set up on a tripod or any convenient rest for a time-exposure, being provided with ground-glass screen, and screw pinion movement for distending and closing the bellows, no focusing-cloth being required.

AS AN AUTOMATIC "PRESS THE BUTTON" CAMERA. The Hawk-Eye will be supplied for $10 extra, or $25, with an attachment containing a coil of sensitised film for taking 100 different pictures, when one has only to wind a fresh portion of the film into position, and press the button for each successive picture. This attachment containing the exposed film can be sent to the factory to have the pictures finished, and a fresh coil of film inserted, and will be returned with the finished pictures.

The Hawk-Eye Camera will be forwarded, carefully packed, with complete instructions, upon receipt of price. Illustrated pamphlet, with sample photograph, sent free upon application.

THE BOSTON CAMERA CO., Manufacturers,
30 India Street, BOSTON, MASS.

'This is the camera [the Hawk-Eye] selected in preference to all others by Thomas Stevens, the famous around-the-world bicycler, when fitting out his expedition to the Dark Continent in search of Stanley and Emin Bey. Our illustration represents Stevens as he will appear in the act of photographing an African Potentate.'

became the standard for 'snapshots', being just fast enough for portrait work without straining the subjects' powers of keeping still. Moreover there was no messing about with plates: the camera came loaded with a roll of film long enough to take 100 pictures. You paid $20 for the loaded camera; when you had finished the roll you returned the camera with another $8 and it came back reloaded together with your prints (except, of course, for those that had failed completely).

Small wonder, then, that Eastman's Kodaks swept the market. The message was carried by Eastman's famous slogan: 'You Press the Button, We Do the Rest'. And as the bandwagon started to roll, other manufacturers rushed to climb aboard. In Boston 'The Hawk-eye' was offered as 'possessing every advantage of the "Kodak" with the addition of greater utility and making pictures more than three times as large'. The greater utility included its 'Use as A Detective Camera', having both variable focus and variable shutter speed.

The photographic industry today has become an outstanding realisation of Francis Bacon's vision — the democratisation of science. Cameras in the developed countries have become commoner than bicycles or boxes of paints. In the United Kingdom alone, amateurs own about thirty million cameras and take close to a thousand million photographs a year. The complex process has been so streamlined that a child can pop a cartridge into the back of an automatic camera and fire away with every probability of success. A Polaroid Land camera will even supply a colour print just moments after the exposure, and sound a buzzer when it is ready. Whether or not this is Art with a capital A is beside the point: clearly, it satisfies a considerable human need for personal records of events, places and people. It offers an entire portrait gallery to those who previously would never have been wealthy or eminent enough to acquire even a single portrait. The liberation that portrait photography brought was apparent to Elizabeth Barrett almost from the start. Writing to Mary Mitford in 1843, three years before her marriage to Browning, she said:

"You press the button
We do the rest"

I long to have such a memorial of every being dear to me in the world. It is not merely the likeness which is precious in such cases – but the association and the sense of nearness involved in the thing . . . the fact of the **very shadow of the person** lying there fixed forever! It is the very sanctification of portraits I think – and it is not at all monstrous in me to say, what my brothers cry out against so vehemently, that I would rather have such a memorial of one I dearly loved, than the noblest artist's work ever produced.

(Sontag, *On Photography*, p.183)

Nearly everyone living in the developed part of the world can now fulfil such longings. In some developing countries the price of an ordinary camera could keep a child alive for a year — a reminder of how far the application of the scientific revolution still has to go.

The heroic age of the development of photography is now over. Progress may be expected in making cameras smaller and easier to use; automatic electronics will simplify the operator's problems — depth of focus, field of view, and so on; ordinary cameras may become able to take pictures underwater, in the dark, or at very high speeds. But all of these are minor changes compared to the giant strides that photography has already taken in the 150 years of its existence. The future of photography lies not in the science, in the narrow, conventional sense, but in the skill with which its products are manufactured and marketed, as well as in the art with which they are used; for

> **Of what use are lens and light**
> **To those who lack in mind and sight?**
> (translation of Latin inscription on a German coin of 1589)

This change in emphasis is reflected in the post-war Japanese industrial success story. Mr S. Fukuoka, Vice President of Nippon Kogaku, spoke recently of the growth of the Nikon camera business. 'Before the war', he said, 'German cameras had all our respect and admiration. After the war we stopped production of precision machines and began work on cameras ... We were trying out one experimental lens after another, never to our satisfaction.' Success came only after a prominent war photographer in Korea stated publicly that he preferred the Nikon to the Leica. After that, Mr Fukuoka explained, 'The fruit of our efforts was recognised and our products began to sell. Now, leaving out toy-like cameras and special cameras such as Polaroid, there is no camera industry in the world except in Japan.'

Special cameras there are, of course, in profusion: cameras for microscopes and telescopes; X-ray or infra-red cameras; television cameras; cameras for spies and stereoscopic cameras. And for the prime patron and big-spending consumer of applied science, the military, there are cameras for photographing every square metre of the opposition's territory, from aeroplane or from satellite. Even before the First World War the German Army had a rocket camera capable of taking pictures from a height of a thousand metres. But perhaps the most dramatic pictures are those taken by very high-speed cameras, using extremely short exposure times. Fox Talbot himself had started the ball rolling with a demonstration to the Royal Institution in 1851. He took a clear photograph of a page of *The Times* attached to a rapidly rotating wheel by using as the source of illumination an electric spark lasting for only about one-hundred thousandth of a second. The military became interested when C. V. Boys in 1892 photographed bullets penetrating plate glass at speeds of around two thousand metres a second; their interest became a major commitment during the Second World War when British specialists went to Los Alamos in New Mexico to build a camera which would photograph the initial moments of the explosion of the atomic bomb.

Thanks to the work of such pioneers as Harold Edgerton of the Massachusetts Institute of Technology, high-speed pictures of such events as the splashing of a drop of milk, a bullet tearing its way through an apple, or a golfer taking a swing, have become widely known and appreciated. Perhaps the quaintest piece of work in this field was that carried out in 1878 by a Londoner, Edward Muggeridge, who developed a passion for things Anglo-Saxon and changed his name to Eadweard Muybridge. He was approached by Leland Stanford, the Californian railroad millionaire and founder of Stanford University, to settle a little problem for him. Stanford was a keen horse-fancier with his own stables, and during an argument he made a bet of $20 000 that there are moments when a running horse has all four hooves off the ground. Rubber was then the wonder material, so experiments were tried: a rubber ball was tied beneath each hoof and connected by a rubber tube to one of a bank of four pointers mounted on a board in front of the rider. When the horse placed a hoof on the ground the air was squeezed out of the rubber ball so that the corresponding pointer was deflected. The rider had to get the horse into a gallop, then watch carefully to see if at any time none of the pointers was deflected. This experiment had failed completely. Here was an ideal situation for some high-speed photography.

At Stanford's request, Muybridge set up a bank of cameras at intervals of about a metre beside the race-track. Each camera had a shutter speed of one-thousandth of a second — not *very* high speed but fast enough to freeze the motion of the galloping horse. Each shutter was released by its own piece of black thread stretched chest-high across the track. The resulting pictures — something between a very high-speed photograph and a motion picture — demonstrated unequivocally that Stanford was right: there were individual pictures showing all four hooves in the air at the same time.

There is still one camera, however, that in several ways is the most special of them all: the pinhole camera. In essence it is no more than a box with a pinhole in the front and some clips on the back to hold a sheet of photographic film or paper. The first and most important thing about it is that it can be made and used by any boy or girl whose creative spirit and abilities have not been blunted by too many expensive toys. In the process something may be learned, not only about photography but also about the wave nature of light and the functioning of the eye. The pinhole camera is really just a small-scale version of the camera

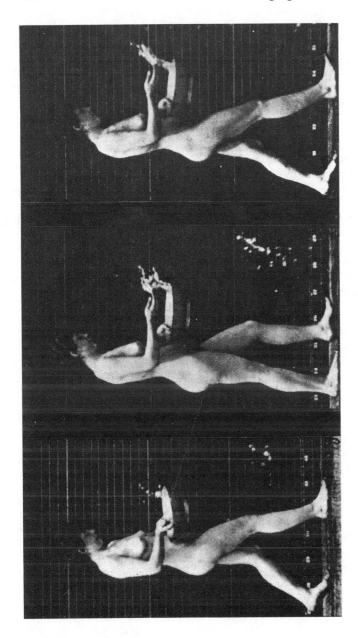

High-speed photographs by Muybridge, 1887

obscura, and relies on the simple principle that light travels in straight lines. Figure 9.1 shows how an image is formed by such an arrangement. Ideally the pinhole should direct the light from each point on the object to a different point on the back of the box, thus building up a sharp, upside-down image. But as the pinhole is not infinitely small, the rays from a point on the object spread out to form a small circle rather than an exact point. The image from a 'large' pinhole is thus blurred by the overlapping of many small circles of light; the picture in Fig. 9.2a was taken with a pinhole of 2 mm diameter, and the exposure time was 0.25 seconds. A smaller pinhole, with a diameter of .35 mm, gives a sharper picture but the exposure time has had to be increased to 6 seconds (see Figure 9.2b). Presumably an even smaller pinhole would produce a sharper picture still, although it would require an even longer exposure.

Figure 9.2c shows the result obtained with a pinhole of only 0.04 mm diameter. The exposure has had to be increased to nearly 7 minutes to match the tone of the previous pictures, but far from being sharper the image is now fuzzier than ever. What has gone wrong? The answer is simply diffraction. When light rays meet any obstacle, such as a card with a pinhole, they display their wave-like nature by spreading out away from their original direction. In most situations this effect is so small as to be unnoticeable. A pinhole half a millimetre in diameter, for example, will spread the light coming from a point on a distant object into a spot only about one millimetre wide on the film of a camera that is twenty centimetres long; a reasonably clear picture is thus obtained with a pinhole of about a thousand times the wavelength of light.

As the pinhole gets smaller and smaller the spreading gets rapidly bigger and bigger. If the pinhole is reduced from one-half to one-twentieth of a millimetre, the light spreads out into a spot about five millimetres in diameter; the overlap between neighbouring spots now destroys all sharpness of the image. A twentieth of a millimetre is only about a hundred wavelengths of yellow light — about the thickness of a human hair. If the pinhole were made a hundred times smaller still — that is only about one wavelength wide — the light passing through it would spread out in all directions; every point on the object would illuminate the whole film and there would be no image at all.

The wave theory of light is thus needed for working out the formation of an image in this simple, lensless system of photography, just as much as it is for computing the most complicated compound lenses in a modern camera. Lord Rayleigh applied wave theory to the formation of images by optical systems and showed how a simple aperture could act

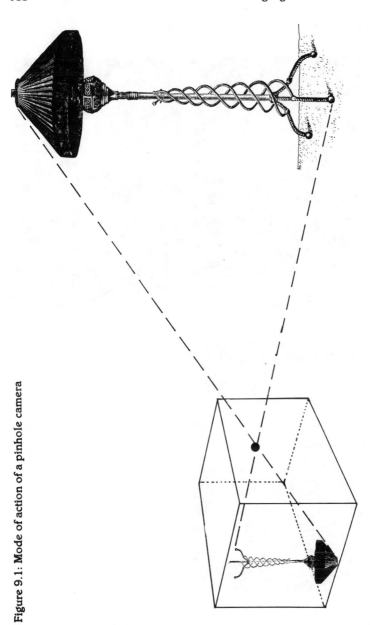

Figure 9.1: Mode of action of a pinhole camera

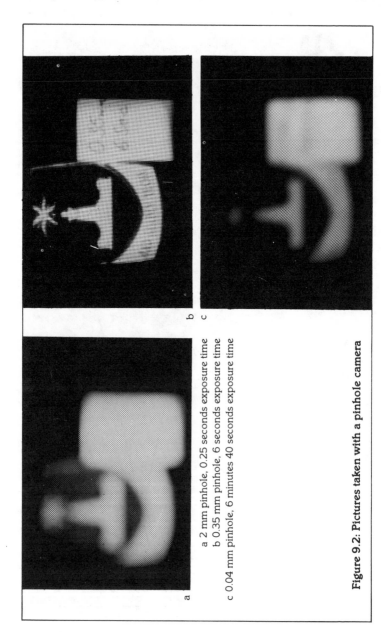

a 2 mm pinhole, 0.25 seconds exposure time
b 0.35 mm pinhole, 6 seconds exposure time
c 0.04 mm pinhole, 6 minutes 40 seconds exposure time

Figure 9.2: Pictures taken with a pinhole camera

as a lens. For such a pinhole camera, he wrote, the size of the pinhole is of critical importance:

If this aperture is too small, the image loses in definition owing to the spreading out of the waves, and on the other hand it is clear that no image can be formed, when the aperture is large. There must therefore be one particular size of the opening which gives the best result.

For an object at a distance d from a camera of length c, he showed that this 'best-result' is obtained when the radius of the aperture r is related to the wavelength λ by the expression:

$$r^2 \frac{c + d}{cd} = 0.9\lambda$$

Taking a wavelength of light of 500 nanometres, an object 10 metres away will be most sharply focused by a 20-centimetre long camera if the pinhole is 0.6 millimetres in diameter. Given a camera of that fixed length, both near and far away objects will also be reasonably sharp. This great 'depth of focus' is one of the particular virtues of the pinhole camera.

Photography without a lens is the oldest method of recording pictures. It is also one of the newest. In 1949 Denis Gabor invented a novel way of forming images that uses no lenses and provides pictures which give a three-dimensional view of the original subject. The process is called *holography* because it makes use of the whole of the optical information coming from the subject being photographed. Nowadays a hologram is usually made by allowing the light from a laser to fall both upon the subject and upon a photographic plate. The light scattered by the subject also falls upon the plate where it forms an interference pattern with the direct beam from the laser. This pattern bears no visible resemblance at all to the subject. It looks more like a random collection of dots, squiggles and blotches until a laser beam is shone through it, whereupon an image of the subject appears looking every bit as solid as the original and capable of being viewed from any side. Production of such pictures is still little more than a party trick, though holograms are becoming useful in technologies such as radar, mapping, or computer-aided design.

Gabor's original aim was not to produce pretty 3-D pictures, but to improve the performance of the electron microscope to the level where it could produce a photograph showing an individual atom. An improvement by a factor of about ten was needed, but unfortunately it could not be attained by Gabor's method because of the difficulty of producing a beam of electrons as pure and homogeneous as a beam of laser light. Resorting to brute force, electron microscopes operating at up to one million volts were built, still without achieving the required resolution – a little better than 0.2 nanometres. Hopes rest with an instrument now under construction in which the million-volt supply is not to vary by more than one-tenth of a volt. Even if this attempt is successful, the pristine simplicity of the early electron microscopes will have been lost: the photographs of individual atoms will be so complex that they will need the help of a computer to interpret them.

A photograph showing the atoms in a specimen will not be as useless as, say, a journey to the moon. It should be valuable for research on alloys, for example, or in the study of biologically important structures such as the membranes of cells. But for most of us the really important pictures will continue to be the films made for entertainment and our personal photographs of family, friends, places or events, the true descendants of George Eastman's first Kodak pictures made nearly a century ago.

The artistically inclined may also feel that more consideration should be given to consider the way that light was used in the development of modern art. To consider, for example, how it was that the Impressionists and their successors broke away from the smooth, pictorial view of classical painting at the same time as the smooth, classical ideas of matter and light were breaking up into atomic particles and photons. 'Impressionism –' wrote Cézanne, 'what does it mean? It is the optical mixing of colours, do you understand? Disintegrating the colours on the canvas and reuniting them in the eye . . . A painting represents nothing, should not, at first, represent anything but colours.' Yet this form of pictorial art, though far more popular than astrophysics, and with probably more influence on our culture, is still essentially a minority pursuit. The great visual art forms of this century came straight out of the science of light – photography, the cinema and television.

10

The Mysterious Rays

The discovery of X-rays

10

By the end of the nineteenth century the properties of light waves were reasonably well understood; and not just of the narrow, visible spectrum but also of the longer infra-red rays and the very much longer 'Hertzian waves', the waves of radio. Ultraviolet light, with somewhat shorter wavelengths, was also known. But was there any invisible light beyond the ultraviolet? Were there electromagnetic waves with shorter wavelengths still? And if there were, what strange properties did they have, and how could they be applied?

Such waves there certainly were, and the drama of their discovery and immediate application would be hard to match. The story really begins in the latter part of the nineteenth century with the investigations of the beautiful coloured lights that were emitted by an electrical discharge in an evacuated glass tube. By 1876 great improvements in the technical part of the apparatus — the vacuum pump to provide a higher degree of vacuum and the induction coil to provide the high-voltage electricity — enabled Sir William Crookes to build the first cathode ray tube, the forerunner of the television tube. With this more powerful equipment he was able to study the peculiar bands of light which formed near the negative electrode, the cathode. Crookes found that these bands could be moved about by bringing a magnet near the tube; this movement, he proposed, showed that the 'cathode rays' which formed the electrical discharge were actually streams of negatively charged particles. English physicists tended to support this view, but the German physicists, following their man, Heinrich Hertz, held that the cathode rays were just electromagnetic waves in some other part of the wavelength spectrum. Science was not exempt from the intense nationalism of that period.

For twenty years scientists worked away feverishly with their Crookes tubes and cathode rays. There was a mystery to be resolved, with national honour at stake; there was the possibility of a new source of light, perhaps to rival even the incandescent lamp; and in any case it was all great fun. The solution to the mystery was revealed one Friday evening in 1897. J. J. Thomson, giving a lecture to the Royal Institution, not only showed that cathode rays consisted of particles, but he even measured their mass and electric charge. These were the particles we now know as *electrons* and that night saw the birth of the subject of electronics.

Impressive though that was, the research into the nature of cathode rays had already produced the most dramatic scientific bombshell of all. Wilhelm Roentgen had been one of those investigating the strange phenomena going on inside a Crookes tube. One day, to his surprise, he discovered an even stranger phenomenon taking place *outside* it. He recounted the scene in a newspaper interview in 1896:

'Now Professor,' said I, 'will you tell me the history of the discovery?'

'There is no history,' he said. 'I have been for a long time interested in the problem of the cathode rays from a vacuum tube as studied by Hertz and Lenard. I had followed their and other researches with great interest, and determined as soon as I had the time, to make some researches of my own. This time I found at the close of last October. I had been at work for some days when I discovered something new.'

'What was the date?'

'The eighth of November.'

'And what was the discovery?'

'I was working with a Crookes tube covered by a shield of black card-board. A piece of barium platinocyanide paper lay on the bench there. I had been passing a current through the tube, and I noticed a peculiar black line across the paper.'

'What of that?'

'The effect was one which could only be produced, in ordinary parlance, by the passage of light. No light could come from the tube because the shield which covered it was impervious to any light known, even that of the electric arc.'

'And what did you think?'

'I did not think: I investigated. I assumed that the effect must have come from the tube, since its character indicated that it could come from nowhere else. I tested it. In a few minutes there was no doubt about it. Rays were coming from the tube which had a luminescent effect upon the paper. I tried it successfully at greater and greater distances, even

at two metres. It seemed at first a new kind of invisible light. It was
clearly something new, something unrecorded.'

(cited in Price, *Science Since Babylon*, pp. 77-8)

Having no idea what these strange rays could be, Roentgen gave them
the 'provisional' name of X-rays. That name is still in use almost everywhere, although in his native country of Germany they are known as
Roentgen rays and a radiographer is a Roentgenographer. Roentgen did
not rush to tell the world of his fantastic discovery. A true scientist, he
worked intensely for the next seven weeks, testing the properties of his
rays in every way he could think of. He showed that they could also
pass through glass or wood; through aluminium, though not through
lead; and even through human flesh. On emerging they would still make
a fluorescent screen glow or a photographic plate go black.

In January 1896 Roentgen was ready. He gave a public lecture on
X-rays and concluded by taking an X-ray photograph showing the bones
in the hand of the grand old man of physiology, Rudolf von Koelliker,
who had stepped up from the audience when Roentgen called for a vol-
unteer. The cheering that broke from the audience gave a foretaste of
the world-wide excitement that would soon be aroused. (Actually he

LA PHOTOGRAPHIE DE L'INVISIBLE

Par M. L. OLIVIER, Dr és sciences
Directeur de la *Revue générale des sciences*.

La nouvelle de la grande découverte que
vient de faire le professeur Rontgen a passé
directement de son laboratoire dans le public,
où elle s'est propagée avec la rapidité de l'éclair
avant même que les journaux scientiques aient
eu le temps d'en parler.

Il n'est bruit, en ce moment, que des « rayons

The first article on the discovery of X-rays to appear in a French medical journal

X-ray machine mounted on a tricycle

had already taken an X-ray photograph of his wife's hand!) On 1 January, Roentgen sent copies of his experimental report, including an assortment of X-ray photographs, to scientists around the world. Then, in his own words, 'Hell broke loose!'. 'Our domestic peace is gone!' exclaimed Frau Roentgen as an amazed world hailed the new discovery. Even in England, still in a state of shock from the Jameson raid into South Africa only a few days earlier and preoccupied with the impending Boer War, space was still found for headlines proclaiming the startling arrival of the X-rays:

The noise of war's alarm should not distract attention from the marvellous triumph of Science which is reported from Vienna. It is announced that Prof. Roentgen of Würzburg has discovered a light which, for the purposes of photography, will penetrate wood, flesh and most other organic substances. The professor has succeeded in photographing metal weights which were in a closed wooden case, also a man's hand, which shows only the bones, the flesh being 'invisible'.

(cited in Schroeer, *Physics and Its Fifth Dimension: Society*, p. 140)

The sensation that the X-rays produced has been matched in our time only by the news of the dropping of the atomic bombs in 1945. Newspapers, magazines and music-halls were full of it. Two ladies in Manchester wrote indignantly to *The Times* that they now felt compelled, knowing what these scientists were up to, to keep their clothes on while bathing. Yet the speed with which X-rays were put into service was astounding. Four days after the news of them reached America, they were being used to locate a bullet in a patient's leg. In May the British Nile expedition set out, taking with it two portable X-ray units. Everywhere Crookes tubes and induction coils were being pressed into service. Physics laboratories were besieged by doctors bringing patients with suspected fractures, or by dentists bringing patients with raging toothaches. Exposures up to an hour long were administered, the possibility of radiation hazards apparently not being considered by the early enthusiasts. Even when Dr Grubbe of Chicago found that his hands itched and turned red, and that the hair on them fell out, he proceeded in that first blissful January to give X-ray treatment for cancer of the breast. The *Lancet* noted his achievement, which actually produced some remission of the cancer, but went on to propose a new X-ray method of shaving: a Crookes tube would be run over the chin for a few minutes before retiring, and washing in the morning with soap and water would do the rest!

Many of the scientists who had been working on cathode rays for years scratched their heads and wondered why they had not made the discovery themselves. They had often found that photographic plates in boxes near to their Crookes tubes had become fogged or even blackened beyond use. Sir William Crookes himself had complained to the makers, the Ilford Photographic Company. And out of the hundreds of scientists who took up the challenge of X-rays in the spring of 1896, none worked more feverishly than Thomas Alva Edison. In February the *Electrical World* reported his activities:

Edison himself has been having a severe attack of Roentgenmania. The newspapers having reporters in attendance at his laboratory did not suffer for copy, as the yards of sensational matter emanating from this source attest, and we learn that last week Mr Edison and his staff worked through seventy hours without intermission, a hand organ being employed during the latter hours to assist in keeping the force awake.

(cited in Schroeer, *Physics and Its Fifth Dimension: Society*, p. 141)

In May, Edison put on an exhibition in New York where visitors could X-ray their own hands and see the result on a fluorescent screen. Eight years later, though, one of Edison's assistants died of X-ray burns; Edison never worked on X-rays again.

Gendarme X-raying passengers' luggage

The ill effects caused by the casual use of X-rays will never be fully known. Even in the 1960s X-ray machines were still being installed in shoe shops so that customers could see the position of their foot inside the shoe as an aid to fitting. This sales technique was unforgivable, although the lure of the rays in the first months after their discovery must have been almost irresistible.

But just what were these world-famous X-rays that offered so much promise, with only a few sinister overtones? The correct answer was given by a number of scientists, among them the old and eminent Sir George Stokes. He had studied the invisible ultraviolet light lying just beyond the violet, short-wave end of the spectrum, and he proposed that X-rays were also electromagnetic radiation but with even shorter wavelengths than the ultraviolet. Roentgen himself thought that they were not transverse but longitudinal waves, like sound, while others still believed them to be another kind of particle. Only a decade later were diffraction experiments carried out with crystals which confirmed Stokes' view of X-rays as an invisible form of light.

And in the glorious flush of that scientific springtime of 1896, there had come the discovery of another quite unexpected phenomenon, revealing the existence of invisible light with shorter wavelengths still. Henri Becquerel found that crystals of the salts of uranium could also blacken a photographic plate while it was still in its black paper wrapper. Further work on this phenomenon of *radioactivity*, as Marie Curie called it, showed that certain elements, particularly radium, were spontaneously giving out energy. They were constantly emitting positively and negatively charged particles as well as sending out electromagnetic waves of very short wavelength, the gamma rays. The grandeur of the whole spectrum of electromagnetic waves could at last be appreciated (see Figure 4.2). From the short gamma rays of radioactivity to the long waves of radio, the spectrum stretched across more than fifty octaves. (An octave is the span from any particular frequency to a frequency twice as great.) A young person, for example, may be able to hear sound waves from as low as 15 Hz up to an almost inaudible hiss of 20 000 Hz, a range of something over ten octaves. But the frequency of violet light is only about 1.8 times that of the deepest red, so that the visible spectrum occupies less than a single octave out of the vast span of electromagnetic radiation.

Such were the events that launched the Second Scientific Revolution. In those two cataclysmic years of 1895 and 1896, the discoveries of X-rays, of radioactivity and of the electron, had shattered the comfortable belief that physical science was largely complete. And more was soon to come. With the walls of the edifice of physical science cracking around them, scientists dropped their belief of completeness and replaced it by a new belief: that there will always be great and unexpected discoveries just around the corner that will transform the whole nature of physical science. While this might be true within the more esoteric branches of fundamental physics, I believe that it is no longer true for the kinds of physical science that affect the lives of ordinary people; it is a piece of wishful thinking with its origins in those startling events at the end of the last century.

At any rate, these revolutionary discoveries certainly influenced the lives of millions. Both X-rays and radioactivity have brought huge benefits to industry and medicine, though both have also brought much suffering, either by accident, by design, or by sheer thoughtlessness. Apart from the tragic fate of many of the pioneers − including Marie Curie − there were countless cases of cancer and genetic damage among those who worked with luminous paints or just bought them for personal use from toy or art shops, or who drank the French mineral waters carrying the proud label on the bottle − 'Guaranteed Radioactive'. Those particular hazards were removed, but meanwhile uncontrolled enthusiasm of the medical and dental professions led to an excessive use of X-rays. In some countries the abandonment of the mass chest X-ray campaigns has partly alleviated the problem of over-exposure. And after the large-scale 'experiments' at Hiroshima and Nagasaki, the designers of atomic weapons have created their masterpiece, the neutron bomb; the radiation from this bomb maximises the ratio of human suffering to property damage − it kills more people and destroys fewer buildings.

Ironically, Roentgen's name appears in all of this as the unit by which radiation exposure is measured. A modified unit, the *rem* (standing for Roentgen equivalent man, or radiological equivalent mammal), is used to describe radiation damage, as it allows for the differing effectiveness of various forms of radiation in destroying human tissues. It is ironic because, although most great scientific discoveries have been used not only for the benefit but also for the destruction of humanity, Roentgen himself was completely dedicated to advancing his science for the good of all. To the somewhat puzzled amusement of Edison, he took out no patents, nor did he attempt to make any money out of his tremendous contribution to science, industry and medicine. Apart from the very appropriate award of the Rumford Medal, and having his statue erected by a grateful nation on the Potsdam Bridge in Berlin, his chief reward came from a quite unexpected source. Alfred Nobel, a Swedish chemist who died in 1896, had written a most unusual will in the previous November, just a fortnight after Roentgen's discovery. Nobel was a rather lonely bachelor whose main contribution to the good of humanity had so far been the invention of dynamite and gelignite. He did in fact design his explosives for peaceful purposes only, for blasting and mining for example, and he showed the way by using them to exploit the Russian oilfields at Baku, making a fortune in the process. Encouraged by his association with Bertha von Suttner, an Austrian baroness and an outstanding pacifist, Nobel indulged his idealism by leaving his whole fortune to create a foundation that would award prizes 'to those who, during the preceding year, shall have conferred the greatest benefit on mankind'. Five prizes were to be awarded each year — one for physics, one for chemistry, one for physiology or medicine, one for literature of an idealistic kind, and one for the cause of peace. The first Nobel Prize ever awarded was given in 1901 to Wilhelm Konrad Roentgen in recognition of the discovery of X-rays.

The gods of war still had one harsh trick left for Roentgen. In 1901 he had presented the substantial sum of money that goes with the prize to his University of Würzburg for the benefit of further scientific studies. The aftermath of the First World War saw the economic collapse of Germany, with inflation raging to a climax in 1923 when the mark reached the astounding level of four million to the dollar. Roentgen, in retirement and living quietly on his pension, was just one of the many middle-class Germans who were caught in the economic blizzard, and he died in poverty in 1923 at the height of the storm.

In the early years of the Nobel Prizes, while the Foundation was still interpreting the conferring of 'the greatest benefit on mankind' in the true spirit of its Founder, the scientists working on light, whether visible or invisible, were duly recognised. Hertz was dead and therefore ineligible, but the physics prize for 1909 went to Marconi for his application of radio waves; the year before it had been given to Gabriel Lippmann for his work on colour photography, and three years later it went to Nils Dalen, a Swedish lighting engineer, for his invention of an automatic lighthouse light that increased the safety of coastal navigation. Many of the other awards were for fundamental advances in understanding the nature of light. The culmination came in 1921 when the physics prize was awarded to Albert Einstein for his explanation of the photoelectric effect. It was at last being recognised that with his photon theory he had written the next — and possibly even the last — big chapter in the story of light.

Einstein was a victim of both the nationalism and the racism of his times. He joined in the exodus of Jews who were able to leave Germany just before the advent of the Fascist government in 1933, and settled in the United States. The Depression was still biting deep, and there was a widespread feeling that the available jobs should go to American citizens only. To that loyal organisation calling itself The Daughters of the

American Revolution, the appointment of Einstein to the Institute for Advanced Studies at Princeton was the last straw and they wrote an open letter in protest to the President. Einstein replied in kind, and pointed out a historical precedent: in classical times, he recalled, the Capitol had been saved by the cackling of its faithful geese.

In 1905, however, when Einstein's paper on photoelectricity appeared, the curtain was just coming down on one of the most bizarre episodes in science, an episode strongly coloured by Franco-German rivalry. Professor René Blondlot, a distinguished French physicist and a member of the Academy of Sciences, had been one of the leading investigators of X-rays. In fact his experimental demonstration of the polarisation of X-rays was probably the crucial step in establishing them as electromagnetic waves just like radio or light.

Then in March 1903 he had an amazing experience. He was detecting his X-rays by observing the brightening of a small electric spark, the effect that had been observed by Hertz' assistants with ultraviolet light. He turned the power on his Crookes tube down and down without apparently affecting the brightening shown by his spark detector. Still the sparks of the detector were brighter when the tube was switched on! Then what *was* coming out of the tube? For a moment Blondlot saw himself as France's answer to the German hero, Roentgen. Yes, that was it, he had discovered a completely new kind of ray. What could he call them? B-rays? No, too presumptuous. They were new rays, *raies nouvelles*, so why not n-rays? Better still, call them N-rays in honour of the institution where he had discovered them, the University of Nancy.

Blondlot carried out further experiments which convinced him that his results were genuine, and he announced his discovery in *Comptes Rendus*, the journal of the French Academy of Science, on 23 March 1903. He went on to show that the rays could be bent and focused by prisms or lenses made of aluminium, and that there were many other sources of N-rays including the sun.

Many other scientists, mostly French, hastened to climb on the band-wagon and in 1904 *Comptes Rendus* published nearly a hundred papers on N-Rays, ten times the number dealing with the more prosaic and Germanic X-rays. But in 1905 the last N-ray paper was published. The bubble had burst.

A group of English, German and American scientists comparing notes found that none of them had succeeded in reproducing any of Blondlot's experiments. They wanted an independent observer to go to Nancy and make an unprejudiced report on what was going on. Ideally the person chosen should be a first-rate experimental physicist, experienced in optics and preferably having an interest in practical jokes, frauds and hoaxes.

In 1904 the man for the job was Robert W. Wood, a world authority on experimental optics and professor of physics at the Johns Hopkins University in Baltimore. Wood's relevant talents were shown in the production of a supposed photograph of a U.F.O., and the exposure of many frauds, particularly in the current vogue of spiritualism. On one occasion he induced a medium who claimed to be in touch with the spirit of the British physicist, Lord Rayleigh, to ask some tricky questions about electromagnetism. There was no reply.

Wood was, naturally, one of those who had tried to reproduce Blondlot's experiments as soon as he heard of them, but without success. He gave up, as he said, 'after wasting an entire morning'. When he reached Nancy he was well-received by Blondlot who showed him all the N-ray demonstrations. The climax came with a demonstration of an N-ray spectroscope. The N-rays from an open incandescent lamp were supposed to be bent by an aluminium prism just as Newton's glass prism had bent ordinary light. Moving the detector into different positions showed the angles by which N-rays of different wavelengths were being bent, and all agreed upon the positions of the detector where it brightened up under the influence of the rays. During the course of this demonstration, which took place in a darkened room, there was a slight scuffle when the assistants jumped forward under the impression that Wood might be interfering with the experiment, perhaps even removing the prism. However all was in order, and the prism was in its correct place. What they did not realise was that Wood had just replaced the prism, having removed it unobtrusively at the beginning; it had been in his pocket throughout the whole 'successful' experiment!

The next day, Wood wrote to the British weekly science journal, *Nature*. He had failed to observe a single demonstration of the existence of N-rays, and he was 'left with a very firm conviction that the few experimenters who have obtained positive results have been in some way deluded'.

That was virtually the end of the N-rays. French scientists were particularly keen to expunge all traces of the debacle, though pockets of resistance fought on, arguing that the phenomena were detectable only by unusually sensitive observers. Irving Klotz relates in the *Scientific American* of May 1980 how some extremists, presumably possessed with an unusually well-developed sense of humour, claimed that 'only the Latin races possessed the sensitivities (intellectual as well as sensory) necessary to detect manifestations of the rays'. They alleged that 'Anglo-Saxon powers of perception were dulled by continual exposure to fog, and Teutonic ones blunted by constant ingestion of beer'.

Blondlot himself never gave his side of the story. He used his Academy prize money of 50 000 francs to provide his town of Nancy with a park and retired into obscurity. The whole strange affair had lasted only two years. It was neither a fraud nor a hoax, but an example of self-deception by scientists making subjective measurements of phenomena which at the best were only barely detectable. Such an occurrence is common enough today, though not on that spectacular scale. The N-ray affair brings back a breath of those heady days at the turn of the century when science was a newly opened treasure-chest filled with brilliant jewels just waiting to be lifted out of it. The electromagnetic spectrum was an uncharted world in which all kinds of rays might be awaiting discovery: death rays, life-giving rays, anti-gravity rays, thought waves, or even rays that would simply make you feel good. Now that we have filled up the spectrum there are (probably) no unknown rays left. The challenge of our time, less dramatic but more certain, is to use the rays we already have in the best possible way for the common good.

11

The Colour Question

Unsolved problems about colour
despite a scientific explanation

Sir,

   To perform my late promise to you, I shall without further ceremony acquaint you, that in the beginning of the year 1666 (at which time I applyed my self to the Grinding of Optick Glasses of other figures than spherical) I procured me a Triangular Glass Prism, to try with the celebrated Phenomena of colours . . .

(from A Discourse of Mr Isaac Newton, containing his new theory about light and colours, sent by him from Cambridge to the Secretary of the Royal Society, 6 February 1671/2. Original in possession of the Royal Society of London)

Thousands of people before Newton had observed the rainbow-like colours produced when white light passed through triangular pieces of glass or crystal, whether in the form of jewellery, a chandelier, or a scientist's prism. None had succeeded in explaining how such brilliant colours could be produced by the combination of white light with a colourless prism.

   The young Newton started off with a very commonplace experiment. He made a small hole in his window blind so that a beam of sunlight shone through it onto a screen producing a bright circular disk, a little picture of the sun. He then interposed his prism so that the sunbeam fell upon it and was bent towards a different point on the screen. The image on the screen was no longer a little white disk; it had changed into a rainbow-coloured spectrum. Newton took a careful look at what was happening: he noted that the spectrum was not a coloured circle but a drawn-out band some five times longer than it was wide. He speculated that it was not that the prism was putting the colours into the light, but that white light was itself already a mixture of colours — the prism was simply separating them by bending them in different directions.

Two further ingenious experiments sufficed to confirm this bold hypothesis. Putting in a second prism the other way round from the first recombined the spreading spectrum of colours and restored the white image of the sun; the mixture of colours had been taken apart and put back together again. The second crucial experiment was to look at the bending action of the prism one colour at a time. Using a piece of wood with a hole in it to screen off the rest of the light, Newton picked out one coloured ray and allowed it to fall on the face of his second prism. He found that each separate colour was pure. In contrast to white light it was bent but not split up into any further colours. Furthermore each colour was bent by an amount different from any other colour; the violet rays were bent the most and the red rays the least.

Newton had certainly fulfilled his promise 'to try the celebrated Phenomena of colours'. He had shown that the white light from the sun, was, as he put it, 'a confused aggregate of rays indued with all sorts of colours, as they were promiscuously darted from the various parts of luminous bodies'. Attention, he said, should be concentrated upon the nature of light of a single colour. Colour was essentially a quality of light and not of any particular object. In a darkened room he examined 'coloured' objects in light of a single colour; a red rose viewed in red light still looked bright red, but in green light it appeared to be dark green, or almost black. Objects, he wrote, have 'no appropriate colour, but ever appear of the colour of the light cast upon them, but yet with this difference, that they are most bright and vivid in the light of their own daylight colour'.

You might imagine that the scientific world would welcome such a clarification of one of its foremost problems. It did not. For there now ensued a real comedy of errors. Newton had made several mistakes, tactical as well as scientific, one of which held up scientific advance for a century while another led to a technical invention of great importance, the reflecting telescope. But he was only twenty-three years old when he carried out his experiments with the prism and rather than being critical, with the ease of hindsight, it is more instructive to look at his actual Discourse, the first paper he published, before considering the storm that it unleashed. It recalls those spacious days when editors did not regard the subjective reactions of experimenters as superfluous. Here is Newton's explanation of his investigation of colour after he had bought his prism:

... And in order thereto have darkned my Chamber, and made a small hole in my Windowshutts, to let in a convenient quantity of the Sun's light. I placed my prism at his Entrance, that it might so thereby be refracted to the opposite Wall. It was at first a very pleasing Divertisement, to view the Vivid and intense colours produced thereby, but after a while applying myself to consider them, more circumspectly, I became surprized to see them in an oblong form, which according to the received Laws of Refractions, I expected should have been circular ...

Comparing the length of the spectrum with its breadth. I found it above five times greater, a disproportion so extravagant, that it excited me to a more than ordinary curiosity of examining from wherever it might proceed.

(The Royal Society of London, R.B.C. 3, 215, 1671/2)

Newton goes on in proper systematic fashion to change all of the variables one at a time – size of hole, position of prism, and so on – then considers the surprising proposition that the elongation of the image may be due to the light travelling in a curved path – by analogy with 'a Tennis Ball, struck with an Oblique Racket . . .' He uses this interjection to drag in his favourite idea that light rays are really streams of some kind of particles:

... if the Rays of Light should possibly be Globular bodies, and by their Oblique passage out of one Medium into another, acquire a Circulating Motion, they ought to feel the greater resistance from the Ambient Aether, on that side where the Motion conspires, and thence be continually bowed to the other. But not with standing such plausible grounds of suspicion, when I came to examine it, I could observe no such Curvity in them.

(The Royal Society of London, R.B.C. 3, 215, 1671/2)

After that honest experimental rejection of his own hypothesis he moves on to describe his crucial experiment, with its conclusion that rays of different colours are bent by different amounts as they pass through the same prism. This was a shattering idea to Newton! A lens is really a prism with curved sides, so his conclusion meant that any lens, however well made, would bring rays of different colours to a focus at different points. *All* optical instruments made with lenses would inevitably have fuzzy images with coloured edges. 'I wonder', he wrote, 'that, seeing the difference of refrangibility [the dispersion] was so great as I found it, Telescopes should arrive to that perfection they are now at'. He measured the angle of separation between red and violet rays and concluded that it was the same for all kinds of glass so that there was no possibility of combining lenses so that the dispersion would cancel out.

He was mistaken in this conclusion. Many years later an instrument maker, John Dollond, combined lenses of different glasses with differing dispersions to make the colour-free 'achromatic' lens that is used in modern optical instruments. Nevertheless Newton's mistaken view stimulated his ingenuity to find another way round the difficulty. Although the angle of *refraction*, the bending as light goes from air into glass, varies with the colour of the light, the angle of *reflection* from a shiny surface does not; reflection in a mirror, whether plane or curved, does not introduce any colouring of the image. Newton was thereby led to the concept of a telescope that would produce its magnification by reflections from curved mirrors rather than by refractions through lenses:

I under stood that by their mediation Optick instruments might be brought to any degree of Perfection imaginable, provided a Reflecting substance could be found, which I would polish as finely as Glass, and reflect as much light as Glass transmits, and the Art of communicating it to a Parabolick figure be also attained . . .

Admidst these thoughts, I was forced from Cambridge by the Intervening Plague, and it was more than two years, before I proceeded further.

(The Royal Society of London, R.B.C. 3, 215, 1671/2)

In those far off days theoretical physicists still did their own experimental work, and Newton actually made two reflecting telescopes with concave parabolic mirrors, the forerunners of the giant telescopes of today.

The storm was about to break. As this was the youthful Newton's first paper, the Royal Society, thanking the author 'for his ingenious discourse', sent it to three referees for their appraisal. Seth Ward, the Bishop of Salisbury, was one referee, the Hon. Robert Boyle another, but the third, unfortunately for Newton, was Robert Hooke, Curator of Experiments to the Royal Society. Hooke was a wide-ranging physicist of great ability who often got into arguments about the proper priority of investigations in the many fields he studied. Asimov, in his *Biographical Encyclopedia of Science and Technology*, calls Hooke an 'argumentative individual, antisocial, miserly, and quarrelsome'. Newton, whose mathematical ability was greater than Hooke's, was described by the astronomer John Flamsteed as 'insidious, ambitious, excessively covetous of praise, and impatient of contradiction . . .' Friendly relations between these two great physicists were less than likely, and hostilities seem to have continued right up to Hooke's death in 1703. 'I was so persecuted', wrote Newton in 1675, 'with discussions arising out of my theory of light that I blamed by own imprudence for parting with so substantial a blessing as my quiet to run after a shadow'. One of the opening shots came, in fact, in Hooke's report to the Royal Society:

I have perused the Discourses of Mr Newton about Colours and Refractions, and I was not a little pleased with the Niceness and curiosity of his Observations. But though I wholly agree with him as to the truth of those he hath alledged, as having by many hundred of experiments found them soo; yet as to his Hypothesis of solving the Phenomena of colours thereby, I confess, I cannot see yet any undenyable Argument to convince me of the certainty thereof. For, all the Experiments and Observations I have hitherto made, nay and even those very Experiments, which he alledgith, doo seem to me to prove, that which is nothing, but a pulse or Motion, propagated through an homogeneous, uniform and transparent medium . . .

I should be very glad to meet with one **Experimentum Crucis** from Mr Newton, that should divorce me from it. But it is not that, which he so calls, will doo the trick . . .

(The Royal Society of London, R.B.C. 3, 231, prob. 1672)

Hooke criticises Newton's haste in abandoning the use of lenses for the telescope: 'since it is not improbable but that he that hath made so very good an Improvement of Telescopes by his own Tryals upon Reflections, would if he had protracted it, have done more by Refraction . . .'

The real thrust of Hooke's attack, however, was not upon Newton's theory of colour nor upon his retreat from telescopes with lenses, but upon his belief that light consisted in a stream of particles. Newton had, rather gratuitously, smuggled this idea into his discourse on colour. Hooke, on the other hand, was already a believer in a wave theory of light. In fact, in his report to the Society, Hooke stated his own conviction in what was possibly the most pregnant yet most neglected sentence of the century:

. . . the motion of Light in an Uniform Medium, in which it is generated,

is propagated by simple and uniform Pulses or Waves, which are at right Angles with the Line of Direction . . .

It is astonishing that when the battle between the wave and the particle theorists was finally joined, about a quarter of a century later, the leading protagonists, Christian Huygens for waves and Isaac Newton for particles, both completely missed the significance of the idea that the waves are waving, like waves on the sea or a shaken clothes lines, 'at right Angles with the Line of Direction' (see Figure 2.4). Without this key concept of *transverse* waves the argument between Huygens and Newton became more like a religious conflict than a reasoned debate. Huygens published his *Treatise on Light* in 1690, while Newton waited until 1704, the year after Hooke died, before publishing his own work, *Opticks; or a Treatise of the Reflections, Refractions, Inflections, and Colours of Light*. The viewpoint of Newton prevailed, more because of his great scientific authority than through the force of his scientific arguments. The wave theory was down and out, and it stayed out for the whole of the eighteenth century.

Yet even in *Opticks* Newton had dealt with another aspect of colour which was a strong clue in favour of the wave theory. He had shown that most things appear to be coloured because they absorb some of the colours in white light and reflect the rest. But some of the most brilliant colours of nature arise in quite a different way. A shimmering film of oil on a puddle of water, for example, or the wing of a dragonfly, a peacock's feather, the iridescent scale of a fish, or a glowing opal, owe their beautiful colouring to the existence of thin layers or films in which the reflected rays interact with the illuminating white light so as to remove certain colours and reinforce those remaining. The 'bloomed' layer on the lens surfaces of a modern camera or a pair of binoculars works in the same way. It cancels out the yellow rays that would normally be reflected from the glass surface and actually allows *more* light to enter the camera than would otherwise be the case (see Figure 2.1)! The residual light after the yellow has been removed gives the characteristic purplish-blue tinge to the bloomed surfaces.

How to investigate such complicated phenomena? Newton used an ingenious arrangement already employed by Hooke. He pressed a shallow convex lens into contact with a flat glass surface and looked from above at the point of contact. This arrangement provided an air gap whose thickness increased rapidly away from the central point of contact. He observed a series of coloured rings, now rather unfairly

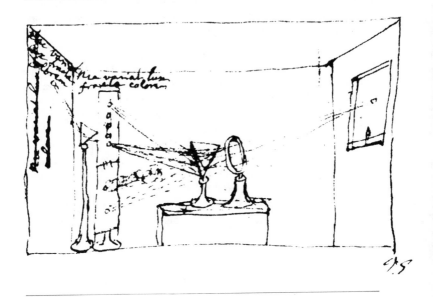

Newton's sketch of his prism experiment

called Newton's Rings, which became closer and closer together the further they were from the centre. The first dark ring occurred where the air gap had a certain thickness, and further dark rings were seen whenever the air gap was two, three, four, or, in fact, any whole number times that first thickness. On Hooke's reasoning, the incident and reflected rays of light interacted so as to cancel each other when their paths differed in length by some multiple of a small but definite distance (see Figure 2.1). If Hooke had only remembered his own idea of light as a transverse wave ('. . . at right Angles with the Line of Direction'), he would surely have recognised the formation of the rings as supporting evidence strongly in his favour. However it was left to Newton, striving desperately to sidestep the wave theory, to give an explanation by attributing 'fits of easy reflection and transmission' to his particles of light, stating that:

. . . every Ray of Light in its passage through any refractive Surface is put into a certain transient Constitution or State, which in the progress

of the Ray returns at equal Intervals, and disposes the Ray at every Return to be easily transmitted through the next refracting Surface, and between the returns to be easily reflected by it.

Such were the lengths to which Newton felt impelled to go to resist the rival wave theory of light. Newton of course knew that two waves out of step by half a wavelength cancel each other out, but his emotional commitment to the particle theory prevented him from applying this fact to light.

By the 1690s Newton was no longer the same person as the young physicist who had made such spectacular achievements in those golden years around 1666 in Cambridge, the time when, as he wrote, 'I was in the prime of my age'. Increasingly his interests had spread in other directions. He spent more time on chemistry, on alchemy — he was a great searcher for a method of transmuting base metals into gold — and on theology.

He was twice elected to Parliament, but his only recorded speech is when he rose to ask that a window be closed because of the draught. In 1692 he had a long-lasting nervous breakdown. Seeking another job, he rejected a suggestion that he should apply for the headmastership of a London school, partly because of the intense competition for the post and partly because of the pollution of the London air. Later he was appointed master of the Royal Mint, organising it with such ability that he became the terror of counterfeiters. In 1703, when Hooke died, he was elected President of the Royal Society, and *Opticks* was published in the following year.

At the end of *Opticks* Newton listed his doubts and speculations in the form of a series of Queries. He set out what he considered to be key questions in physics and in biophysics — the interaction of light and matter, the retina and the brain, and the action of muscle, for example — and even implied some association of light with vibrations. This hint was overlooked in the universal acceptance of his assertion of the particulate nature of light. Newton seemed not inclined to reconsider the matter. The last words that he ever published, the conclusion of his book, may suggest that he was devoting himself to other considerations:

And if natural Philosophy in all its Parts, by pursuing this Method, shall at length be perfected, the Bounds of Moral Philosophy will also be enlarged. For so far as we can know by natural Philosophy what is the first Cause, what Power he has over us, and what Benefits we receive from him, so far as our duty towards him, as well as that towards one another, will appear to us by the Light of Nature. And no doubt, if the Worship of false Gods had not blinded the Heathen, their Moral Philosophy would have gone farther than the four Cardinal Virtues; and instead of teaching the Transmigration of Souls, and the worship of the Sun and the Moon, and dead Heroes, they would have taught us to worship to our true Author and Benefactor . . .

As the new century wore on, however, there was a romantic reaction against the hard rationalism of science, and an alienation from the machine civilisation as the Industrial Revolution got under way. The romantic poets were keenly aware of the separation of the heart from the intellect. Blake wrote powerfully of the 'dark Satanic mills' and gave a concrete illustration of what he was talking about:

> . . . intricate wheels invented, wheel without wheel,
> To perplex youth in their outgoings & to bind labours in Albion
> Of day & night the myriads of eternity: that they may grind
> And polish brass & iron hour after hour, laborious tasks
> Kept ignorant of its use: that they might spend the days of wisdom
> In sorrowful drudgery to obtain a scanty pittance of bread . . .
> (cited in Schroeer, *Physics and Its Fifth Dimension: Society*, p. 104)

Meanwhile Germany's supreme poet, Johann Wolfgang von Goethe, launched into a direct and personal attack upon Newton. Goethe did not believe that a pure thing like white light could possibly contain all of the colours. He saw the formation of colours as the result of a battle between the conflicting forces of light and darkness. The experiments that Newton put forward to prove his theory were anathema to Goethe because they had deliberately tried to reduce the part played by the observer to a minimum. The observer is the sole reason for the experiment, argued Goethe. Seizing a prism he viewed a white object through it and saw, not a rainbow-like spectrum, as he wrongly imagined Newton was claiming, but a white image with red and blue edges. He made more experiments and even wrote his ideas up as a book, *The Theory of Colours*, which he rated higher than his own masterpieces including *Faust*:

As for what I have done as a poet, I take no pride in it whatever . . .

Excellent poets have lived at the same time with me, poets more excellent lived before me, and others will come after me. But that in my century I am the only person who knows the truth in the difficult sciences of colours – of that, I say, I am not a little proud, and here I have a consciousness of superiority to many.

(cited in Schroeer, *Physics and Its Fifth Dimension: Society*, p. 111)

For some strange psychological reasons, which we can now only dimly perceive, Goethe persisted in attacking Newton on his own ground where he was virtually unassailable. Newton's clear, reproducible experiments with his prism were about as objective and certain as anything could be. Newton was indeed the epitome of the physicist, possessed of that supreme tunnel vision which strips away all complications, all human values, until the original problem is so simplified that it can be solved. He had already demonstrated this technique by crystallising out his laws of motion and solving the riddle of the solar system. Goethe's strategy should have been to keep right outside the battlefield of simplified experiments such as the single beam of light and the prism, and to concentrate on the colourful situations that a human being actually sees. This was the strategy that came naturally to that lateral-thinking individual Edwin Land, the 'Mr Polaroid' of the 1930s.

Edwin H. Land is listed in Asimov's *Biographical Encyclopedia of Science and Technology* as 'American inventor'. In the 1930s, while he was still an undergraduate, he lined up a suitable microcrystalline paste by an electric field and fixed it in that oriented state by pressing it between two sheets of clear plastic. The product provided a cheap and easy way of polarising light, whether for research purposes or sunglasses, and Land dropped out from his university to market his invention under the name of Polaroid. As with Edison, his only science degrees were honorary ones. In 1937 he consolidated his commercial success by forming the Polaroid Corporation, becoming President, Chairman of the Board, and Director of Research. The Corporation made or developed many of Land's subsequent inventions, such as a plastic lens for devices used at night, a ring sight for bazookas, a camera for use on U-2 spy-flights, and probably his most famous invention, the Polaroid Land instant camera.

Edwin Land has continued throughout his career to sparkle with unorthodox ideas, ideas not confined to the scientific field but concerned equally with the social relations between scientific production and society. He wrote a personal letter to his employees in 1970:

This is no ordinary company that we have built together. It is the proved pioneer that set out to teach the world how people should work together ... Polaroid is on its way to lead the world – perhaps even to save it – by the interplay between science, technology and real people.

Land's entry into the field of colour vision was characteristic. He launched a direct attack upon the trichromatic theory of vision. What was that theory based upon? The classical experiments of Newton, with his prism and spectrum, and of Young, who shone red and green lights upon a screen, producing yellow where they overlapped, then added blue to produce a pure white. Land proceeded to demonstrate that these experiments were inadequate. 'The great investigators', as he called them, had proved lots of things by typical physicists' experiments, but their determinations have little to do with colour as we normally see it.

Land repeated some of the colour mixing experiments of Newton and Young, but using more complex, realistic sources than circles or slits. For example, he took two black-and-white photographs of a commonplace scene, one photographed through a red filter and the other through a green. From each photograph he made a black-and-white positive slide suitable for projection. Each slide projected by itself gave a picture of the original scene, though the balance of greys was of course different. By using two projectors Land was able to superimpose the pictures on the screen to give a clear picture, again in black and white. He next put a red filter on one of the projectors. Instead of the picture simply appearing to be tinted red or pink, it appeared in a range of colours, all rather dilute but including green! More surprising still, if each slide was projected with a pure *yellow* light, one of wavelength 579 mm and the other very close in the spectrum at 599 mm, the picture on the screen, though still somewhat washy, showed a wide range of colours, with red, yellow, orange, green, blue, black, brown and white all in the right places! Quite impossible, the ordinary physical theory would maintain, but there it was.

As far as I am aware, these matters have not been fully resolved, nor would I expect them to be in the foreseeable future. The complexity of the brain, the interactions and the feedback loops, are such as to preclude much hope of a complete solution to the question of colour vision, despite the rapid progress in optical neurophysiology and psychology. Physical theory gives a useful approximation, but it cannot deal with such elusive factors as the positions, colours and intensities of other objects in the field of view. Even more elusive is the influence of the expectations we may hold of what the colours ought to be. Here we enter the realm of optical illusions, phenomena which are real enough but which a traditional physicist prefers to ignore.

While Dr Land was stirring up the foundations of colour vision theory, he did not neglect social and human affairs. Soon after its formation, the Polaroid Corporation had developed a lucrative trade with South Africa which has continued ever since. It attempted to play the role of an enlightened employer of the Blacks, paying the maximum wages permitted under the South African labour laws, awarding scholarships to promising young Blacks, and so forth. In 1971, with apartheid falling increasingly into disrepute, it spent $100 000 on an advertisement in major American papers entitled 'An Experiment in South Africa'. It claimed that its investment in that country and the employment opportunities it was creating could only be of benefit to the Blacks, and in fact that it was quite proud of its involvement. It spoke up publicly about changes to the system of apartheid.

But some of the Corporation's 10 000 employees in the United States claimed that the advertisements were hypocritical. In South Africa the Corporation was still paying Blacks 20 per cent less than whites for the same job. They pointed to the fact that the newly developed Polaroid ID-3 system provided an instant colour portrait and data card which was to be linked with an I.B.M. computer in the South African government's planned racial control system. So when Edwin Land rose to speak at the American Physical Society's meeting on Physics and Society, held at the New York Hilton in the tense, wartime atmosphere of 1971, there was little surprise when the platform was taken over by Polaroid workers who spoke against the company's involvement with apartheid. (Land didn't deliver his address on 'The Retinex Theory of Colour Vision'.) Two Black employees were subsequently fired for advocating that Polaroid products be boycotted until the Corporation's professed opposition to apartheid was given some practical effect. But whether or not you believe that the Polaroid Corporation was on its way to saving the world, Edwin Land was certainly justified in quoting this episode as an outstanding example of 'the interplay between science, technology and real people'.

There was no union at Polaroid to take up the workers' case because the Corporation had, in the true American business tradition, set its face against unionism right from the start. Likewise there was no union at Kodak when Saul D. Alinsky arrived on the scene in 1965. Before the war Alinsky had been a protégé of the C.I.O. leader, John L. Lewis. In

The colour problem

1939 he had organised the Black communities, the victims of the canned meat industry living behind the Chicago stockyards in the hideous and unsanitary conditions exposed by Upton Sinclair's shattering novel, *The Jungle*. This, and similar experiences, prepared him for his encounter with the American optical industry in 1965. The scene was the great optical centre of Rochester in the state of New York, known familiarly as Kodak City. Alinsky was called in by the City Council of Churches and by members of the Black ghetto to help them campaign for equality of treatment in jobs, housing and education. Only the previous summer, Rochester had exploded in a bloody race riot, resulting in the calling out of the National Guard and much loss of life and property. Alinsky described the city as being numb with shock: 'A city proud of its affluence, culture, and progressive churches, was dazed and guilt-ridden at its rude discovery of the misery of life in the ghetto and of its failure to do anything about it'.

Alinsky found that the dominant company of Eastman Kodak, founded by the photographic pioneer and philanthropist George Eastman, was unreceptive. Its attitudes to the public, he said, made paternalistic feudalism look like participatory democracy. When asked at the airport why he was meddling in the Black ghetto, after everything that Kodak had done for the Blacks, he replied that, as far as he knew, the only thing Eastman Kodak had ever done on the colour problem was to introduce colour film. He realised that Kodak, a great multinational concern, would not be susceptible to demonstrations and confrontations confined merely to Rochester, nor would an economic boycott have any chance of success. It would amount to asking the American people to stop taking pictures, while babies were being born, children growing up, getting married, going on holidays and so on.

Alinsky hit upon the idea of obtaining proxy votes from large holders of Kodak stock — church organisations, trade unions, pension funds, for example — and using them to persuade the management to deal with the dwellers in the ghetto. He also worked closely with Senator Robert Kennedy, preparing the grounds for an investigation by the Attorney-General if necessary. But the immediate battle was won: Kodak and the other corporations recognised the representatives of the ghetto, and negotiated with them to improve their conditions, particularly by helping with employment. A factory owned and operated by Blacks was set up in collaboration with the Xerox Corporation. The scientifically progressive company of Kodak had at last made its contribution to this other colour question, though even these events did not lead to the establishment of a labour union.

12

New Discoveries and Powers

Atomic energy, lasers, electronics —
but the power of science is still
not matched to human needs

"DON'T YOU SEE, THEY HAD TO FIND OUT IF IT WORKED . . ."

12

G. H. Hardy, the mathematician, once looked out at the wicked world from his ivory tower in Cambridge and consoled himself with the thought that pure mathematics is a relatively useless subject. It cannot be used, he said, either for killing people or for increasing the present inequitable distribution of wealth.

Such comforting assurance, even if it were true for pure mathematics, is far from true for science. Science is, above all, useful.

The science of light, in particular, has become an essential ingredient in modern life. Imagine the world tonight if every electric light were to be extinguished, if all cities became dark, if all cars, trains and aeroplanes came to a stop at sunset. No invisible waves to bring radio or television to the homes lit by candlelight; no theatres or cinemas to go to. And, on the other side of the coin, no guided missiles poised to wipe out half the world's population. Science is intimately bound up with the totality of this progress, and it is of no avail to invent a big word such as technology in an attempt to shift the responsibility, or to claim that science and technology are neutral, merely being misused by politicians and industrialists. Science, economics, warfare and politics have been inseparable corpuscles in the bloodstream of society for well over a century now. An example of the connection between them is the study of the interaction of light with matter — in modern language, of what happens when a photon meets an atom.

A ray of light can travel along happily through space for a million years, but not until it strikes an atom in a piece of matter do we know anything about it. The reds of the ruby and the sunset, the blues of the sapphire and the sky, the greens of the emerald and the grass, all have their origin in such an encounter. And even if we are only staring at a black and white television screen or reading this book, our sight is ultimately the result of a photon of light hitting a retinal molecule and releasing an electron.

The classical, pre-Einstein physics of the last century could already account for some of the more colourful interactions of light with matter. One of its particular successes was in explaining the colours of daylight. Think of the brilliant blue sky of a summer's day. Something has scattered the sunlight away from its direct path — otherwise the sky would be black! It had long been thought that the scattering was due to dust in the air, but Lord Rayleigh was able to show, using the wave theory, that air molecules alone were sufficient. According to this theory the shorter the wavelength the more the light is scattered. The scattering varies inversely with the *fourth* power of the wavelength. Thus a blue component of sunlight at 440 nanometres would be scattered more than five times as much as a red component at 660 nanometres

$$(\frac{660}{440})^4 = 5.06$$

This predominant scattering of the blue light, which gives the colour to the sky, was actually demonstrated in the laboratory by some characteristically elegant experiments of R. W. Wood, the American physicist who demolished the cult of N-rays.

The sunlight loses blue light by scattering as it travels through the Earth's atmosphere, so even at midday the sun looks redder than it would appear to be from outer space. At sunset or at sunrise the effect is even more pronounced. The sun's rays passing almost horizontally through the atmosphere encounter many more air molecules and also, frequently, more dust and pollution. As the sun approaches the horizon it loses more and more of its blue light by scattering and it goes down in a glorious, blood-red sunset.

But far and away the most common cause of colour in the world around us is the absorption of particular wavelengths of light by electrons. This phenomenon produces the red colour of blood. It gives us the green of the countryside, of plants, trees and grass, the green that we find so restful and that perhaps stirs primeval memories and a deep awareness that this is the source of life. This green is produced in a rather strange way. The electrons in the chlorophyll molecule absorb light strongly in the red and violet ends of the spectrum, leaving the yellow and green to be reflected. But sunlight is most intense precisely in these yellow and green regions, so as far as the plant is concerned most of it is wasted! Can it be part of the Grand Design to use a very inefficient solar energy collector just so that we can enjoy the beautiful greenery? It seems more likely that the chlorophyll structure evolved as a highly efficient instrument for *using* the energy it collects to make food and to liberate oxygen. The relative inefficiency of *collecting* the energy is compensated, in nature's profligate way, simply by having masses and masses of it all over the place, just as thousands of seeds may be produced so that one of them may grow.

And what about the colours of the gemstones, the deep red of the ruby or the vivid green of the emerald, for instance? These precious stones are crystals which, to the mind of a solid-state physicist, have a disease, just as an oyster may have a disease — a pearl — which is valued by anyone other than the oyster. The perfection of their crystal structure is disturbed by some small impurity or defect so that photons with wavelengths in the visible region are absorbed and the crystal appears to be coloured.

Although this action was not understood during the Second World War, certain crystals became not just pretty ornaments but agents of life and death. Large prisms of quartz, perhaps twenty centimeters long, were sliced up with a diamond saw into thin plates the size of a small coin. Squeezing such a plate produced an electrical charge, and this coupling between the mechanical and electrical behaviour meant that it would oscillate both mechanically and electrically at a very precise frequency, determined mainly by the thickness of the plate. Enormous time and skill went into the grinding and polishing by hand of these crystal plates to produce the exact frequencies needed for vital military equipment — radar equipment or communication sets for invasion armies, for example.

Towards the end of the war an alternative method of adjusting the frequency of a quartz crystal was developed. It was already known that the attractive colouring of a type of quartz, known as smoky quartz, could be produced by exposing ordinary colourless quartz to an intense beam of X-rays. The structural reason for the colour change was not known, but there was a simultaneous change in the mechanical properties, which meant a corresponding change in the frequency of a crystal plate. All you had to do was to shine a beam of X-rays on an oscillating crystal until it reached the exact frequency required and then switch off.

Since the war, the application of quantum theory has produced a deeper understanding of the electrical, thermal and optical properties of solids — in particular of their colouring. Quartz, for instance, is a form of silica. It is a transparent crystal made from silicon and oxygen atoms (SiO_2), looking like a piece of glass, but having its atoms in a perfectly regular three-dimensional structure. There is also often a small amount of aluminium present, which changes the electrical environment of some of the oxygen atoms. X-rays cause electrons to be ejected from these oxygen atoms, thereby creating 'energy levels' in the structure which allow photons of visible light to be absorbed. The quartz then becomes 'smoky'. If the impurity is iron, instead of aluminium, the different energy levels produce a different colour, and the crystal is then called amethyst.

A ruby is a crystal of corundum (aluminium oxide, Al_2O_3) in which about half of one per cent of the aluminium atoms have been replaced by chromium. The resulting electrical changes produce an absorption of broad bands of wavelengths in the violet and green-yellow regions. All of the red and some blue passes through the crystal, giving the characteristic colour of the ruby. Similarly, emerald green is produced in a crystal of beryllium aluminium silicate ($Be_3Al_2Si_6O_{18}$) by the substitution of some chromium for aluminium; in this case the energy levels are modified so that the red and some of the yellow light is absorbed.

There is a temptation to rebel against the cold analysis of a scientist seeking to pin down the smouldering beauty of a ruby in such terms as 'energy levels', rather like a naturalist pinning down a lovely butterfly. But in what lies the beauty of the ruby? In its form and colour? Or is it partly in its rarity and, therefore, its price? The ability to mass produce cherished objects, from motorised carriages to television sets or jewels, gives a view of science as a powerful social force that is democratising our age. If diamonds as big as your thumb were to be made or exact replicas indistinguishable from the paintings or sculptures of the Great Masters, all at the cost of a day's wages, that would be part of the same process. Would the beauty thereby be lost?

Science is often used against the interests of humanity, but one must suspect that those who see science only as dehumanising are already in comfortable possession of the benefits that it could make universally available. To make the full use of science it is necessary to understand and to deal with such concepts as the energy levels in atoms or groups of atoms which are evidently the key to the interaction of light with matter. This particular concept emerged in the early part of this century when the structure of the atom was being worked out, an exercise that led to dramatic results.

The story goes back to the fine black lines crossing the spectrum of

light from the sun, as mapped out by the young Joseph Fraunhofer while
Napoleon was riding to his Waterloo. Fifty years later two other German
scientists, Robert Bunsen and Gustav Kirchoff, devised the technique of
spectroscopy. They used a prism to spread out the light from an illuminated slit, and a telescope to measure the position of each line in the
spectrum precisely. If they heated ordinary salt, sodium chloride, in their
Bunsen burner, the spectroscope showed a number of bright lines, but
especially two very bright yellow lines, close together, with wavelengths
of 589.0 and 589.6 nanometres. This same pair of lines was observed
by heating other substances that contained sodium. This pair of wavelengths was evidently a fingerprint for sodium. Fraunhofer had
measured exactly the same wavelengths for a pair of black lines in the
solar spectrum and he concluded that the sun contains sodium. Somehow that sodium must be absorbing its own characteristic wavelengths
from the continuous spectrum of the sun's white light.

After several other elements, including gold, had been identified as
being in the sun, Kirchoff's banker asked him skeptically 'What is the
use of finding gold in the sun if you can't bring it down to earth?' Some
years later, Kirchoff was awarded a medal and a prize of gold sovereigns
for his discoveries. Handing the sovereigns over to his banker he dryly
remarked, 'Here is gold from the sun'.

How was it, though, that sodium could emit two very precise colours
in the yellow region and under other conditions absorb exactly those
very same colours? Some systematic mechanism was evidently at work,
but what could it be? No atomic explanation was forthcoming. Many
scientists didn't even believe in atoms, while those who did thought of
them as miniature billiard balls, without any internal structure that could
generate or absorb exact wavelengths of light.

The mystery deepened as more regularities were found in the spectra
of individual elements. The spectrum of hydrogen, glowing in an electric
discharge tube for example, showed a red line at 656 nanometres, blue
lines at 486 and 434 nanometres, and a violet line at 410 nanometres.
Apart from the fact that the lines were getting closer and closer together
there was no obvious numerical relationship between their wavelengths, nothing that might possibly give a clue as to what was happening. Any proposed formula would be put to a severe test indeed to fit
very precise data, as the wavelengths had been measured to about one
part in 100 000. Yet just such a formula was discovered in 1885 by a
Swiss schoolmaster, the sixty-year-old Johann Jakob Balmer, quietly
teaching mathematics and physics at a girls' school in Basel.

Balmer announced to an astonished scientific world that the wave-lengths of the four visible lines in hydrogen spectrum all fitted the expression wavelength = 364.56

$$\text{wavelength} = 364.56 \left[\frac{n^2}{n^2 - 4}\right]$$

The n had to be a whole number, and it had to be greater than two for the expression to make sense. For n = 3 the expression gave a wave-length of 656.208 nm, corresponding to the red line in the spectrum. Balmer calculated the wavelengths of the four visible lines and compared them with the observed values (see Table 12.1).

The calculated values differ from the observed values by only about one-thousandth of 1 per cent! Balmer had hit upon the most accurate empirical formula ever put forward. And as measurements of lines further and further into the ultraviolet range were made and found to fit the formula just as closely, it became apparent that he had touched upon the secret of how atoms radiate and absorb light. But how could the full secret be revealed?

The answer lay deep inside the atom. By 1913, just before the out-break of the First World War, the atom was no longer quite so unfathom-able. Rutherford had fired radioactive particles right through thin sheets of gold and shown how open the atomic structure really is. An atom is not 'solid' like a miniature billiard ball, but is more like a globe with over 99.9 per cent of its mass concentrated into a tiny speck at the centre. This speck, the *nucleus*, takes up only a million millionth of the volume of the atom, the rest of the space being occupied by electrons.

	Calculated (nm)	Observed (nm)
(red)	656.208	656.210
(blue)	486.080	486.074
(blue)	434.00	434.01
(violet)	410.13	410.12

Table 12.1 Wavelengths of light from the hydrogen spectrum

In 1913 Niels Bohr had returned to the University of Copenhagen from Manchester where he had been working with Rutherford. Bohr was both a first-rate physicist and a first-rate soccer player. He developed the first theory that could explain the spectrum of hydrogen, by combining the ideas about the nuclear atom he had learned from Rutherford with Einstein's concept of photons of light.

For simplicity Bohr applied his theory first to the atom of hydrogen, which has only one electron. This electron, he said, was flying round and round the nucleus in an orbit at a relatively enormous distance from it, a bit like the Earth going round the sun. It could jump out instantaneously to one of a number of possible wider orbits by absorbing a photon of exactly the right energy for the 'blast-off' into the orbit with the higher energy. Conversely an electron whizzing happily round one of the larger orbits could spontaneously drop back into a lower energy orbit nearer to the nucleus, simultaneously emitting the energy difference in the form of a photon of light. The appearance of fine lines of exact wavelengths in spectra could thus be explained, and by choosing the right levels of energy for the different orbits, actual observations such as the series of lines Balmer studied could be fitted to the theory. All very neat and elegant, but had the theoretical framework merely organised observed data, Bohr's theory would have attracted little attention.

The thunderclap came when Bohr worked out the Balmer expression, getting the right answer *without* any reference to spectroscopic data at all. As Banesh Hoffmann points out in his delightful book, *The Strange Story of the Quantum*, Bohr really wrote a recipe for the hydrogen spectrum. The ingredients he used were:

> Planck's constant
> the speed of light
> the mass of the electron
> the electric charge of the electron.

Combining these independently measured quantities in the way his theory indicated, he arrived at this expression for the wavelengths in the Balmer hydrogen series: wavelength = 364.5

$$\text{wavelength} = 364.5 \left[\frac{n^2}{n^2 - 4} \right]$$

The astonishingly accurate agreement with Balmer's empirical formula brought wide acclaim to Bohr's theory. At last a plausible mechanism underlying the absorption or emission of light had been proposed: an electron could 'jump' between different energy levels in at atom. In the same year, H. G. J. Moseley, perhaps the most brilliant of all Rutherford's young associates, discovered regularities in the X-ray spectra of elements which showed that X-rays were also produced by electrons jumping between energy levels, though these electrons lay deeper in the atom than the outer electron or electrons which produced visible light.

In 1914 the first dark shadow fell across the scene. Moseley went off to Gallipoli and was killed amidst that frightful waste of human life. Einstein, now a Swiss citizen, still managed to keep working at the Kaiser Wilhelm Physical Institute in Berlin. He completed the general theory of relativity, showing how light rays are bent by gravity, and produced the theoretical basis for the existence of energy levels in atoms. His theory of energy levels provided the basis which led to the atomic clock and to the laser.

For another ten years the Bohr model of the atom held the field, until, with the advent of the new quantum mechanics in 1925, it was swept away into the museum of scientific history. But the idea of electronic energy levels in the atom lingered on, and it is as potent today as it ever was.

Although Bohr received a Nobel Prize in 1922 for his work, that was far from marking the end of a distinguished career. His adventures had scarcely begun. He became head of the Copenhagen Institute for Theoretical Physics and made it into one of the scientific centres of the world. In January 1939 he travelled to the Washington Conference on Theoretical Physics, taking with him the momentous news of the discovery of nuclear fission. On Christmas Eve, Otto Hahn and Fritz Strassman in Berlin had revealed the astonishing fact that bombardment of uranium by neutrons did not produce the heavier atoms that they had expected, but yielded instead atoms of barium, only about half the size.

Over the Christmas holidays, Lise Meitner, an exile from Nazi Germany and now working in Stockholm, solved the riddle. Her nephew, Otto Frisch was working in Bohr's institute at Copenhagen, and he recalls the event as clearly as if it were yesterday:

There is one Christmas I shall never forget – in 1938. I was in Denmark, and had obtained permission for my father to enter Sweden . . . But my father was in Dachau, my mother worried sick in Vienna.

My aunt, Lise Meitner, had accepted a position at the Nobel Institute in Stockholm and was trying to start nuclear physics research there . . . One Swedish family she knew invited her to Christmas dinner; they had invited me as well, so I travelled over from Copenhagen and joined Lise Meitner at her hotel.

When we met for breakfast the next morning she was poring over a letter from Otto Hahn, reporting a result which seemed so impossible that at first I didn't take it seriously . . . Hahn's discovery was, of course, that bombarding uranium with neutrons produced barium . . .

The sun was shining, and Lise and I sat down on a log and argued. It was clear that an atomic nucleus could not just be cut across by the impact of a neutron. Gradually we realised that we had to think of a nucleus as a kind of liquid drop, as Niels Bohr had done . . . I knew that the surface tension of a droplet was reduced by electric charge, and of course the uranium nucleus is very highly charged; a simple calculation made it seem possible that the slight disturbance by an incoming neutron might cause that almost unstable drop to wobble itself in two. Lise Meitner knew by heart a formula for roughly computing the energy that would be freed in such a process. I verified that much the same value could be computed for the kinetic energy of the two newly formed nuclei, by allowing for their mutual electronic repulsion. This is how the concept of nuclear fission was born.

(cited in Karplus, *Physics and Man*, pp. 303-4)

Bohr's fateful announcement produced consternation among the scientists at the Washington meeting. It was barely three months since Hitler, without serious opposition from Britain or France, had started carving up Czechoslovakia, and the threat of war was heavy in the air.

The idea of building an atomic bomb to unlock the tremendous energy in the nucleus had been bandied around as a remote possibility for years, but this atomic fission of uranium made it suddenly seem a lot more plausible. The reporters were abruptly excluded, and at the end of the proceedings, scientists rushed back to their laboratories to repeat the calculations and experiments. The race was on.

Bohr himself went back to Copenhagen but a year later the peaceful life at his Institute was shattered by the sound of jackboots as the German army of occupation moved in. In 1943, on the point of being arrested, he escaped to Sweden and was flown to England in the bomb bay of a Mosquito fighter-bomber. He failed to put on the headphones through which the pilot told him when to turn on his oxygen, so he was unconscious for most of the trip. Soon afterwards he was taken to the United States, under the code name of Nicholas Baker, as probably the most eminent adviser to the Manhattan Project, which was to build the atomic bomb. In May 1944 he returned to England and obtained an interview with Churchill, hoping to persuade him that nuclear weapons should be taken seriously; that the Russian allies would certainly develop their own in due course; and that the interests of post-war stability would best be served by open collaboration from the start. Churchill, however, held the lofty attitude, which persisted among the establishment even after the hydrogen bombs had been exploded, that the atomic bomb was no more than a very big bomb. He became impatient with Bohr's academic manner of qualifying and hedging all of his statements, and decided that he was either a confused thinker or a Russian agent.

Bohr returned to the atomic science factories of the Manhattan Project, Los Alamos, to the company of what the Director, General Groves, called 'the biggest bunch of crackpots ever assembled'. By quite a coincidence, the German physicist James Franck was one of those crackpots. It was a minor coincidence that both Franck and Bohr had, independently, hidden their gold Nobel medals by dissolving them in acid before taking flight from Hitler; after the war they precipitated the gold and recast their medals. The greater coincidence was that it was Franck, working in Berlin with Gustav Hertz, who had carried out the crucial experiments which clinched Bohr's theory of the atom. They provided direct evidence of the energy levels in a mercury atom and of the emission of light when an electron jumped from a higher to a lower level.

Probably most of the scientists of the Manhattan Project were too occupied with solving their own piece of the puzzle to give much thought to how the bomb was going to be used. But Franck was as worried as Bohr about the long-term effects on the peace and security of the world. On 11 June 1945 he, with six other distinguished scientists, sent a memorandum to the Secretary of War recommending that the atomic bomb not be used in an unannounced attack on Japan. This 'Franck Report' warned of the impossibility of keeping a monopoly of the bomb once its existence was known. It should either be suppressed or openly demonstrated in an uninhabited place with the aim of achieving international control of all nuclear weapons. For 'if no efficient international agreement is achieved', they prophesied, 'the race for nuclear armaments will be on in earnest not later than the morning after our first demonstration of the existence of nuclear weapons'.

The committee advising the President came to a different conclusion. On July 16 at Alamogordo in the New Mexican desert the first plutonium bomb was exploded, and the scientists watching from a distance saw the transformation of matter into light. Robert Oppenheimer described the sight by quoting from the sacred Hindu epic, the *Bhagavad Gità*,

If the radiance of a thousand suns
were to burst into the sky,
that would be like
the splendour of the Mighty One,

while the military mind of Brigadier General Thomas F. Farrell was, in
its own way, just as impressed by the optical effects of splitting the atom:

The effects could well be called unprecedented, magnificent, beautiful,
stupendous and terrifying. No man-made phenomenon of such tremendous power had ever occurred before. The lighting effects beggared
description. The whole country was lighted like a searing light with the
intensity many times that of the midday sun. It was golden, purple,
violet, gray and blue. It lighted every peak, crevasse and ridge of the
nearby mountain range with a clarity and beauty that cannot be
described but must be seen to be imagined. It was that beauty the great
poets dream about but describe most poorly and inadequately. Thirty
seconds after the explosion come the air blast, pressing hard against
the people and things, to be followed almost immediately by the strong
sustained, awesome roar which warned of doomsday and made us feel
that we puny things were blasphemous to dare tamper with forces here-
tofore reserved to the Almighty.

An equally dramatic, though less rapturous, account was given by the
crew of the B29 aircraft that dropped the first uranium bomb on Hiroshima three weeks later. Seen from above, the great city seemed to disappear in a sea of boiling smoke and flame. Many impressions have
been published of the view from below, though none, perhaps, more
telling than a series of accounts given by children of Hiroshima a few
years afterwards but only recently translated from the Japanese. One
boy, who was five years old on that morning in August 1945, wrote:

I was playing outdoors when I saw a sudden flash. Fire broke out everywhere. Our house and gate burned down before I knew it. I felt very
sad. Then we went under a bridge. There were many people there dying
from burns. Then we went to the other side of the river and stayed there
overnight.

    The next morning, we were hungry. My sister went to the school near
Misasa Bridge where there was an emergency relief squad and she
brought back some boiled rice balls for us to eat. While we were wan-

NEWS CHRONICLE, Tuesday, August 7, 1945

RELY ON THE QUALITY..
ballito
STOCKINGS

News

No. 30,958   TUESDAY, AUGUST 7

On this Bank Holiday the course of

FORCE OF NAT

PUT ASIDE HIS TEACHING

ATOM BOMI

Power equal to 20

ALLIES BEAT GERMANS IN
BATTLE OF SCIENCE

From ROBERT WAITHMAN, News Chronicle Correspondent

WASHINGTON, Monday.

IT MAY BE THAT THIS BANK HOLIDAY WEEK-END TH
COURSE OF WORLD HISTORY WAS CHANGED. FO
AT 11 A.M. IN THE WHITE HOUSE TODAY PRESIDEN
TRUMAN ANNOUNCED THAT BRITISH AND AMERICA
SCIENTISTS, WORKING TOGETHER, HAD "HARNESSE
THE BASIC POWER OF THE UNIVERSE," AND THAT
FEW HOURS EARLIER THE FIRST ATOMIC BOMB HA
FALLEN ON A JAPANESE CITY.

This is something so much bigger than any of the storie
of war-time scientific discoveries that have yet appeared; it
implications, for both good and bad, are still hidden.

President Truman says that "further examination" is necessary
"the possible methods of protecting us and the rest of the world from th
danger of sudden destruction." More reassuringly, Secretary of Wa

SIR JAMES CHADWICK
Professor of Physics at Liverpool University, put his teaching aside to take part in the experiments.
In 1935 he received the Nobel Prize for physics

dering around with our sister, we met Daddy and Mummy. Mummy had burns on her hands and feet. Daddy looked as if he would die any moment. I was so unhappy I started to cry. I was very, very sad. We did our best to take care of him. He was on the verge of dying. When I brought a glass of water for him to drink, he seemed to get better.

Then we went to our relatives' and stayed there for some time. In a few days, they built a shack for us to live in.

One day, I went to the hill to play. When I came back, Daddy was

Chronicle

LATE LONDON EDITION

ONE PENNY

world history may have been altered

RE HARNESSED:
ON JAPAN
)00 tons of T.N.T.

Next step is to control the force	

—Sir John Anderson

News Chronicle Re...rtcr

THE discovery of the atomic bomb is the greatest step forward ever made by man in his efforts to control nature.

Sir John Anderson, speaking as a physicist, told me this last night.

"It far transcends that of the discovery of electricity and makes steam something of the far past," he said.

"It has opened a new door to physics which has hitherto defied all approach.

"It means that man has at last found the way to release the forces of the atom.

"That is a tremendous task because it is only because that great store of energy is so difficult to release that we are able to carry on our normal lives.

"The preparation of the matter which has enabled

LATE NEWS

'IT CAN BE DONE," HE SAID IN 1941

British and U.S. scientists pooled skill

"THIS revelation of the secrets of nature, long mercifully withheld from man, should arouse the most solemn reflections in the minds and consciences of every human being capable of comprehension."

These serious words are contained in a statement on the new bomb which had been prepared by Mr. Churchill. The statement was issued by the Prime Minister, Mr. Attlee, from 10, Downing Street, last night.

"We must indeed," says Mr. Churchill, "pray that these awful agencies will be made to conduce to peace among the nations, and that, instead of wreaking measure-

---

dead. We put him into a coffin and carried it to a crematory. The next day, we brought back some of his ashes and buried them in the cemetery.

A few days later, Mummy died too. We put her into a coffin and carried it to the cemetery the same as Daddy. My sister and I buried ... my Mummy beside my Daddy. We prayed kneeling in front of their grave and cried to ourselves.

(cited in Rotblat, 'The Threat Today', in *The Bulletin of the Atomic Scientists*, 37 (1981), pp. 35-6)

Back in Copenhagen after the war, Bohr laboured incessantly in the

Atoms for Peace movement while Franck in Chicago turned his hand to the vital and exciting problem of finding how chlorophyll works in photosynthesis. But their lasting monument was the concept of electronic energy levels in atoms. The newer quantum theory of solids has left the original Bohr model of the hydrogen atom far behind, but it still envisages the interaction between light and matter as the interchange of energy between a photon and an electron, the simple event that puts the colour into this colourful world of ours. And it still uses the idea of energy levels, not just in a hydrogen atom or heavier single atom, but even in a complicated molecule or a crystal containing many atoms.

The concept of atomic energy levels underlies the design of lasers, those sources of light, superficially resembling fluorescent lighting tubes, that could only have been invented in the twentieth century. They depend upon a way of exciting the electrons in atoms that could hardly have been discovered by chance. In an ordinary fluorescent tube, electrons are lifted into a higher energy level by the electrical energy of the discharge. As they fall back into the lower levels they emit photons of light quite randomly in all directions, so that the tube is equally bright all round. Einstein showed that a different kind of emission of light could be produced if the atoms were so highly energised that the *majority* of the electrons at a certain energy level were excited into a higher level. In this situation, a photon emitted from one excited atom 'collects' another photon from a neighbouring excited atom and takes it along with it, in step and in exactly the same direction. These two collect two more, and in this way a chain reaction can proceed through the material, whether in the form of a solid crystal rod or a long tube of gas. If the tube is one metre long, the photons travel down it in a 300-millionth of a second; by putting a mirror at each end of the tube to reflect the light back and forth an enormous intensity can be built up in a very short time. One of the mirrors is made only partly reflecting, and the narrow, parallel, intense beam that emerges from it is the new form of light, the laser beam.

Laser optics is one of those rare instances, such as the development of nylon, atomic fission or genetic engineering, where an important technology has sprung directly from scientific theory. Its importance is starting to show in many fields — surveying, range finding and welding, for example. It is in routine use for repairing retinal detachment in eye surgery, and it has already saved thousands of people from blindness. It is, of course, under intense development for many forms of military application, but fortunately the wilder dreams of death rays and anti-satellite beams seem likely to stay in the province of Flash Gordon or Superman for many years to come.

A more constructive potential lies in the field of communications, where the capacity of cables for carrying electrical signals imposes considerable restrictions. The modulation of light beams offers a way round this limitation, and laser beams travelling through underground pipes may one day carry one of the few unfulfilled dreams of science fiction, the domestic television telephone that lets you see the person you are talking to (and, maybe a mixed blessing, allows that person to see you!).

This brings us back to vision as the central theme of the story; after all, the most important aspect of light is sight. How far is modern science helping with the world-wide problems of eyesight? Spectacles have been improved by the development of bifocal and trifocal lenses, and more recently of lenses whose focus varies continuously from the top to the bottom. Contact lenses have been developed, first of glass and then of a soft, water-compatible plastic. A good solution to the problem of decreasing accommodation as the lenses in the eyes of middle-aged people become harder has not yet been found, but when the lens itself deteriorates badly, as with cataracts, it is now possible to replace it with a substitute.

The wonders of solid-state physics have been harnessed to produce spectacle lenses which darken as the outside light gets brighter, thus protecting the wearer from excessive glare. Such sophistication sits strangely with the basic but still unsatisfied needs for optical protection of the underprivileged and the oppressed. For example, a four-year survey by the Royal Australian College of Ophthalmologists reported in 1980 that 38 per cent of the Aborigines examined in the rural areas of Australia had trachoma, an eye disease that commonly leads to blindness. The corresponding figure for non-Aborigines was about 2 per cent. The survey teams in this National Trachoma and Eye Health program included Aborigines and carried out surgery and remedial treatment as they went. Their final report, however, included proposals not only about the narrowly scientific and medical aspects but also about housing, water supply, refrigeration and sewerage. This is surely the advancement of science in the way that the early pioneers of modern science intended. 'What end are you scientists working for?' asks Galileo in Brecht's play, and goes on to answer his own question:

To my mind, the only purpose of science is to lighten the toil of human existence. If scientists ... confine themselves to the accumulation of knowledge for the sake of knowledge, science will be crippled and your new machines will represent nothing but new means of oppression.

(Brecht (trans. Mannheim),
The Life of Galileo)

The new machines' in Galileo's time were pumps, metal-working instruments or telescopes, though Brecht himself, with the echoes of Hiroshima ringing in his ears, was thinking of atomic energy. The new machines of today are computers, guided missiles, digital watches, electronic games, radio or television sets, the high technology of the electronic revolution. In the Santa Clara Valley of California, the ubiquitous silicon chips which lie at the heart of these devices are produced. After they have been processed, the finished components are tested with equipment costing something like half a million dollars per worker. But between these two steps comes the business of bonding the electrical leads on to each chip, fine gold wires thinner than a human hair. With present techniques, this step is relatively labour intensive, the main requirement being a microscope costing about $2000 for each worker. And who better to perform this delicate task than the women of South-East Asia?

The manual dexterity of the oriental female is famous the world over. Her hands are small and she works fast with extreme care. Who, therefore, could be better qualified by nature and inheritance to contribute to the efficiency of a bench-assembly production line than the oriental girl?

(from a publicity brochure,
Malaysia: The Solid State for Electronics)

There are, however, other reasons for the practice of flying the wafers from California to South-East Asia and flying the assembled chips back again for the final tests. The *Wall Street Journal* of 20 September 1973 (p. 36) observed that

Electronics companies depend on hundreds, sometimes thousands, of young girls to do the painstaking job of assembling tiny parts that are shipped home for use in computers and other products. Labor sometimes represents as much as half the cost of these parts, so the cheaper the labor the higher the profit.

A woman who gets a job as an assembler must have perfect 20/20 vision. She may have to bond a hundred chips an hour throughout an eight-hour day, peering down her microscope as she bonds perhaps several dozen leads on each chip. After two years' employment she can

Victims of the electronic revolution

expect a moderate wage, maybe $80 a month in the Philippines for instance. A few years later, her vision begins to blur; her quota is reduced, but she is expected to marry soon and then to retire from the industry. By this time, though, she may have become the main bread-winner for her family. In an attempt to maintain the family standard of living, many of these women are drawn into the rapidly growing 'hospitality industry', a euphemism for the prostitution which is estimated to employ over a hundred thousand women in Manila alone. This is part of the price being paid for the jobs and the wealth that the big corporations are bringing to South-East Asia.

The definition of science which Brecht put into the mouth of Galileo, an activity to lighten the toil of human existence, has been criticised for being not what Galileo actually said, but merely what Brecht wished that he had said. It is, however, close to the view expressed by Francis Bacon, founding father of modern science: 'The true and lawful goal of the sciences is none other than this: that human life be endowed with new discoveries and powers.' The science of light has indeed brought many new discoveries and powers, but the haunting faces of its victims, from the lacemakers of old to the silicon chip assemblers of today, tell us how far we have to go before we can be truly proud of our achievements with the Light Fantastic.

Bibliography

Abbe, E., *Gesammelte Abhandlunger*, G. Fischer Verlag, Jena, 1906.

Arons, A. B., *Development of Concepts of Physics*, Addison-Wesley, Reading, Mass., 1965.

Asimov, I., *Asimov's Biographical Encyclopedia of Science and Technology*, Allen and Unwin, London, 1964.

Auerbach, F. (trans. R. Kanthack), *The Zeiss Works and the Carl Zeiss Foundation in Jena*, Foyle, London, undated (ca. 1936).

Baily, L., *The Gilbert and Sullivan Book*, Cassell, London, 1952.

Barker, T. (ed.), *The Long March of Everyman*, Penguin Books, Harmondsworth, 1978.

Bence Jones, H., *The Royal Institution*, Longmans, Green and Co., London, 1871.

Bernal, J. D., *The Extension of Man*, Weidenfeld and Nicolson, London, 1972.

Buckle, H. T., *History of Civilization in England*, I, Henry Frowde, London, 1857.

Cantor, G. N., 'Thomas Young's Lectures at the Royal Institution', in *Notes and Records of the Royal Society of London*, 25 (1), June 1970.

Chirnside, R. C., *Sir Joseph Wilson Swan F.R.S.*, The Literary and Philosophical Society of Newcastle-upon-Tyne, 1979.

Clarke, A., *The Coming of the Space Age*, Gollancz, London, 1967.

Coe, B., *George Eastman and the Early Photographers*, Priory Press, London, 1973.

Eliot, T. S., *Collected Poems, 1909-1925*, Faber, London, 1926.

Gamow, G., *Biography of Physics*, Hutchinson, London, 1962.

Gregory, R. L., *Eye and Brain*, Weidenfeld and Nicolson, London, 1966.

Hobsbawm, E. J., *Labour's Turning Point, 1880-1900*, Harvester Press, Hassocks, East Sussex, 1974.

Hubbard, R., and Kropf, 'Molecular isomers in vision', *Scientific American*, 216 (1967), pp. 64-76.

Hughes, T. P., *Thomas Edison, Professional Inventor*, H.M.S.O., London, 1976.

Hurd, D. L. and J. J. Kipling (eds), *The Origins and Growth of Physical Science*, II, Penguin Books, Harmondsworth, 1964.

Karplus, R., *Physics and Man*, W. A. Benjamin, New York, 1970.

Koestler, A., *The Sleepwalkers*, Penguin Books, Harmondsworth, 1964.

Lucretius (trans. R. E. Latham), *On the Nature of the Universe*, Penguin Books, Harmondsworth, 1951.

Moore, P., *Sun, Myths and Men*, Muller, London, 1968.

Parker, D., *Radio, the Great Years*, David and Charles, Newton Abbott, 1977.

Price, D. de Solla, *Science Since Babylon*, Yale University Press, New Haven, 1961.

Rotblat, J., 'The Threat Today', *The Bulletin of the Atomic Scientists*, 37 (1981), pp. 33-6.

Royal Astronomical Society, 'Nicolaus Copernicus, De Revolutionibus, Preface and Book I' (trans. J. P. Dobson, assisted by S. Brodetsky), *Occasional Notes*, No. 10 (May 1947).

Royal Society of London, R.B.C. 3, 215, A Discourse of Mr Isaac Newton, 1671/2 (original in the possession of the Royal Society of London).

Royal Society of London, R.B.C. 3, 231, Consideration by Mr Hook [*sic*] upon Mr Newton's Discourse of Light and Colours 1671/2, prob. 1672 (original in the possession of the Royal Society of London).

Schroeer, D., *Physics and Its Fifth Dimension: Society*, Addison-Wesley, Reading, Mass., 1972.

Sherrington, C. S., *The Endeavours of Jean Fernel*, Cambridge University Press, Cambridge, 1946.

Sontag, S., *On Photography*, Allen Lane, London, 1978.

Sparrow, W. J., *Knight of the White Eagle*, Hutchinson, London, 1964.

Talbot, Fox W. H., *The Pencil of Nature*, facsimile edition, Da Capo Press, New York, 1969.

Taton, R., *Reason and Chance in Scientific Discovery*, Hutchinson, London, 1957.

Volkmann, H., 'Ernest Abbe and his work', undated pamphlet.

Whitman, W. (H. W. Blodgett and S. Bradley, eds), *Leaves of Grass*, New York University Press, New York, 1965.

Young, T., Notebook 16 (original in possession of University College, London).

Acknowledgements

Producing a book, like carrying out a piece of scientific research, reflects the contributions, direct and indirect, of many people. Most immediately I wish to thank Brian Johns, Helen Semmler, Carla Taines and Chris Wilder, of Penguin Books Australia, for their encouragement and patience even during the darkest hours. I also gratefully acknowledge valuable inputs of various kinds from Ernest Clegg, who was with Marconi's in the early days of radio, Queen Finlay, Zdeněk Horský, Sheila Mason, Wolfgang Pfeiffer, Arthur Pryor, Martin Schade and Phyllis White who first suggested writing a book on the ramifications of the light fantastic. The librarians of The Royal Institution, The Royal Society, and University College, London, kindly allowed me to consult original documents, and I owe a special debt to my students from whom I always learn more than I am able to impart.

Illustrations and poems

Every effort has been made to trace copyright holders, but if any have not been acknowledged, the publisher would be pleased to be informed.

p. 2 British Crown Copyright, Science Museum, London.
p. 7 Reprinted by permission of Faber and Faber Ltd, London, from *Collected Poems 1909-1925* by T. S. Eliot.
p. 8 The British Museum.
p. 13 British Crown Copyright, Science Museum, London.
p. 16 Library of Congress, Washington D.C.

p. 21   The Museum of Street Lighting, Concrete Utilities Ltd, Ware, England.
p. 30   Herr Retzer, Landeshaupstadt München, Fremdenverkehrsamt, München.
p. 48   Leonard Craven Hill and Punch Publications Ltd.
p. 56, 58   GEC-Marconi Electronics Ltd, Chelmsford, England.
p. 79   Courtesy of the Archives, California Institute of Technology.
p. 86   Reprinted from *Leaves of Grass* by W. Whitman (H. W. Blodgett and S. Bradley, eds), New York University Press, New York.
p. 112   Reproduced from *The Rubaiyat of Omar Khayyam*, Avenel Books (Crown Publishers, Inc.), New York.
p. 136   Zdeněk Horský and the National Technical Museum, Prague.
p. 146   The Royal Society of London.
p. 147   Reproduced from the catalogue for the Exhibition for the Second International Congress on Cell Biology, Berlin, 1980, under the auspices of the European Cell Biology Organisation.
p. 161, 164   Carl Zeiss Company and Martin Schade.
p. 175   Reproduced from *Early Photography* by Patrick Daniels, Academy Editions, London.
p. 176, 177   Brian Coe and Kodak Ltd.
p. 209   The Bodleian Library, Oxford.
p. 215   Associated Press.
p. 218   Vicky and the *London Express* Features Service.
p. 230-1   *The Daily Express* News and Features Group.
p. 235   Stephen Lavender and Australia-Asia Worker Links.

Index

gasworkers, 22, 23
  see also unions, trade
General Strike, British, 23, 61
glass, 150-2
  for optical instruments, 154-7
  refractive power of, 156
  Schott's experimental, 156-7
  types of, 154-7
globe
  celestial, 115
  Eudoxus', 114-15
Goethe, Johann Wolfgang von, 211-12
gravity, 138-9
Greek (ancient) science, 114-22

Habermel, Erasmus, 133, 135, 136
Hahn, Otto, 226, 227
Halley, Edmund, 138, 139, 140
Hardy, G. H., 219
Hertz, Gustav, 228
Hertz, Heinrich, 4, 53-6, 58, 66, 73,
  189, 197, 198
  interference experiment, 55
Hipparchus, 114, 115, 119-20, 133
Hoff, J. H. van't, 94-5
hologram, 26, 185
holography, 185-6
Hooke, Robert, 24, 35, 42-3, 145-6,
  147, 206-10
Hoover, Herbert, 59, 60, 61
horoscopes, 117, 133
Hughes, David, 55
Huygens, Christian, 42-3, 84, 208

Ikhnaton, *8*, 10, 45, 113, 114
  see also Amenhotep IV
infra-red detection, 66
instruments
  astronomical, 133, 134-5,
    139
  manufacturers, 151-66 *passim*
  optical, 133, 141, 151-6 *passim*,
    205-6
interference of light, 36, 38-9, 44, 55,
  77

experiments 36, 38-9, *39*, 41, 55,
  80-2
International Standard of Light
  Intensity, 24
Islamic science, 120, 122-3
isoprene, 95

Joos, Georg, 165
Jupiter, moons of, 83, 141

Kelvin, Lord, 19, 56
Kepler, Johannes, 133-8, 139, 141,
  142-4, 146
Kirchoff, Gustav, 223
Kodak, 174-6, *176, 177*, 186, 216
Koestler, Arthur, 133, 137, 171
Kolbe, Hermann, 94
Krakatoa, 116, 117
Küppenbender, Heinz, 165

lacemakers, *2*, 3-4, 6, 235
Land, Edwin, 110, 212-14
Laplace, Pierre, 86
laser, 26, 166, 185-6, 232
Leeuwenhoek, Anton van, 5, 144-5,
  146, 158
lenses, *2*, 3, 122, 133, 139, 171, 205
  achromatic, 154-5, 156, 206
  artificial, 122
  camera, 102, 212
  colour correction of, 146, 154-5,
    156, 157, 205-6
  hollow, 155
  in human eye, 95-6, 99-100, 102
  magnifying glass, 123-4
  manufacture, 153
  spectacles, 5, 42, 44, 100, 101, 102,
    124, 233
  in telescopes, 133
  theory of, 127
  water-immersion, 153
  see also microscopes; telescopes
life, origins of, 90, 92
light, 197, 219
  absorption, 225-6